SOME PLACE QUITE UNKNOWN

Works by Jane Lazarre

Fiction

Some Kind of Innocence
The Powers of Charlotte
Worlds Beyond My Control
Inheritance *

Non-Fiction

The Mother Knot
On Loving Men
Beyond the Whiteness of Whiteness: Memoir of a White Mother of
        Black Sons
Wet Earth and Dreams: A Narrative of Grief and Recovery

Poetry

Bodies of Water *

[* not yet published]

Some Place Quite Unknown

A Novel

By

Jane Lazarre

H \s

HAMILTON STONE EDITIONS

This is a work of fiction. Names, characters, places, and incidents either are the product of the author's imagination or are used fictitiously. Any resemblance to actual persons, living or dead, events, or locales is entirely coincidental.

Library of Congress Cataloging-in-Publication Data

Lazarre, Jane.
  Some place quite unknown : a novel / by Jane Lazarre.
      p. cm.
  ISBN-13: 978-0-9714873-9-0 (alk. paper)
  ISBN-10: 0-9714873-9-1 (alk. paper)
  1. Middle-aged women--Psychology--Fiction. 2. Women authors--Fiction. 3. Fiction--Authorship--Fiction. 4. Psychological fiction. I. Title.
  PS3562.A975S66 2008
  813'.54--dc22
                                    2007050848

Cover by Lou Robinson

For my beloved granddaughter, Aiyana Grace, for whom, as for all of us, history, both outside and inside, will matter.

And for the young writers I taught over the years. You all helped me write this novel though you could not have known it at the time. It is filled with your voices and your words.

H \s

HAMILTON STONE EDITIONS
P.O. Box 43, Maplewood, New Jersey 07040

SOME PLACE QUITE UNKNOWN

"For really, what did she feel, come back after all these years and Mrs. Ramsay dead? Nothing, nothing – nothing that she could express at all."
    Virginia Woolf, *To the Lighthouse*

"My conversion involved rethinking, refeeling, rather than life changes. Yet the division between before and after is, emotionally, a chasm."
    Sara Ruddick, "New Combinations: Learning from Virginia Woolf"

Shadows, *familiar and vague; still, then moving, but never out of sight. A woman bent over a narrow wooden desk covered with notebooks, pads filled with writing, a pile of manuscript pages in neat print, a packet of letters yellowed with age and covered with small script in black ink — elegant and even except for a* **c** *breaking out of conventional penmanship standards with a long tail that arcs over the whole word, an* **f** *made nearly illegible by intricate lines and loops. The woman is reading the letters closely, then reading the notebooks, then the pads of writing, then the pages of print.*

A woman in her fifties begins to have unbidden, compulsive suicidal fantasies. She indulges them even though she has no conscious wish to kill herself, despite certain recent disappointments, despite the defining fact of her emotional life: her mother killed herself when this woman was a child of eight. Then one day she is crossing the street and is nearly hit head on by a car. She knows she saw the car, that the near "accident" was somehow intentional.

She is walking around the room, looking in the mirror. She takes her finger and tries to touch the reflection of her face, but her finger meets its own reflection where she places it against the glass. Only by touching her actual flesh can she see what she wants for some reason to see: her reflected finger touching her reflected mouth, her reflected eyes staring back at her.

A woman is writing. As she writes she thinks of her ordinary life as if she has left it for a time: her grownup son who lives far away but whom she talks to and corresponds with regularly, who visits frequently; her husband who is almost never far away; the women friends she loves, one since the earliest days of childhood, another serving a prison term of twenty years to life; her sister, their conflicted, sentient love; the acute pain and few remaining pleasures of her teaching position. (Just that week one of the best students she has ever taught wept at the end of term, crying, Oh, what will I do without this class! When she tells the story, weeping herself, to her son Khoby over the phone, he laughs affectionately. "You think everyone is the best student you ever had," he says. "Well, not everyone," she tells him, "but this one really is.")

All these thoughts and emotions toward her actual life fill her and then pull back again to dark, safe borders. In the center she is trying to map a journey backward in time in a realm other than ordinary life, the realm of barely conscious memory, of conscious secrecy, of imagery and feelings beyond words, of dreams.

And now she reads aloud the words from one of the old letters: "I have the strangest, most detached feeling — it's like a dream — I'm in the middle of nowhere with a huge amount of utter strangers surrounding me going ahead to some place quite unknown — holding fast only to one sure fact — that I'll be coming home to you, to the children, to all the dear, familiar routine."

They are her mother's words. Now they are her own.

1. Refraction

1.

I imagine my mother singing a love song, one she must have sung to my father at an earlier time since when they met she was married to someone else. Later, my father would sing it to me, calling it her song, and only in the fragile, vague space opened by his words did I recover the sound of her voice.

Once, I thought I knew
My love then I saw you
My love, you changed
My life, forever more.

Someone beautiful, passionately loving, but then suddenly remote, perhaps angry, dismissive, resentful at being intruded on. (That is how I would describe it now.) Someone vulnerable, yet also in some way impenetrable; a fearful shyness in certain aspects of life – the story, for example, about her social reticence on the ship when she journeyed to Paris, how "Lucille," she said, "would have had all the guests gathered around," but she held back, found it hard to speak. Yet, in spite of this shyness, an unmistakable sexual confidence, almost haughty in her know-ledge of her own beauty and magnetism.

People have told me stories all my life. I have memorized the suicide note I found among my father's papers when he died more than twenty-five years ago: *I love you all, darlings, but I can't bear the emptiness any longer. There is nothing to live for, and I can't make you suffer any more. I have no more words.* And now I have the few old letters written in her elegant hand, including the one from the ship to Paris where she wishes she had the social grace of her older sister, Lucille.

Is it imagination or memory at work? At some barely known con-fluence in the past, are they the same?

So many of my memories of her are locked in songs. She sang all the time, popular love songs, old spirituals, and after she died I somehow recorded them mentally, word for word, so that many years later, despite all I'd forgotten since then, I could sing her songs to my own child when he was tucked in for the night. I was never confident like they say she was, or like Liz, about being beautiful, but I did think I could see things beneath the surface. I am a noticer, a writer down of what I see – just for the record, my own, and the one I seem to be constructing so obsessively for the world. Do I continue this labor because I have such faith in what I see, what I want the world to see with me? No, I'm afraid the opposite is the truth.

> *Down in a green and shady bed*
> *A modest violet grew*
> *Its stalk was bent, it hung its head,*
> *As if to hide from view.*
> *And yet it was a lovely flower,*
> *So young, so fresh, so fair,*
> *It might have had a rosy bower,*
> *Instead of hiding there.*

I am sitting in my uncle's car since my father can't drive. I am in the back seat near the window, and the wind is blowing into my face as I sing the song about the poor violet, keeping my words soft, blowing them into the wind in a whisper so no one in the car will hear. She has been dead only a year or two, and at nine or ten years old I can still hear her voice singing the song to me. I can still hear its low, throaty tone. That she must have understood something so true about me is what makes me cry, the memory of feeling understood and then, the feeling of being incomprehensibly alone.

Only now, decades later, beginning this record of my extraordinary experiences with Dr. Daniels, do I suddenly realize she must have been singing about herself. Not only because of the line in the old letter where she described herself as shy and compared herself negatively to the more socially confident Lucille. But my mother's name was Violet, the very flower itself the autobiographical heart of the song.

2.

It is the week of my last session before the summer separation. I am told by the doorman that the main elevator is broken and I must take the service elevator to the kitchen entrance of Dr. Daniel's apartment, which is connected to his office. I step out of the elevator into a tiny hallway, and, although I know I am behind a door which will lead to the kitchen (this is the design of most of the old apartments in this neighborhood), as soon as the elevator door is snapped shut and I am alone in the small space, I become frightened that I am in the wrong place. I look around and see there is no staircase, no escape. If I ring for the elevator to return, the operator may not hear me for some time. Panic rises into my throat just as Dr. Daniels opens the door and says jovially, "Yes, yes, you're in the right place, I'm sorry the main elevator is broken and you had to come through the back," and he leads me through his narrow kitchen, past the living room decorated in greens and golds, and down a corridor whose door opens into the familiar room where I sit twice each week waiting for the previous patient to emerge. Today, she is a woman in a green dress that leaves through the door to his apartment, down the back way. Obviously, she knows her way out. I breathe a sigh of relief, but that day I refer only in passing to the anxiety I felt in the hallway, then following him through the rooms of his home. "Like Eurydice following Orpheus," I say, thinking of the graceful way his back moved beneath his white shirt, the slope of his shoulders, the roundness of the back of his head. Later, when I am on the street going home, I remember that if he were Orpheus and had turned to look at me, I would have sunk back into the underworld for all time.

It is strange and unsettling to feel the child so close again after so many years, so present in the second half of life, as if in the first awareness that death is no abstraction, no symbol, but a reality that must be prepared for, one has to try again to understand the fundamental themes and trace the controlling images. My sad profile in the posed photograph with Liz; my exuberant smile in the one where our mother surrounds both our naked, sunburned shoulders with her arms. But the pictures are only reminders. They stand for the real thing, and the real girl is with me again. Inside, in some place once remote, now merely secret, she fills me with hunger. My stomach lurches and growls. All the holes are gaping, all the openings dark. The line between actual experience and imagination has been shifting all summer.

I know I remember I wanted her to love me, my truest, most actual, unfictionalized self. I suppose it has always been my actual life I wanted to infuse with erotic intensity. No translation could match that ecstasy. In one realm I am working, working, working at this labor. In another realm, I sharpen my tools, trying as best I can to discover the most elegant harmonies of language I am capable of imagining. Does the seamless, well-constructed story undermine my first and most passionate desire, or does it clarify, provide proportion by giving it shape? I keep writing not because I know the answer but because I am repeatedly compelled to try to find out. Old embers smoke, ignite new fires. I am unsettled, fanning the flames beneath a deceptively calm surface. It will be this way all summer.

3.

Throughout this summer I have been drawn to mirrors. I do not pass them by with a quick glance, as has been my habit for many years. Nor do I sit and stare into them like I did as a child searching for evidence of Violet's features shadowed in my own. I look at myself. My face, my body, clothed and naked. I focus on my shoulders, my neck, my thighs, sometimes on the full reflection, hair to toes. I don't cringe at the lines, the skin loosening around my jaw, the age marks that have appeared here and there on my skin. I hear my father's voice admonishing me long ago – Stop admiring yourself in the mirror, Celia. During those years of childhood and adolescence when a beautiful young girl looked back at me I was incapable of what Frank accused me of. I was always looking for Violet, and if there were days when unexpectedly, mysteriously, I looked beautiful to myself, it was she whose beauty I marked, she whose beauty that day, that hour, I had somehow achieved. Most of the time I found no reflection of my mother in the mirror, and without that layer of her face visible beneath my own skin, I was hopelessly inadequate, worse than ordinary, like a many-layered portrait in oils that has been painted so thickly translucence has turned to mud. I seemed ruined to myself.

Now, Frank, more than forty years later, I am admiring myself. In the beautiful old Cape Cod house where I stay for a few weeks each summer with my oldest friend, Judith, I shower outside under a large tree and admire my aging thighs. In my quiet room at night, one small light near my bed casting a soft glow, I stand before the large mahogany framed mirror and admire my face.

"Isn't there a Jewish custom about covering mirrors during a period of mourning?" Dr. Daniels asked me when I described my surprising shamelessness, this new conceit. Yes, I told him, during *Shiva*, the initial period of grieving for the dead, you have to keep the mirrors covered so you won't give into vanity when your thoughts should be focused on your loss. Humility, not pride, is what's needed for acceptance and eventual emergence from the trance of grief. Hours later, when I was home and looking in the mirror again, I finished the sentence. "And when the sheets are taken off and you can look in the mirror again, the first phase of ritual mourning is done."

It has taken forty-seven years, but this summer I finally experience the complete absence of self-loathing. It does not engulf, does not threaten from around the bend. It is not replaced by an image too perfect to hold its shape for long. Like a polluted tide cleaned up by ecological rebalancing, for an hour, even for an entire day, it disappears.

Each morning, I wake in my lovely room in a state of surprise. I am unused to this new person who is comfortable night after night, alone. During the day I crave solitude, but at night I have long required the safe nearness of Luke's body. I have slept beside him for nearly thirty years, the feel of his flesh the most consistent security I have ever known. I begin the night with my back curled into his chest. Soon I move away to my own side of the bed when he is fast asleep and I am in that luxurious state of slowly fading consciousness. At some point every night I dream, and by dawn I am hugging his back like some shadow on a wall.

Here, this summer, I walk downstairs to join Judith at the old wood table near the window that faces a wild-looking stretch of grass and announce – It happened again. I felt calm alone in the room. I slept well. I don't really understand why. Ordinarily, I would try to analyze every possible thread in the fabric of this remarkable shift, but lately I am intrigued by the mysterious ambiguities that surface when familiar words become suddenly insubstantial, as if reduced to arbitrary sound.

I was both frightened and attracted by this mystery when I was a small child, between the time language opened up the world of meaning to me and five or six years later when Violet killed herself and key words lost their meaning. Words in the dictionary. Words I could no longer comprehend. *Forever. Dead.* Like *elephant* had suddenly turned from solid sign into a mysterious drifting sound in an extraordinary moment when my mother – perhaps unknowingly – enabled me to see, by experiencing it myself, the precariousness of meaning, its constructed fragility.

Knock, knock, she said, having taught me the routine.

Who's there? (I might have clapped in excitement. I was only four or five.)

Ella. (I think I recall her dark eyes twinkling, or she may have shaken her head, displacing her carefully shaped short dark hair.)

Ella who? I whispered, obedient and aroused.

Ella-Fant, she said.

It took a few moments for me to grasp it. Ella-Fant. What was that? For what seemed a very long time I repeated the words over and over searching for the double meaning I knew must be there, and finally the strange name slipped back into the image of the familiar animal I saw nearly every Sunday in the Central Park Zoo. I would hold Frank's hand as we watched the huge creatures lift their trunks with dark holes at the end which seemed to stretch and constrict rhythmically around peanuts, leaves, the air.

When it was *elephant* again, I stared at my mother in silent amazement, but she may have had no idea what was happening inside me as I stood there repeating, *elephant, ella-fant*. The long gray trunks, hard and erect and opened at the end. My father's hand in mine. My mother's voice, her laugh – as I stood there falling in love with the indefinite plasticity of words.

After she was dead – (but I never said *dead*, not until much later when I was in my twenties; I said *died;* she died; the action suggesting a possible re-action, a lack of definite ending) – I kept saying elephant to myself, meaning, I think, that the word *dead*, which I wouldn't say, might have within its mysterious sound the same magical ambiguity.

Violet had a mirror on her dressing table, which folded into three sections, or was actually three individual mirrors attached in a row. The two side mirrors angled toward you so you could see your face from three different perspectives at once. There was no frame, but cut glass flower designs curved around the edges. I sat at her dressing table looking at my triple self – left view, front view, right view – my skin brown from the summer sun on a beach where I swam with her. On the rocks that stretched like a long bridge back from the bay, she had shown me how to find a place to rest so that one rock supported your back, another your legs, and in between the two supports your backside rested lightly on air. Looking at all three of me at once in the angled, three-part mirror, I felt an odd vertigo. There I was. Yet, I was also the odd fourth – the most real – sitting on a chair facing the other three. I touched my face and saw my hand touch my face in the mirror. But when I touched the reflection of my face in the glass, my finger touched only its own reflection, leaving an intriguing space between itself and the tripled face that stared back at me.

During the first year of my work with Dr. Daniels, I had a recurring dream about three women. They sat on the shore while I rode the waves, watching in awe as a huge, dark sea creature dove and surfaced before me. When I became frightened that it was getting too close, I leaped out of the water to find the three of them waiting for me and I touched each one's face with my finger. One was dressed in a gown of flowing white gauze, and she was pregnant. Another wore a black tunic over black tights and had some disease signaled by large black moles on her face and neck. The third wore black also, and she looked over the water, longing for someone; she is too much in love, I thought as I pulled my hand away from her sad face. The three mirrors, the three women, reminded me of three women characters I imagined in the story I have begun for Dr. Daniels, an allegory of the voices speaking in his room. I wonder about the desire to split the self into parts that is one of the paths to fiction. Are we trying to be purer and thus more comprehensible than we are in reality to ourselves? Are we trying to exorcise ghosts or become something new? I have always wondered about the meaning of fiction, a way of telling stories that seems enviably comprehensible to most of the other writers I know. For me, something ominous lurks in the notion of making things up. I seem to crave a naked plunge into real experience, each time from a different angle. I imagine all sorts of interior geographies, during good times believing that I will discover something with all this diving worthy of giving to someone else. During the bad times, I am afraid I will lose all grasp on the truth; that truth – solid, elegant and elusive – is mocking me.

After my outdoor shower, before Judith and I make our early dinner so that we can get to the bay before sunset, I put down my gray notebook and stand before the mirror again. From the end of the road outside my window traffic noises intrude on the silence. Even late at night, Route 6 is alive with cars. On the other side of my room the window faces trees, a wide expanse of grass ending in an old barn whose windows and door are bolted so tightly we sneak around it, peering in through cracks, imagining mysteries. Crickets cling to the screen, chirping loudly enough to compete with the cars. Imagining the three-part mirror as I look into this mirror, I whisper again what is becoming a kind of chant, teasing myself with the very specters that once would have made the night terrifying. Knock, knock, I say bravely, no notebook in my hand. Let the chaos in. I look hard at my features remembering my father's voice narrating stories in the dark, stories about Frank and Celia and Liz, where they went that day, the places the three of them would go tomorrow. No Violet around to complete us into four, and at times I wondered if she had ever been here at all. Had she lived with us in fact? I had long forgotten the actual sound of her voice. And sometimes in my fantasies of her return I'd suddenly see a nightmarish, featureless face, smooth flesh with nothing particular to distinguish it from any other face; an inhuman blankness.

Then I am in the present again, the cars on Route 6 whizzing, the evening coming on, and I find I am whispering it out loud, Knock, knock, who's there, Ella, Ella who, Ella-fant. Only now the Ella coming to mind is the fictional character Anna Wulf created in *The Golden Notebook* to represent herself in the novel-within-a-novel Doris Lessing wrote (Doris, Anna,

Ella) as if she had some cross-Atlantic vision into my particular life, or, it would be true to say, as if she were writing me into a life of translating experience into stories, finding ever new versions of myself staring into not three but an infinite series of attached mirrors. As I keep repeating the old knock-knock joke in my head, trying to capture a single note, a trace of Violet's voice speaking, I remember also the terror that the very things I thought I knew with certainty were not real; I had made everything up.

4.

I am a small child, dressed in some ruffled, stiff thing Violet liked. I cannot see its pattern because it is under my coat, which is wool, navy blue, with a pretty indented waist. My defective feet (weak ankles and arches, turned-in toes) are pushed into smart patent leather dress shoes, Mary Janes. Under a thick red plaid woolen blanket that reeks of animal flesh and hair, I cuddle next to Violet in an old-fashioned open carriage being pulled by a tired-looking black horse around Central Park. This is a special date, an *excursion* – the word my mother uses and I have come to love. We are on an excursion together, only the two of us. Frank is someplace else. Liz is not even born. I notice the weariness of the horse's movements, his mangy mane threaded with what looks like gray dust, a great sadness in his eyes. As with the twin worlds of elephant (in one the word meaning something perfectly comprehensible, in the other nonsense) I imagine twin worlds of a different sort for the horse. I can see he is an exhausted animal in ordinary life. But held in Violet's arms, my aching feet warmed by the stiff wool and my cheeks icy from the cold, I can feel the saliva of excitement gather in my mouth and I am certain the horse is really majestic, powerful, his coat glistening. I see him lift his hooves high off the ground, prancing. His mane grows long and shines like I imagine midnight might if you were alone on a dark sea reflecting a sky full of stars. And that is how I come to remember the horse that pulled our carriage around the park. Years later, when Frank takes Liz and me for a ride one afternoon, trying to replicate Violet's excursion and, perhaps, preserve a bit of her dramatic nature for her daughters, I will be shocked by the sickly appearance of the black horse and, despite my previous insistence, refuse to go for the ride.

Many years after that, I will dig out my old books about black horses for my son, Khoby. He loves the *Black Stallion* series so much he reads all the novels in one summer, and then, curled up on his bed, he reads the Classic Comics version of *Black Beauty*, the story of a powerful young colt who is orphaned, sold here and there until he becomes a carriage horse that is overworked, whipped, underfed and generally so mistreated he is eventually retired to a farm. Khoby disliked the story, insisting it was too sad. I gazed at the comic book drawings of the ill-used, exhausted horse and tried to push behind my falsified memory to a vague uneasy familiarity where I recognized that worn-out animal from someplace in my past.

In time for the sunset, Judith and I go for a long walk on the bay. Later, when I am alone in my room in the back of the house, the past will stretch out before me, reversing the conventional direction of time, and ordinary life will fade in comparison with the interior. Solitude, sleep, dreams, private thoughts, obsessions will dominate and pull, and I will sink into them like my feet sink into the mud of the lowest tide of the day. Long trekked journeys are being remapped to begin again. A fantasy love affair may hold me for an hour or more as I wait for sleep, and the realness of what is imagined easily supercedes the realness of real life. But first, Judith and I walk over the bay, large sandbars surrounded by gentle, shallow water moving in tiny waves in various directions. The sea pulls back and exposes its private interior – shells, stones, creatures, wide islands of damp sand. Above us, the sky stripes orange and pink through white clouds, but the brilliance of the colors fades by the second until the stripes are muted, slowly vanishing, and the whole panoply of magnificence is edged with loss.

5.

The next morning, as I wait in the car to go to the ocean, Judith stands in the driveway saying goodbye to her daughter Anna. They are looking at each other in an unbroken gaze of intimacy when no shame for intensity of desire can make you turn away. They'd had a small fight the night before over the phone. Anna, who has her own apartment on the Cape this summer, wanted to come visit us for the evening, but her car was in the shop, and though she had a ride to the town we stayed in, her mother would have to drive her back. Judith felt too tired to make this trip late in the evening, and rather shortly, she said, "No, let's just forget it. Come for breakfast in the morning." Almost as soon as Judith hung up the phone, Anna called back to say she felt hurt. Why did Judith not want to see her? And knowing Anna since she was born, listening from the other end of the room, I knew she'd reacted to a sharpness that comes into Judith's tone when she feels conflicted or overwhelmed, unequal to some task she either wants to fulfill or feels she ought to want to fulfill. Judith apologized, assuring her daughter in soft tones of her love, of my love for her, how much we both wanted to see her. It was only that the drive on Route 6 up to Provincetown seemed too much to ponder late at night, but she looked forward immensely to seeing Anna in the morning. Her goodbye sounded warm, passionate. "Is she okay?" I asked, closing my book. "Yes, I think so," Judith answered. "I think she's fine." And she returned to her chair in the living room and picked up her journal where she had begun constructing a narrative about her life.

I watch the swiftness with which she returns to the solitude of her own thoughts. I love the lines around her eyes, the slight roundness of her shoulders left over from a girlhood marked by blows to her confidence – hunching over books when life proved far too complicated and dangerous for a child to comprehend. I remember the two of us giggling as my Aunt Lucille, who lived across the hall from Judith and was Judith's mother's best friend, walked naked from her bedroom to the bathroom, her long, thick, gray hair brushing against small, lovely breasts, her dark pubic hair climbing her thighs like mossy seaweed on large rocks at the bay. Later, Judith and I would play with paper dolls, pretending the painted on bathing suits were not there, once bravely drawing and cutting out naked bodies complete with nipples and actual vaginas, attaching these instead of a dress to the dolls' cardboard bodies with tiny tabs.

Even then, Judith's head leaned a bit forward on her neck, stiff and fragile. Even then, I was plagued by a rounded, loose-fleshed belly no matter how thin I became.

Lucille would smile at us, call us *Dahling* when she reappeared dressed for work or a casual evening at home, her hair braided into a bun or a crown. She seemed so beautiful then it was hard to believe in the other Lucille, who called Judith ugly, told Liz her mother hadn't loved her, who appeared to me as a two-headed dragon in the long mirrors bordering the elevator in the lobby of the building, so that each time I came to visit Judith, or Lucille and her family, I had to close my eyes and find my way into the elevator as if I were blind.

The next morning Anna and her current lover Janine arrive with bags of rolls and sweets from the over-priced gourmet shop in town, and we feast on Portuguese muffins with homemade jam, chocolate pecan squares and rich coffee. Later, while Janine and I wait in cars, mother and daughter stand in the driveway saying goodbye, Judith warning Anna to be careful this afternoon on her drive to Boston. I am magnetized by the passion between them, watching their locked eyes, and remembering another scene recently witnessed; myself the outside observer, the one who is not herself seen.

Khoby had moved to Los Angeles some years before and had recently begun living with his lover Mariama, a name chosen by her Ghanaian father who died only three years after his daughter was born, shortened to Mari by her mother, born and raised in Ohio, who now made her home in L.A. In her enthusiasm to create a beautiful home, Mari had hand-sewn a spread for their bed. It was constructed of many large colored patches of green and pink satin and velvet, some patterned, some plain, each reflecting the one next to it in a harmony of color and design. Bordering the spread were stitched stripes of green, then pink velvet, and these were outlined finally by a narrow ridge of delicate lace. When I saw the magnificent spread on the bed she and my son share, I was as moved by its beauty as I might be by any work of art. Later in the evening, after we ate the delicious dinner Khoby had cooked, Mari stood before the bed exhibiting her handiwork to her mother, Karen, the two of them framed in a large archway that separated the two main rooms. They bent their heads together. The mother leaned over and traced her daughter's delicate stitches with her finger, complimenting their tiny symmetry, smiling and shaking her head at the way Mari had designed the related patterns and fabrics of pink and green. Khoby walked up behind me and whispered, "Karen is an expert seamstress. She passed on the craft to Mari." Mother and daughter stood next to each other, their similarly shaped, slim bodies clad in similar clothes, sleek black pants, a lovely silk blouse on the mother, a tight black velvet shirt tucked in at the daughter's waist. Karen's skin is fair, silvery rose highlights emphasized by well-applied makeup. Mari's skin combines her father's dark brown with her mother's beige in a rich tan she wisely adds no highlights to at all. Her lovely cheekbones shine. Her wide lips are colored just slightly with a dark purple tint. Her eyes, like small black currants, seem to see beneath the surface of things. Staring, to the point of rudeness I feared, I walked out to the front porch and heard my sister Liz's voice over the phone, talking to me several weeks before.

She had been feeling very sad, and physically unwell too, a kind of flu, she thought, which seemed to come on the tail of a period in her work as a sculptor in which all her images were about loss, absence, shapes framing what was gone. She knew, of course, she was sculpting Violet in a way, and the old emotions she could barely remember – she was only four when Violet died – seemed to blow around within her, swirling like wind in dark skies with no rain. Finally, she succumbed to a fever, a backache, a headache which made her sleep so long she felt like the drowned. One morning she was awakened by a fluttering feeling around her eyes, and she came out of her drugged slumber to the smell of steeped tea and the feeling of her daughter's lips on her eyelids. "Lia was kissing my eyes awake," Liz told me, and her voice cracked. She almost cried.

My sister only said, "I was feeling so bad, and when I woke up Lia was kissing my eyes." I have added the rest. The scene comes to me like a film clip I have actually seen and I copy it down. As I write it, I am thinking about Liz naming her daughter after me, giving her half my name, Lia for Celia, as I was given half of my Aunt Lucille's. And I am amazed that Liz has carried on a family tradition symbolized by the aunt she has hated for good reason all of her life.

I remembered my niece kissing her mother's eyelids as I stood on the porch of Khoby's house picturing Mari and Karen bending their heads together, leaning over to trace the edge of lace with similarly polished, carefully groomed fingernails, and I recall both scenes as I sit in the car and watch Judith and Anna gaze at each other, then embrace and kiss each other's cheeks and lips in the driveway to our house on the Cape. Anna comes over to the car, leans inside the open window and puts her arm around me. She kisses my cheek, and whispers in her typically passionate way, I love you Celia. I return the kiss, touch her dark brown hair, stroke her sunburned cheek. She is trying not to leave me out, and her kindness gives a name to my emotions in the series of scenes. Language disperses ambiguity, and I try not to make a sound.

And yet, I don't believe it is simple sadness, or envy, or even longing for something never to be had that the driveway scene generated in me at the beginning of this day. I am thinking this as I attempt to immerse myself in the frigid water of the ocean, where Judith already swims her strong stroke back and forth over the high-tide waves. There is this strange, unfamiliar feeling of goodness that accompanies even the sadness and loneliness, and I am able to do nothing except let these feelings settle, inactivity itself suddenly not dangerous – anything may emerge. The layers of feeling pull back like bay water, exposing the creatures beneath – crawling, slimy, muddy, tiny crustaceans and seaweed of the most slippery texture, the most complex designs. I know that in one way and another I have been dreaming and thinking of Violet all summer. I dive into the cold water. There is no ground. For the first time in years I am comfortable, or at least not frightened, in the ocean. I swim behind Judith, a crawl, a breaststroke. I turn onto my back and rock on the waves. Then, from several yards out, I ride a wave into shore and suddenly my feet hit wet earth. I have been lifted by the wave over a steep ridge onto a shallow sandbar. If I stand up the water reaches only to my knees.

And all summer it is like this as I try to imagine how to tell this story. I make notes, read them over obsessively, but I am not confident enough to begin to formulate actual sentences. I'm afraid I shall never be able to convey the intensity, the mystery, the extraordinary combination of the magical and the mundane. The emotions could so easily fall into cliché. I may be too limited in my ability to describe. All summer, this paradoxical combination: flooded by emotion, even my dreams feeling wet at the edges, my body wet with sweat each morning when I awake; and a sense of balance which itself enables the feelings to keep rushing in this most naked form. An image: the archway through which I viewed Mari and her mother, or a daughter kissing her mother's eyes, and I am completely exposed. Past fears and present judgments part effortlessly, like a theater curtain lifting, like thighs opening; and some faith, if only in the power of my own desire, allows the stories in.

6.

Violet and Frank ate an elegant meal each night after Liz and I were bathed, fed and waiting for bed. Nearly fifty years later I can call up the feeling of peering in at them through the squared-off arch that separated the kitchen and dining room. Sometimes, we were allowed to join them at the gleaming dark wood table for dessert, and on special occasions, I was allowed to present them with a drawing, which would be placed carefully in the frame that hung on the dining room wall. With each new season, holiday or birthday, I made a new drawing, all the old ones collected in a large brown envelope Violet had given me to keep them safe. For several years after her death I kept the drawings – a perfectly depicted black horse I had copied from the comic book version of *Black Beauty*; a long lush braid with a red ribbon running through it; and the one I would never show anyone of my body naked, drawn one secret, exciting night as I looked into my mirror, which was lit up by an unusually bright moon; all of them still protected by the large brown envelope with the elastic attached to the side. Several months after her death, I was in my room dressing – actually in between being undressed and dressing – I was naked and weaving my hair into braids as I sat on the bed. I was completely engrossed in this braiding since only recently, and with great pride, had I learned to do my own braids, reaching behind my head to start them and then pulling the hair over my shoulder so I could look down at the pattern forming out of the three separate brown strands. I was so engrossed in and proud of the braiding I forgot where I was, forgot I was still naked, forgot the soft voices of my Uncle Max and another man I had heard coming from the room adjacent to my own. But suddenly I heard my uncle call my name. I must have been in a reverie between dream and awake, because it was mechanical, the way I got up, still holding my left braid in both hands as I began to weave a bright red ribbon carefully into the bottom third, ready to tie it into a delicate bow above the loose part the way I remembered my mother teaching me to do a year before. Then I heard him call my name again. I let go of the braid – I must have, and it must have been done too loosely after all, because I remember that afterward it had come apart again all the way up to the first layer of woven hair – and I opened the door, just a crack, but a crack big enough for my nine-year-old body to be visible.

"That's the one," my uncle said. And there were my drawings – but how did he get them? – strewn over the table, and there was the brown envelope lying on the floor, its taut rubber band thrown backward, hanging over the flap. They were looking at the one of the kitchen table, the one I hated because I hadn't gotten it at all right, the top looked like it was hanging vertically instead of sitting flat on the legs, I had only kept it because I didn't like to throw anything away, but I hated the way I did that table; and he was holding that one in his hand, showing it to his friend. With his other hand he was pointing at me. The two men laughed softly, not harshly, but laughed. I stared, one hand holding the large wooden door opened, the other resting on the pale blue wall of my room, my braid slowly uncoiling over my shoulder. It was the red ribbon falling out onto my foot, tickling it, that broke my trance. I slammed the door and only then remembered that I had also been stark naked.

"That's the one all right," I heard again through the door. And again, a laugh.

Where were you, Frank, when this incident occurred? Why, in my memory, are Lucille's husband Max and the strange man the only people in the house? Had you left with Liz to go some place without me? I was never close to my uncle, never even comfortable with him. I was afraid of his gruffness. You knew that. Or is this elaborate story false, a small mystery created to hide ones far more profound: the memories I seem to have recovered this year as my love for you came back to me, sitting in Dr. Daniels' office journeying back to some unexamined depth of feeling guided by the stark and shocking imagery of my dreams: how, like twins attached by bone and flesh, the terror of exposure was coupled with the desire to be exposed.

Earlier this summer, before my Cape vacation with Judith, Luke and I traveled to northern California to visit Liz and her family. Khoby came up from L.A. and we were all in the same house nestled behind the dunes of a beautiful stretch of the Pacific coast. One morning, Liz and Lia were lying next to each other in Liz's large bed in a room that looked out at the ocean. "Hi, Celia," they both called girlishly when I poked my head into the room and asked the ritual morning question of the northern California coast: Do you think the fog will lift?

Thick damp fog rolls around the house, over the enormous hills behind us, stopping like some solid mass over the water. On certain days it will suddenly part, a blue stripe will spread over the beach and everyone will run out to worship the sun. An easterner and city-dweller, I still had months of August heat ahead of me, so I hardly minded the fog. It emptied out the beach creating a pattern of grays, tans and smoky blues that suited my need for this vague, uncertain contemplation. I sat under a cotton blanket in a beach chair, my notebook on my lap, recording descriptions, images, the trail of numerous nightly dreams, the anxiety that I would not be able to find a way to tell the story I wanted so much to tell.

Still, in the morning I joined the hopeful exchange: Will the fog lift? I think it might. See the blue over the hill? And when I found my niece and my sister cuddled together in bed despite Lia's twenty-three years, my eyes stung with tears because the feeling of distance I could not seem to cross with anyone was coupled with desire so primal I had no words to blunt the pain.

As the week moved toward Khoby's departure for his home in Los Angeles, I tried to keep my mind from its habitual leaps into future loss – counting the days until I will see him again, *not until late autumn* – and focused on his face and words as closely as I once did when he was a little boy and his mind seemed mysteriously kin to my own. I asked him once why he thought we both loved the night. "Maybe it's a time for troubled souls to rest," he told me in his quick, insightful way. Now, I seemed to see him from a perplexing distance. We watched the fog move back and forth in the sky over the beach, pulling back to expose an hour of sun, then curtaining the sky again with damp, cool grayness. In the late afternoon, driving over the mountain to a movie in a nearby town, we saw its topmost layer and drove above it into the hot sun, witnessing it alter the weather pattern for all those below. When we returned over the mountain in the dark of night, the fog reduced visibility to a few inches, veiling everything but the shining yellow reflectors in the road. Then suddenly it was gone again, the night dark and clear, the black sky gleaming with stars. Once we had crossed the mountain and returned to the tiny village at the shore behind the dunes, the alternating atmospheres were behind us. Fog clung to us like an enveloping cocoon.

Lia, Khoby and Liz's younger child, Ben, often stayed up into the early morning, watching the stars at the beach or a video on the VCR. There was an easier atmosphere between Liz and me, perhaps due to this uncharacteristic remoteness of mine; we kissed good night and went to bed early. On our twin beds pushed next to each other, Luke and I found the farthest corners to sleep on, and I wondered why we had pushed the beds together at all.

Two days later, Khoby was preparing to leave, and as he pulled me to his broad chest whispering, I love you, Mom, I remembered how I used to cry each time I left Liz in the early years of her move to the west coast, and I was afraid of that sorrow as Luke and Khoby drove down the road heading for the airport. I tried to breathe it out of my body, escape its hungry clutch, but I was afraid of losing it too.

It is a year before, a hot summer like this one, and as usual, my family is visiting Liz's family in California. One morning she tells me she has been working on a new piece, part of the series she's been sculpting for several years – rounded helmet shapes, or skulls, which surround sensuous folds, crevices and tunnels, vaginal shapes where – if the outer layer were a skull – the brain would be. "The mind-body problem," Liz said when I asked her to describe the meaning of the work. "Words can be so dangerous," she added with an odd chuckle. "Shapes and colors seem so much safer to me." She was folding the wash the morning she told me I could go into her studio and look at the new piece myself if I wished. I crossed the small yard to the cottage-studio welcoming the chance to view unobserved the images and designs of her work that often spoke almost as closely to my life as to hers.

In the middle of the room on a tall white pedestal was another of the skull series. But this one was painted shades of red so dark that in the layers and crevices the color verged on black. And protruding from the interior shapes that suggested a uterus and a vagina to me were two rounded ovals, the tops of thighs, I thought, chopped off well above the knees. Suddenly I saw it as a portrait of our mother, and the power of the image was so violent and painful I reached over to trace my finger gently down the pitiful bleeding folds. Escaping into Liz's office in an adjoining room, I sat at her desk writing down the experience as fast as I could, trying to regain a sense of balance. When I had filled several pages of a pad, I breathed more easily and looked around. On the large bulletin board to my left was a collection of photographs. Liz and I locked in an embrace at different occasions over the years – a Christmas reunion, my fortieth birthday party, hers. Her children when they were young, arms awkwardly reaching around each other's shoulders as they posed for the camera. She and I as children – a famous family photo of the two of us dressed up in Swiss peasant costumes Violet had brought back from one of her trips to Europe. And a beautiful photograph of Frank, tall and lean, standing on a beach, holding Liz's small body on his shoulders, his hands grasping her calves, her hands holding his head as she grins at the sky.

The next day we took a long walk in Point Reyes National Park, on a trail that led from the road through a long meadow to a rough coastline two miles in. As we walked I described my reaction to her work in a slightly more detailed way than I had been able to in the studio.

"From the time she died, when I was four," Liz said, "Lucille told me Violet never loved me. I know you felt grief-stricken and abandoned by her death, but I felt I was never even on her mind. I was Frank's child. You know that. Now I'm trying to retrieve some of the memories I must have somewhere inside. But often it's all a blank, Celia. I can't get back there, and I don't even know if I want to rake it all up again. Except through my work, in these shapes, in paint."

"For me it was the opposite," I said, repeating the difference in our histories she knew as well as I did. "Lucille told me all the time that Frank didn't really love me." But my words caught in my throat. I felt exposed, ashamed to feel such sharp emotions when childhood was so far away, so I tried for a certain flatness when I said, "My mother was all I had."

And why didn't I stop there? Why, I wonder now, did I not see the futility of my need to repeat and repeat, the cruelty, the danger? Liz did not respond but kept walking. The hike was longer than I'd expected, but I was determined not to falter, and not to be the first one to break the silence that had followed my remark about our mother. I kept so close to Liz's heels I knocked into her once, nearly causing her to trip by falling against her heavy backpack from behind.

On both sides of us meadows stretched to the horizon. Cows wandered behind fragile fences and stared at us curiously. When we had first entered the trail, we'd read a large sign: *Beware of Sneaker Waves which rise as high as 20 feet on this shoreline and are caused by Rip Tides so powerful even the strongest swimmers cannot resist their pull. Do not swim. Even wading is dangerous. Keep a safe distance from the surf at all times.* I thought the language oddly poetic for a warning sign. The resonance of *cannot resist their pull.* The obvious, yet somehow earthy symbol of the name: *sneaker waves.*

"This way," Liz said, turning a sharp left onto a narrower trail. Soon the air began to smell salty, the wind to pick up, but despite the excitement nearness to the ocean always brings, I was reticent, unable to speak – though I wanted to speak to my sister's back, broad and slim under a pale blue t-shirt folding out beneath the large back pack. Short, white socks rolled thickly around her ankles. Her graying blond hair picked up drops of sun, as if the light were fluid, or jeweled. The silence was thick, full of thoughts unable to be spoken, too layered for easy translation into words.

"Here it is," Liz said, and the dust-covered hills ended abruptly in a smooth white beach curving around a dark green lagoon. Surrounding the lagoon on three sides were enormous dunes, shell pink blending into sandy white. "That path goes right to the ocean," Liz told me, pointing to a shadow stretching around the largest dune. We could hear the drumbeat rhythm of the rise and fall of the waves, gathering sound then crashing, the eerie moment of silence when the tide pulled the water back from the shore.

Here in the lagoon, the only waves were tiny ripples capped by a sliver of silver foam, and we walked in, ankle deep, kneeled down letting water run over our thighs. I longed to find the perfect words to force Liz to respond to me, but it was always like this, a tension that thickened and spread from unanswered questions and unspoken desires. And I knew that if I spoke to her about the tension between us, silences I interpreted as indifference or anger, or of my discomfort as I waited for her response, she would say, "What tension? I'm just looking at all this magnificence."

"Did you have any reaction to what I said about Violet back there? To my response to your sculpture?" I finally asked.

"I'm glad you found it powerful," she said. "It means a lot to me."

We left the lagoon, retrieved our packs, and trudged through gravelly sand into the shadow around the dune. Then geography, light, weather and sound changed dramatically.

Now the beach was made of rock – smooth, rounded, sharp; grays, pinks, whites. Against enormous boulders the surf slammed and battered, its white foam showering rock and beach with several feet of dark water. "My god," I said, stunned by the power and the contrast. "I know," Liz laughed. The waves were gigantic, and cutting across the rising walls of water were other, faster tides moving without break or pause. The effect was of an impermeable power as the sneaker waves cut across the primary tide, yet of something permeable too, because it was water, after all.

"You could be sucked into that and be gone," Liz said, both of us holding to a precarious present as the past, like the wild ocean, slammed at our knees. I sat beside her as we began unscrewing our thermoses of coffee, unpacking our cheese and tomato sandwiches. I wanted to but could not reach around my sister's shoulders and pull her to me in a tight embrace, as I might do easily with Khoby, she with Lia or her son, Ben. I began to picture us at other times, passionate embraces after long absences caught in the photographs above her desk; sharing jokes that touched off something old yet forgotten so that long after our children and husbands had stopped, we were still laughing so hard tears rolled down our cheeks, but when asked what was so unusually funny we could never explain; the few times disaster had struck – an illness to one of us or one of our children, a loss in Luke's family or her husband David's, each of us rushing to the other's side. But memories of conflict dominated that summer, full of anger so violent its undercurrents might have equaled this ocean rolling before us now. And perhaps, I would say now, though I would not have thought so then, she was right to keep it all at a distance from the inescapable distortion of words.

I leaned over and patted her thigh. She began to talk about her sculpture series, thoughts about form, space, the nature of materials, the great expense of tools.

The afternoon after Khoby's departure, Liz and I went for a walk down the beach, and I reminded her of my reaction to her sculpture the summer before. "Yes," she said, repeating herself a year later almost word for word, "I'm so glad you found it powerful. It means a lot to me." But I was not satisfied. I wanted her to see Violet's older daughter gazing at a sculpture of her mother's bloody uterus and amputated thighs. She, of course, saw a viewer of her own work of art. Generations gathered around us, robbing us of intimacy, closing in. "I always felt she was all I had." I said it again, pressing her. "I loved Frank, like you did, but his love for me was never simple – nor mine for him."

"Yes," she said, "I know. But about my sculpture? You turned it into something else, something wrong. Or maybe it's not wrong, but something of yours. But it's mine. I don't see it the way you do. Not at all." After a long pause, she said, "I remember standing in Lucille's apartment, and being frightened, feeling like I didn't belong, then going over to wherever Dad was sitting and standing next to him, putting my hand on his leg, and feeling I was safe. Nothing could hurt me. He always made me feel perfectly beautiful. Beautifully perfect."

When I gasped out loud, as if I had been punched, she put her arm around me and said, "I'm sorry. I can't help it. It's true. And it's sad in a way, because you were the beautiful one. Everyone says that."

I felt her shoulder just above my own. I touched her back. I wanted to touch her hair as I breathed in the smell of perspiration mixed with the aloe cream she rubs into her dry skin and the shampoo tinted with a delicate lemon grass perfume she uses on her hair. She was right about her perspective on the making of art. I was right about the artist's loss of control of meaning once the work moves out of the private realm of creation. But we were not talking about art. My tears were invisible thanks to the fog, which had dampened my forehead and cheeks. We could not see more than a few feet ahead of us, or more than a few feet behind us, thanks to the fog.

7.

A light rain mutes and softens the pink of the rose hip blossoms, the browns of the sandy cliff overlooking Long Nook, where Judith and I sit staring into the rough surf below. A cold day on the Cape.

"All these years later, I can still feel the excitement when my father entered a room," Judith says, slipping easily between the present and the past we have shared since birth. The evening before I had recounted the story of Liz's sculpture to her, of our walks and the sneaker waves. She told me how, since her mother's death two years before, she had been recalling with all the early passion of her childhood how much she'd loved that harsh, competent, funny, providing woman, how injured she was by not being cherished in return, how angry that Lucille's criticisms of her (clumsy, ugly, awkward) were never challenged by her own mother, how even after years of a good marriage, successful work, strong, grownup children, she felt damaged by it all.

"And I can still feel Frank's passion, too," she said, switching back to my story. "His warmth. How it felt to be taken into his arms, as if you were suddenly at the center of the world. He may have felt easier with Liz. But he certainly loved you too, whatever distorted myths Lucille has been perpetuating over the years."

I wanted Judith's version to cover and soften my own memories, but battles with my father, when Violet was still alive and after she died, were still vivid stories in my head. I could never forget the certainty that I had to earn or bargain for his love, and underneath that endless haggling lurked something awful and dangerous I could attribute only – since Frank was my beloved father – to myself. But I remembered too my occasionally successful efforts to please him and earn his pride.

And through the thick, vague, roving consciousness of this summer, twenty-five years after his death, Frank becomes visible, audible, as clear and obvious as if he were walking up the dune: his worn face, its lines and creases, the sadness in his eyes; his philosophical smile as he tells stories; his grief-stricken, dumbstruck misery after Violet's death. And for some reason, instead of my usual memories of Frank as a union organizer, years when he seemed powerful and strong, I am remembering later years when he was depressed and feeling hopeless, working in a cleaning store where his friend Morris was an expert spotter. When he held a dress in front of him for inspection, determining whether or not the stains could be extracted from the cloth by even the most expert hand, he assumed a certain elegance, I thought. He knew which spots could be sent on to Morris and which were a waste of money for the customer to bother with.

"You can dye it a darker color," he would advise them, holding the piece of material before him like a map of the world, "or you can throw it out. No point in spotting. Even Morris can't get this out."

And he would put the piece of clothing down definitively, spread his palms across the old wooden counter, his arms opened wide, and look the customer straight in the eye. If she was a good-looking woman he might wink and make a cute little clicking sound with his mouth, but he would never lie.

"What, for an extra two dollars?" he would say impatiently to Morris's brother-in-law, the businessman, the success, the small-time profi-teer – the owner of the store – whenever he began to lecture my father, the romantic, on the facts of business life. "You see, baby," he would tell me as I sat perched on a stool nearly lost among curtains of plastic-covered clothes – "it's not the two dollars. It's not a question of business. It's a question of values. Human values. I could no more recommend a dress for spotting which I know cannot be cleaned than I could recommend a car for sale when I knew the steering wheel was faulty. And that's why I won't last here, sweetheart," he'd add, stuffing soiled shirts into a carefully labeled bag. "I'm no businessman. My days as a cleaning store clerk are numbered. You mark my words."

I remember observing him closely, listening carefully, learning to admire what I eventually came to know was his integrity, and at the same time feeling terrified of our uncertain future, wondering how the three of us would live if he didn't have a job. At times I wished he could be more protective, not so incapable of hiding a feeling or telling a soothing lie. I dreaded the night when he would lope along, back and forth in the kitchen right outside the room Liz and I shared, singing his haunting, funereal songs. Perhaps this quality of naked submission to misery was formed on the long trip by train and foot from the old country, even the Atlantic Ocean months away, let alone the eventual goal of America. But when he finally arrived, he would tell Liz and me over dinner or breakfast or a before-bedtime snack, there were unimagined riches to behold, and he'd begin the story of seeing an orange for the first time in his life. He would hold the fruit up for us to admire, looking at it as he must have years before, and I would imagine the taste of real orange juice emerging from succulent, dripping crescents outlined in delicate edible white thread, all meeting in his mouth for the very first time. The orange came to represent all the possibilities one might hope for even at the most hopeless times. The story about the orange became a tonic for our grief.

Even working all day in the cleaning store he could not shut off this basic quality of imagination. He made up stories about the people he met every single day as he stood hour after hour behind the counter receiving the soiled clothing of the neighborhood, giving out pink tickets in return, and all the while asking the customers questions about their lives, only his passionate nosiness nuzzling aside for a moment the unending boredom of his work.

When he spoke of work he certainly didn't mean what I do when I say *my work*. I work in a shop, Frank would say. I work for a wage. When he said shop instead of store, when he said wage instead of salary, I was drunk with the intoxicating aroma of his identity: a working man.

He elaborated on his stories as the years went by. The Lady with the Pinkish Hair. The Kid Who Always Took the Dime Off the Counter. The Young Woman with the Beautiful Sad Face. And these Stories of Ordinary Life, as he called them, took their place beside the older bedtime narratives about our *excursion*, that morning, to the playground where Liz learned to pump herself on a swing for the first time; or our ride in the Central Park carriage drawn by an old but still strong black horse; or our Sunday trip to the zoo where we stood holding his hands at the fenced border of the elephants' cage and watched in wonder as those powerful trunks threatened to ingest the whole world. He was weak, perhaps. Lucille has assured me of this for as long as I can remember. And she is right in a way. He was a man riddled with anxieties – as unable as I was to sleep through the night, beset by "the creeps" each Sunday afternoon when, I suppose, solitude and inactivity lifted habitual veils in his mind and dangerously unformed stories began to float and rise. He jerked me roughly onto sidewalks at the sound of a car screeching two blocks away. He gasped if I broke a dish, certain that something lethal was falling upon me. I never felt safe with Frank.

But if Violet's laughter introduced me to mystery, it was Frank's voice that taught me how stories might be a railing when the chasm seemed to fall too far and steep below. Of course, he would no more approve of these mirroring sequences of my life I call stories than he liked me constantly looking in the mirror. Nevertheless, he has bequeathed the obsession. When Ella-Fant finally becomes elephant, it is Frank's large hand I feel pressing around mine, the hardness of his thigh against my cheek.

8.

The last heat of the summer beats down onto concrete, Cape breezes and waters a memory without the respite I always imagine memory will provide. For days at a time, I venture out into the neighborhood only at dusk. Humidity gathers in sweat across my forehead, between my breasts and legs. Heat flashes across my neck and back. At times, I don't go out at all for days, turn on the air-conditioner, watch the white haze of sky through a locked window.

These are the unbordered weeks between the summer work of writing and family reunions, and the start of the school year. Dr. Daniels is away on vacation, so even sessions do not structure my days. Layers of experience settle into conventional sequence, then unsettle again. Time has lost its familiar linearity, which, after all, is comforting in a way – the past behind you, the future, with all its uncertainty, not yet here. Now, the frames are overlapping, colliding.

One night I wake from an instantly forgotten dream and once again I am behind the back door of Dr. Daniels' apartment in the tiny hallway, only this time all the feelings are stretched out, magnified, and the action is somewhat changed. The elevator operator leaves. There is no staircase. I am in a tiny place. I can't tell what is real, what might be a nightmare I am caught in. I ring the bell. Dr. Daniels comes to the door, but by then I am in a panic. He sees this and says, "Come in," but the sight of his home through the doorframe panics me even more. I cannot move. "Can you come with me if you close your eyes?" he asks, and I do. This time, he takes my hand and leads me to the familiar waiting room. I go quickly into the bathroom so I won't have to see the patient before me, her brightly colored outfit, her broad, attractive smile. Finally he calls my name, and I go into the office. Then he says, "Can you tell me what happened?"

I begin to relate the experience as I have just imagined it. I recount it stretched out and magnified to him. "What were you afraid of?" he asks. "That I would see your home, perhaps your wife, a daughter," I say. "And if you did?" he asks. I am clutching my dress the way I've seen dying people clutch the sheets around them, as if they are holding on to a cliff they are about to fall from. "I am left out," I say with an odd flatness, feeling blank, feeling a dangerous nothing. "This has been all my imagination. Our relationship, everything we've been through together. I am really only watching you through the frame of an archway. I haven't really felt your love. I have made it all up."

Lying in bed I think: In a few weeks I will actually be telling him about this experience of reliving the day in his hallway, of the stretched-out fantasy, and then I begin imagining myself a few weeks hence, recounting the story of this night. "The feelings which in reality passed through me in an instant became larger, slower, clearer," I will say. "You come through the door. I cannot walk without closing my eyes. You take my hand. I cannot sit in the waiting room for fear of seeing the beautiful woman in green. I go to the bathroom and finally you call my name. I go into your office and begin telling you the story. You say, as you did in the previous fantasy, and what if you did see my family?"

And I say again, only this time without the flatness, this time with intense emotion, "Then I imagined the feeling that you love me. It is a fantasy. A scene I concocted. I made it all up." And as I say those words I am once again clutching the material of my dress, thinking, this is what I have seen people do who are dying, clutching the sheets when they are slipping away.

As I lie in my bed thinking about my triple reality, the experience itself, then imagining it in the past, then in the future telling Dr. Daniels about it, I realize the reason I am clutching my dress, although I almost never wear a dress, I almost always wear pants, is that lying in bed I am clutching my nightgown, and I am sobbing so loud Luke begins to wake and reaches over to stroke my hair. I suck in the cries, pat his hand to reassure him and return it to his own pillow. What amazes me, and even gives me a certain strength, is that I am not crying in response to a sentimental fantasy, like some melodramatic depiction of love or loss in a bad movie when you know all along your tears are somehow fraudulent and manipulated, that you can turn it all to laughter in an instant. I am crying from the real feeling, the weird vertigo of fiction. It is all happening right now, not back then or out there but right here, right now. I have imagined a story in the past more clearly than it occurred in real time, and the imagining has led back to the real thing.

Perhaps it is meaningless or dangerous to try to comprehend in language where certain stories began, presumptuous or arrogant, like a woman writing a story of her own life over and over, as if anyone might be as interested as she is herself. Yet the compulsion outweighs any restraint or humility I possess. I remember her body when it was strong. She stands in the bathroom, naked, skin tan and glistening, just emerged from the water. As she pulls her towel back and forth across her back she looks at her face in the mirror over the sink and she is lost to me, staring into her own eyes with a disinterested focus, observing herself. My eyes drop down past her breasts and slightly rounded belly to the thick black hair between her slightly parted thighs. Then she notices me staring, she smiles and wraps her towel around her body, tucking it into a tight line above her breasts.

All through that summer after the first period of my work with Dr. Daniels, I dreamed repeatedly of a large, damp, moss-green triangle growing in the corner of a room. I am afraid to walk onto it with my bare feet, the dark water will seep up between my toes. I dreamed of a wild young girl who looks like Anna, or perhaps Lia, riding naked on a black horse down a foggy beach. I saw my mother's blood-red uterus, her sculpted, amputated thighs. *Knock, knock. Who's there? Ella. Ella who? Ella Fant.* A fantasy. A fiction. The incomprehensible truth. I dreamed of two riverboats, one much smaller than the other. I leap from the large one onto the small one, climb below where I discover long corridors, narrow hallways, crates and boxes full of provisions. I want to stay there in the dark interior of the small boat. This small boat is a lifeline, I think. A riverboat captain is using a large pole to keep the boat in place, to keep it from drifting away from the main craft. Back on deck, I breathe in the black night, smell the dank life in the dark gray river.

In imagery it all connects, I would think, waking from the haunting dreams. Like being lifted by a high-tide wave onto a sand bar, I was lifted for a precious passing moment out of a past half-forgotten yet perfectly preserved. I was unaware that this summer was itself a prelude to even more surprising fragments of overlapping histories that would never, in the end, be complete. I thought I saw all the contours of the narrative clearly in my mind, a series of images, a sense of distilled emotion. I had not yet come to appreciate the distortion, the fragmentation inherent in refractions of all kinds. I wondered only if I would be able to find the language, if it was possible to translate this story into words.

2. Down Here

1. The Horse and the Elephant

I felt pushed down into an old story, where I could be my truest self. At the same time I was a witness to my own journey, and I wondered if I could use this double vision to find a comparable double tone – not a split voice, one explicating the other; rather, an echo in a related but different language from the first. In the end, neither voice sufficed. Language itself came into question. In order to get to the bottom I had to abandon my faith in words.

How can we escape the narrative clichés of our own time? The story of childhood recreated in psychoanalysis. The compulsion of women writers before the end of the century to shed veils and give their stories to the world. How imagine a structure to hold a truth that seeps in and out of conventional time frames? There were times when I feared I would shit all over the chair. That's how fast things were pouring out of me. And no translation could match that dangerous ecstasy. Old embers smoked, ignited new fires, and I grew increasingly unsettled beneath a deceptively calm surface.

"What makes us go on?" (Virginia Woolf, in *Mrs. Dalloway*, a novel about suicide.)

"I confess I am broken only by the source of things." (Anne Sexton, in a poem called "Said the Poet to the Analyst.")

Two women writers, miners of the language of the interior, both using traditional forms to break out of traditional forms, differently attuned to confession (one tactful and elegant, the other primal and blunt.) Both compelled to refashion old stories as a way of staying alive, yet both suicides in the end. Bibliotherapy, Dr. Daniels called it once, a long time after the beginning. And it was true that I had always sought answers in books, other people's well-crafted language, as if I believed I could will or think my way into change if only I could find the perfect words.

Recollection of the First Period and How I Came to Be There:

It was a kind of laboratory. But no – that sounds too scientific. A retreat. A place where I was determined from the very first to reveal everything. Where there would be no wall between me and my most private, even shameful and complex thoughts. Yes – complex is the right word. I promised myself not to shrink from complexity. It was a kind of temple, if I can use that word without too much mystification. I was amazed, from the first weeks, even the very first few days, by the intensity between us. Inner channels were opening. Some delicate instrument was moving through layers of thick, dark mud, making a tunnel, or a road.

Journal entry: June, 1995: There is no difference any longer between my art and my life. Not in terms of this story about the three women. There has always been something with no name, something with no words, something needing, hungry, something horribly lonely, pulsing with desire and shame. I keep it down; I deny it is there; I know it is there but I lie about it – to others, occasionally to myself. It is too big. It is big. And repulsive.

Rats have always appeared suddenly, eating their way out of walls. I see them, make other things into them. Even going to the park is difficult. But I will not tell him this yet.

His room: decorated in dark pinks and light browns; the walls a kind of beige; a thick rose-colored rug – all the colors of flesh beneath the skin. I looked around the room until familiar shapes – a desk, a couch, a telephone – lost their realistic meaning and became just shape and color. (A large brown thing. A wide expanse of rose. A series of shapes in light and dark tan.) The way a representational portrait, of a woman let's say, might become increasingly abstract in a series of paintings over time. I felt the need to blur the actual functions of things and notice their color and shape in order to lessen somewhat the intensity of my instant connection to him, the fear that I . . . the desire to open myself completely.

Each night for hours, I wrote down every word that was said, every thought, then went to my computer and translated the chaos of that handwritten record into a somewhat more orderly form. Sometimes I'd recreate the same story in a vocabulary as close to the heart of the first as possible, yet somehow beautifully veiled, I thought, by well-chosen language, the deepest illusion of all. Soon a very different story began to emerge, though I knew it was really the same underneath; a translation, a fiction, as close to the real thing as a ritual changing of names.

In the first week of our work, I told him Violet's story, the same one I had told and retold a thousand times, now new and threatening again. The day I found her dead on the bathroom floor, blood streaming from pale wrists in two narrow, shining red lines. At first I could not comprehend what I was seeing, although I was nearly eight years old and perfectly capable of understanding the facts: A woman was lying on the white tiled bathroom floor. Her glazed eyes stared at the ceiling. Her wrists turned up revealed two deep cuts like cracks in the earth, and narrow rivers of beautiful crimson water moved over the small bony hills of pale gray wrists onto white tile. I saw it all, and thought – what is this? Why is she lying on the floor? Why did she spill that thick red paint on her arms? Why is her skin so white?

Later, Frank constructed the original fiction. She had an accident, he told me, staring at me with dazed, desperate eyes. When I was much older and reminded him of his deception, left uncorrected for years, he denied having told the lie. "Don't be ridiculous," he said. "Maybe we told you that at first, to lessen the shock of it. You and Liz were so little. But soon afterwards we told you the truth."

I love you all darlings, but I can't bear the emptiness any longer. There is nothing to live for, and I can't make you suffer any more. I have no more words.

When I recited Violet's last note to Dr. Daniels, he looked stricken. "Terrible words," he said. "Angry and tragic and terrible." "Desperate and tragic," I repeated. But angry? I didn't think angry was the right word.

Two women: One in the beige, pink interior, letting the story flow out like blood flowing from slit wrists. The other leans over a wooden table in a white walled room a mile away recording everything she said, then translating it into a different language. And the split works some kind of power that enables me to get at the deeper stories, the ones that have been winding around beneath ordinary consciousness since the beginning, presumably, when the actual beings of Violet and Frank met up with my temperament, my genes, my life.

I have no idea why these deeper stories have to be uncovered by me so obsessively, but it has always been this way. I don't always like it, but I have learned to accept it, if not before the day I was killed, then certainly after.

Not killed. I had obviously not been killed. I had almost been killed.

I had just passed my fiftieth year. Khoby was living thousands of miles away in Los Angeles where he was completing graduate work in a clinic for disturbed children, and I had never gotten used to it as everyone promised I would. Longing for him could overwhelm me at any time, unexpected and fierce, like a sudden hailstorm in the summer. Luke and I were in one of those periods common to long marriages when chronic distances patterned over decades descend like some elaborately sewn net and both people are caught under it, able to see but not touch each other. We shared our domestic chores as usual. We slept together every night, although we tended to seek our own sides of the bed. We communicated about necessary things – news of Khoby, our jobs, family events, planning a weekend dinner with friends. The distance was all the more marked by the continuation of daily intimacy. I felt as if I had donned a mask that looked exactly like my face but was not my face. Then I was denied an important promotion at the university, one I felt I deserved which would have given me a sense of accomplishment as well as a less demanding schedule. I was offered a variety of generic explanations. All promotions were to be frozen for some time. We were in an enrollment crisis, a state funding crisis, a global economic decline. I'd worked for years to earn a respected place in that institution, and even if I understood the fact that my experience was reflected in that of many others, I was devastated. I felt I hadn't been given my due.

One night, I found myself imagining suicide plans, a recurring fantasy of my youth I thought I had long since overcome, discarded as so much self-mystification from the time I became pregnant with Khoby and felt I had something to live for besides myself, which never seemed enough. I imagined taking enough pills the next morning after Luke went to work so that by the time he came home eight hours later there would be no question of a reversal. They would assume I'd had a heart attack. No one – certainly not Khoby – would suspect anything other than an accident. A heart attack at a young but not a tragic age. I realized I was having the fantasy as I became conscious of my increasingly specific elaborations. And suddenly a line from one of Anne Sexton's poems came into my head: "But suicides have a special language. / Like carpenters they want to know *which tools*. / They never ask, *Why build*." I got up and washed my face. Drank water. I had wrestled with a death wish through intense psychoanalysis in my late teens, again in my middle thirties when I approached and passed Violet's death age, determined not to leave Khoby the legacy she had left to me. Still, I thought, it was only a fantasy, and because I called it that, I permitted myself to return to it regularly, after a while almost daily for about a year, and began to emerge from it strangely refreshed. It was an indulgence, I thought, and the relief, like that of any indulgence, was a sense of escape from everything mundane and controlled to something exciting, essential. I elaborated details about which pills would serve, imagined the slow stopping of my heart, the relief of unconsciousness. I'd be lying in bed, not on the bathroom floor. There would be no ribbons of blood to distress anyone's dreams for years afterward. And I was over fifty, not thirty-eight, as Violet had been. No one would presume a connection. Besides I had no intention of making the fantasy real. It was a fantasy, not a plan.

Then one morning I was walking to the subway on my way to my class at the college downtown. I remember noticing the sky. It was striped with color, as if an artist, layering the space behind a landscape, had become so involved with the background it almost became foreground. Stripes ranging from pearly silver to nearly black, and in between each stripe a brilliant blue. As I stepped off the curb, I just missed getting hit by a taxi rounding the corner at high speed.

I saw him begin the turn. In a split second, I thought – I remembered this clearly later – that bastard – he's going to kill somebody one of these days. Years of crossing streets anxiously, always afraid of cars making those swift, unhesitating turns, of grabbing Khoby's hand when he was a child and I still felt able to protect him if I were sufficiently vigilant – all the fear and vigilance gathered into anger in that split second when the driver, speeding up the avenue, began to turn onto the street I was about to cross. I thought: I'd better back up, out of his way. But then I stepped off the curb, right into the path of the taxi.

It swerved just in time, and I was not hit. I missed getting killed by a hair, the woman who helped me up told me. I might have been knocked down by the edge of the car, or I might have fallen on my own. I was in the street on my knees, not exactly sure for a moment of where I was. I must have blacked out for a few seconds. The woman who reached me first put her arm around me. Then a young man leaned over and between the two strangers I got to my feet and hobbled back onto the sidewalk. "You missed getting killed by a hair," the woman said. And instantly I remembered that I'd seen the cab turning, knew the danger, thought about stepping back out of his way, and then stepped into the street.

The old story was against me, and I had known it, without admitting it, for nearly a year.

After that, I fell ill with a long flu or virus of some kind. Luke tended me maternally, worried about what he called my lethal distraction. I would be lying in bed, drifting in and out of sleep, and I would hear him tiptoe into the room. Opening my eyes a crack, I watched him as he lowered the shade to darken the room the way he knew I liked it, then looked at me with an expression of love and concern. I pretended to be asleep, but he always knew, and would ask if I wanted something to eat, straighten the sheet or make a joke about my lazy desire to be a child again. The net lifted to a place just above our heads. We didn't talk much, but we made love gently, frequently. When my fever was gone, I began a search for therapists and found Dr. Daniels.

Journal entry: September, 1995.

Everything I tell him seems to border on cliché, a story told so often and so melodramatically it threatens to lose its meaning – stories of childhood loss, of erotic passion, even of psychoanalysis itself. *Her mother commits suicide when she is eight years old. She adores her mother, but now she has a clearer path toward her father whom she also adores. And her mother has always been so moody, her dark despair ruining countless events; a party, looked forward to for weeks, destroyed; a summer vacation spoiled before they hit the road by her obsession with her own comfort, her intolerance of any inconvenience or demand.*

I described this reticence today in a clinical tone, as if I were delivering a paper at a conference, and he said, "Well, it is a cliché in a way, a generalized story told many times. But each time an individual discovers their own particular version of the story, it is as if the discovery is happening for the very first time." He paused. He looked at me with an intensity I have already come to depend on. His eyes seem to darken. He laces his fingers together and holds his hands remarkably still in front of his mouth, as if he is keeping himself from speaking precipitously, or he keeps his hands immobile on the arms of his chair, as if he too is on a dangerous ride. I imagine he thinks carefully about everything he says – a quality that provides me with a sense of safety and at the same time some of the worst frustration I have ever known. In his silence, the pit of my self-loathing threatens, the sudden fall where I doubt even – no most of all – the quality of my own voice.

One day I am drawn to an old weathered copy of HD's *Tribute to Freud*. Instantly, I find the page on which she speaks of religion, art and medicine being joined in ancient times.

A sudden recollection of a past reading, recovering the perfect words. A brief passage, but enough to remind me of a kind of faith in this direction I have chosen comprised of reading, writing and medicine of the spirit, a last ditch effort to save my life.

Of course, there is another thing about H.D. and her famous analyst that kept me reading her words. They became friends. He wrote to her. She visited him in London when he was an old man. She brought him gifts, which he accepted. And he reciprocated her feelings of admiration, of love.

During that first year I told him countless stories of my childhood, alternating with stories of my life with Luke, raising Khoby, about my writing and my teaching job, back and forth in time like a classically structured fiction. One day the word *refraction* kept coming into my mind. I looked it up in the *Columbia Encyclopedia* and found the definition: "A lens uses refraction to form an image of an object for many different purposes, such as magnification. A prism uses refraction to form a spectrum of colors from an incident beam of light. Refraction also plays an important role in the formation of mirage and other optical illusions." Then I began gathering all my emotions and images into a story about three women. At first I had only three lines: Melissa is big. Bettina is smart. Leza is wary of the task ahead. The three of them took shape in my notebook between sessions, and all along I knew there was something different about this story from anything I'd written before. I was risking something, exposing something, and could name neither the full danger, nor, for a long time, the revelation itself. I had the sense of a door of some kind to a future I could not yet describe. Or perhaps my so-called story (three fragments really) was a door to the past, because the night I finished the first draft I had the horse and the elephant dream.

I was standing at the edge of the ocean when waves began to grow large and powerful, as if the bottom were churning up sea storms, mud slides, and suddenly, as if out of nowhere, two large, magnificent animals emerged – a black horse galloping, his mane whipping backwards in the strong wind, and a grey elephant, his trunk lifting as he brayed loudly at the sky. I wasn't afraid. They were galloping but at the same time remaining in place, always at the edge of the water, never moving onto shore. I looked up at them and felt a surge of excitement, something like relief, but not of a serene kind, more as if I had come to a point of rest after an arduous climb, but the rest itself was ecstatic, orgasmic.

2. The Reading

When I brought Dr. Daniels the parts of my story, I hoped they would contain clues for him, and he would know that with his ardent listening and floating attention he had enabled me to write it in the first place. But he said no, he did not think it would be helpful for him to read it. He had no crystal ball as to its meaning. He was not a literary critic. And it was more important to our work (the use of the word "our" saved me from an awkwardness that could instantly envelop me in that room) that we talk about why I wanted him to read it, what that desire meant to me. We did talk about this off and on for months, but I remained so immensely disappointed that finally he suggested I might like to read it to him, out loud. Anything that happened between us in the room itself, he reasoned, could be useful to our work. Stung by his refusal and my inability to penetrate the walls of his consulting room into the spaces of his ordinary life, I was nevertheless excited by the suggestion of reading aloud to him. It was a fantasy of mine, in fact, one I'd called up several times, guiltily.

Even now, I look back on that experience as if I am myself and at the same time someone else. Not a fiction in the sense of a made up or distorted story; not a disguise, unconscious or intentional; neither a pathological nor an intentional creative split. Rather, I see someone come into clear focus in the distance – like a nearsighted person putting her glasses on.

As she walks to his office ten blocks downtown from her home, she feels the old, familiar ache in her calves, muscles tightening from walking too fast. She has plenty of time to get there, over twenty minutes to walk half a mile, yet she is certain she is late. Anxiety rises to the surface like silt, pollution kept at the bottom for years with now disintegrating nets. She remembers this particular ache in her calves, sharp and punishing, but she doesn't remember when it began. Once she is in her place in the tiny waiting room, the relief is palpable. She is there. Nothing can happen without her. Yet it is also true that she hates to wait, the waiting becomes intolerable as minutes pass, and by arriving too early, here, everywhere, she condemns herself to a life of waiting.

The night before, she'd had the dream about the little girl with the wild red hair again. She tells him the dream but does not try to interpret the images, and this gives her a certain satisfaction. "This time her hair is full of lice, and her mother is picking through the red curls, washing them with Quell, that special anti-lice shampoo." But she does tell him the dream characters come from a film she has recently seen. The little red-headed girl knows herself to be a writer, even at the age of ten. The mother looks like Anna, Judith's daughter, a beautiful, dark haired lesbian. For some reason this reminds her of Violet's drawings of women – always the same pretty, comic-book looking face, a three-quarter view, pointy chin, full wavy hair, a precise drawing Celia was allowed to color in, carefully, always staying within the lines.

She rereads Freud's *The Interpretation of Dreams*, recent articles on dream theory. She feels the vertigo of a new realization – there is no one interpretation, seamless and defining. Rather, images in dreams are thick and layered, sometimes not even explicit, like a piece of music, or a poem.

She does not keep conventional footnotes when she transcribes these excerpts from articles, essays, fiction, and pieces of poems into her journal. She has no intention of writing her own critique. Rather, she is experiencing a phenomenon she has begun to call associational continuity. She is so sure of its existence she tells her students about it when they embark on a fiction project strongly rooted in their own life experience. You will begin to see connections to the story everywhere, she tells them. You will find things, or see things in what you read that fit into the pattern of your work. Your mind will collect things for you, she tells them. And she requires them to write it all down. She is trying in every possible way to keep a record, to face up to the complexity of matters, not to shy away.

She is in her chair in the room of interior flesh tones facing Dr. Daniels. Behind him, large windows look out on a park, then a lake, a clear view of the sky – a rare privilege in the city. She puts on her glasses and begins to read, aware as she speaks the topmost story shaped into language, that she is telling many different stories, especially here, in this place, and that the others are layered closely into this top story, like neatly pressed and folded clothes.

"Refraction," she says, then takes off her glasses to repeat – "Remember, this is only the beginning, a fragment . . . The first part is spoken by Bettina, a law professor whose sister, Melissa, has been hospitalized for many years with an unnamed disease of the mind, probably some form of schizophrenia. Bettina writes to their old friend, Leza, asking her for a favor."

He smiles, opens his hands, waiting for her to begin. And so she does.

"Dear Leza, Recently, I discovered the enclosed pages in one of the boxes I took home after Melissa was hospitalized and would never, I knew, return home. In all these years I thought I'd gone through all her things, but I was cleaning out the closet in Tony's old room and I found all this on the shelf. Maybe I had conveniently forgotten they were there. Naturally I feel quite guilty about the memory lapse – but what can I say? It has always been difficult having a sister whom so many people thought brilliant, and I suppose I did too, but who always needed me to take care of her in every way. And then there must have been all the classic sibling passions, envy, rage, all mixed in with a kind of maternal love, all of it made disastrous by our mother's death. It's long over with now, of course. I am left only with missing her. I find myself talking to her, sometimes out loud, as if she can hear. But I'm getting away from the reason for my letter. I found these notebooks, Leza, and I hope, since you are a writer, you can make some sense of them, edit them, decide if we should try to do anything more, since she'd begun publishing her work before she became ill. It could all be called a novel, I suppose, but like all the writing she did before that final break, it kind of floats around. A meditation, I thought as I leafed through the pages before packing it up to send to you, intruding, I know, on your month of solitude. Sometimes I think back to those days so many years ago, when we all first met. You were a very different person then, Leza, wracked with self-doubt and broken confidence.

Melissa had plenty of doubt of her own, as we both know, but also a – well, an arrogance, or strange pride, was how I always thought of it, and I think you would agree. First the sense of her own powers. Then the despair. Back and forth for as long as I can remember. And I – well, I was always after understanding, some place outside of emotion where I could figure things out. I didn't want to be destroyed by grief, eaten up by longing until, like Melissa and my mother I start force feeding or feeding on myself. My mother was shrunken to nothing when she died, refused food for weeks. I rarely saw her in those last months of her life, but I remember clearly the frail body, legs so thin they couldn't hold her upright. Face so small she looked like she'd become a child again. So she found a way to kill herself in the end. No one could have stopped her, I am told, though you and I, Leza, certainly stopped Melissa, admittedly for a price. But the point is – I don't want to go over these notebooks myself, and so I am imposing on you to try to get it all straightened out, if that is possible at all. Please, Leza, for friendship's sake, see what you can do. As for me, I don't enjoy being drawn into that famous murky borderland between genres that scholars and artists find so fascinating in recent years. I don't like authors intruding themselves into stories meant to be fiction. And when I read essays about texts or experience I am looking for clarity more than "interrogation." Perhaps I am avoiding certain complexities as you have always thought, and now I hear the same thing from Tony, my own son. Well, nephew really, but you know, after all these years perhaps he is my son more than Melissa's. I leave the mistake in hoping to intrigue you. You like the confusion these layers suggest whereas I – well, I am a woman who likes to feel in control. That is how I survive. Even that word – layers – reminds me of her and makes me cringe. I remember her saying to me during one of her break-downs – her tone that mix of pride and confession I never liked – I see the world in layers and I hear a thousand voices, each with a different point of view. Do you still think that was her strength, Leza, her gift? Or have you come around to the view that it was the madness that destroyed her in the end?"

As Celia reads, her voice becomes increasingly controlled and resonant, as if she is Bettina, speaking in Bettina's voice. This part is familiar. She has experienced the sudden change into a stronger voice at many public readings. But there is something else, something much more surprising; her words are becoming her body, and it is shapely; they are making her face beautiful, and she is proud. When she stops reading the first time, she begins to remember all the stories about horses and elephants – the black stallion, Black Beauty, the old, nearly dead horse in Central Park, the powerful creature in the zoo with the long gray trunk, the knock-knock joke. The three women in her story are real to her. She can see them – Bettina, Melissa, Leza. But like the triple reflection in Violet's mirror, she knows they are all herself.

During the first few times she reads the unconnected parts of Bettina's narrative, she pauses between sections. She is silent and looks away. "Where did you go?" he asks. "What came to mind?" And she has no choice, considering her vow, but to say it. She whispers, "I feel proud – as though I am loved." Dr. Daniels stares at her and nods. Then she feels ashamed. She looks behind him, at the trees, the lake, the sky. "Now I feel ashamed," she says. "I must have just made up that feeling because I wanted it so much, and when she says this, looks down, shoves her work back into her purse, she breathes more easily, a threat recedes. Here she is, a woman over fifty who teaches students, writes books, who has raised a son, who is a listener and support to her friends and here she is, a child again. Dr. Daniels tells her many stories of children he has treated. The little boy caught in the middle of a custody battle whose mother suddenly died in a car accident. The little girl who invited him to her birthday party and instructed him to bring his toys.

It is obvious he loves children. Perhaps that is why then.

That night, and each time after she reads, she will dream of shit – overflowing toilets in public places, pouring out of rooms, sinks, herself. Sometimes the bathrooms are beautiful, shining crystalline enclosures of white tile and pale green glass. Sometimes they are dark and wooden, the smell of shit seeping from the walls, like in an old outhouse.

The week before she had attended a concert where her friend was playing his saxophone, then speaking the songs he wrote as poems, a one-man musical duet. He always seems dangerously exposed when he performs, and, sitting in the audience, she is nervous at first. But very soon she relaxes because as soon as he begins to play or speak, she remembers his confidence, his excellence – the words precise, the notes clear, exposure rendered into careful, blissful purity through his art. His work is about longing, anger, a roaring hunger for life, the weird power of sex, the mystery of love kept still for a moment, incomprehensible but sensual and sweet. She feels the poetry of his words, the music fills her body, and she wonders about cellular biology, the microscopic nuclei of her cells. Do they shift beneficially when she is so "moved"? Do their delicate, mobile outlines liquefy into more graceful shapes? Dr. Daniels smiles when she wonders this after she tells him about the concert. His face looks flushed. When she is back out in the street, she feels uncomfortable, as if she is a child who has behaved very badly.

At night, she rereads her highly dressed yet naked words and the words are too much, too intense for any ordinary listener. He won't be able to breathe, she thinks. He will have to ask me to leave while he recovers. I will drive him away. She dreams of three women again and again, and they become more familiar. "There is my niece, Lia, who is not quite my daughter. My friend Judith, who is not quite my sister. And someone named Sonia – who is not quite myself."

During the weeks she is reading aloud, her obsession with time begins to shift somewhat. She notices it because she leaves later than usual for her sessions. When she walks, she is aware of the absence of the pain in her calves. "I have as much time as I need," she tells him. "I am in the right place at the right time. I am not keeping a vigil."

"What's the vigil?" he asks, fully attentive, like a child eager to hear the rest of the story.

She looks behind him, out the window at the lake.

"I am always visiting my Aunt Lucille." Celia hears a slight change in her tone, her slower, deeper voice, tense and uncertain. "She lives on 16th Street. I walk the six blocks from my home on 10th Street several times a week so I can play with my older cousin, Beth, Lucille's daughter, or my friend Judith, who lives across the hall, and their slightly wild and funny younger brothers. Sometimes Liz comes with me. I have to hold her hand the whole way, especially crossing 14th Street, a major thoroughfare. Sometimes I go alone. Either way, at some point in the visit, Lucille is sure to take me aside, sometimes right in Liz's hearing, and tell me I am the best one of all. I was Violet's favorite daughter, and now I am *her* favorite niece. If I point nervously to Liz, or take her hand while she stands shifting uncomfortably in her polished, white saddle shoes in the doorway, Lucille says, Oh, don't worry about her, darling. She's too young to understand. She puts an arm around me and laughs. She croons into my ear. Sometimes I ask her directly if my Daddy loves me, partly because I need to know, and partly because she's told me before he loves Liz the best and this helps to dry up the dirty pool of guilt and shame Lucille is shoving me into. Oh, *Frank*, she would be sure to say sarcastically, as if his name itself called up images of inadequacy, a foolish, pathetic sound. He doesn't know what to do with you. That's why your mother always made me promise to take care of you if anything happened to her, and I remembered it when she died."

Celia switches back to her ordinary voice. "I suppose I liked being the prettiest, the best in a way, and when Liz ran out of the room, it was her I got angry at." She looks directly at Dr. Daniels, confessing what retelling the story has made her see. "But I felt exposed too — for being conceited, for being the best."

"You remind me of little girls complaining about their friends," says the father of three grown daughters, chuckling at his own memory and giving an ordinary caste to hers. "Oh, she's so conceited, I always used to hear them say."

"Conceited," Celia says, forcing a smile. Conceited Celia. Full of herself. Then she completes the story. "It's when I walk home from Aunt Lucille's that the pain in my calves begins. I don't run, but I walk very fast. My feet slam hard onto the sidewalk. If Liz is with me, I have to drag her along, and if I am alone I have to drag myself. For all the six blocks, I am picturing Violet lying on the bathroom floor, the blood rivers are staining the white tile. If I walk fast enough she may still be there, although I know perfectly well over a year has gone by since her death. If I walk even faster I may get there in time."

"In time for what?" he asks, wanting the actual words for some annoying reason, because it seems perfectly clear.

"In time to save her." She pauses. She lets her breath go.

"Your mother," he says, and she is confused for a moment, as if he has uttered a non sequitur.

"Violet."

"You always call her Violet, never Mother."

She keeps her eye on her watch. She had stopped her reading in time to talk about it before she had to leave, but instead she has talked about all these other things, and now the words she'd hoped would come to her in perfect specificity are completely elusive. She remembers only how happy she'd felt reading before, how strong. He stares at her. She looks down. This hunger has no words. Lia is kissing Liz's eyelids. A man is speaking passionate love to a woman. Obscene words. Swelling, liquefying words.

She and Luke are visiting friends in the country. The house is small, and so is the bed, a double bed, not the queen size they have at home. Trees surround the house and the wind moves the leaves filling the room with a wonderful wind sound. The friends and the friends' parents sleep in rooms right next to them and right across the tiny hall. Nevertheless, they begin making love in the cool, gray dark. For the first time in many years she feels no resistance, only the desire to be as open as she can be. She moves slowly, luxuriously, around him, over him, lying on her back on top of him, curved away from him while he penetrates her, then on her back spread out wider than the world. She keeps her mouth closed so no sounds will come out and he is never a noisy lover, but she hears the old bed creak and thinks they might be heard. No matter, she can't stop this, her need to be loved is gigantic, her need to love devouring. She is three women having sex. The one in bed with him, opening and closing, moving and then held still as light. The one in the flesh-colored room speaking beautifully shaped words. And the third one who is perfectly alone with this rapturous self-losing sex that would be threatening in its intensity if the man leaning over her now were not Luke, the one she trusts above all others, Khoby's father, at other more ordinary times an ordinary man.

The next time she reads aloud, it is a portion of the section about Melissa, the most difficult voice to reveal to a listener. She is ashamed of the rage she has put into Melissa's voice. Still, she begins:

Melissa: For almost as long as I can remember I've had the desire to kill myself. It began when I was a child of six and my mother was suddenly, mysteriously ill. One day she seemed fine — her normal, volatile, beautiful difficult self. The next day she took to her bed, lay in the dark, could not speak to us, seemed at times hardly to remember who we were. Weeks passed and she got worse and worse. The room remained dark. The sheets, even when my aunt began coming over daily to attend to things, smelled musty. Then my mother would sit in a chair in the corner, staring into space, watching my aunt sweep, air things out, change sheets. There would be a moment (I watched it, sniffed it, saw a certain light pass through the room as I stood in the doorway) when the sheets smelled fresh and inviting, yet the room still reeked. And so I came to know it was not the sheet that smelled, but my mother. Nearly six months passed like this I think – though it may have been three, or twelve. Past time distorts, and my aunt and my father rarely told the truth about anything. They were liars; let's use the harsh, honest word. During that time I became fat for the first time. Before that I had been an agile, lanky child. But the smell was nauseating, and nothing alleviated the sickening feeling but food. It was a sort of hunger I have felt again only in the first trimester of pregnancy. I gained over twenty pounds in three months. I wasn't even hungry, not that I was aware of. But I was so nauseous and only food could make the sour rumbling in my stomach settle down.

And then one day she was gone. To a nice hospital for a rest, my aunt and father said, my father's misery obvious in his drawn face and vacant eyes. She never returned. We were never taken to visit her – of course not, in reality she was dead – and much later, when I was eighteen, we were informed that she had died. During all those years – twelve of them – I worked on pictures of her, some on drawing pads with pens and pencils and paints, some inside my head. After I completed a drawing I'd place it in a frame my mother had given me and hang it on my wall. There it would remain until I was moved to draw a new picture, the new one more skillful as my capacity for realistic accuracy in drawing grew, and also closer emotionally to my feelings somehow. Each time I replaced the old drawing in the frame with a new one, I thought I'd captured something essential at last. I kept all the versions in a large, brown oak tag envelope my mother had given me so that now I can take them all out, a linear record of my ever-elaborated memory.

At first I begged my aunt and my father to allow us – I always managed to enlist Bettina in my pleas – to visit her. But after years of their refusals (or perhaps months) I finally gave up. And yet it was difficult knowing she existed somewhere, that if I could convince them to allow me to go to her I'd be able to touch her actual body, hear her actual voice, even smell her. I'd have been happy for the dank rotten smell of unwashed flesh now, anything better than this absence I've carried around with me all my life, unfillable with food, or sex, or even love. The only time the emptiness was filled was when the baby was inside of me, and eventually, well, of course I had to let him go. Now, I try to understand their fears – my mother was unreachable, lost in her own world, either silent for months at a time or screaming, terrified and unintelligible until some primitive tranquilizer finally worked. Still, I think they were wrong. We should have been allowed to visit her – to see and touch and smell her. Perhaps our voices, I have sometimes thought, might have reached her in there, might have called her back to us.

But I'm getting confused, back in my child's mind, thinking she was alive all that time. I am writing this story as if she were alive all that time, as if my fantasy and the lies were the truth. But she was dead. Through all the years I thought if I drew the right picture I could bring her back home, through all the years there was nothing I could do.

After about a year I stopped drawing and began the inside stories. I'd picture her, imagine reunions, or we'd be back in the past, the two of us tucked under a scratchy blanket in an old-fashioned carriage pulled by two sleek black horses. Sometimes I even risked actual memory – the dark room with its nauseating smell, her face, blank or worse, ugly, my aunt snapping the white sheets in the air, letting them float down onto the mattress, then smoothing the sides, tucking in corners, fluffing pillows while my mother sat in the corner, cruel and mocking – as if my aunt were involved in something ludicrous beyond description.

When the actual memory came I'd reach back for one of my constructed stories to escape my anger. It would be a cool sunny day, or a dark stormy night, but in either case I would be finding her, helping her escape, saving her. Only if my imagination failed to take hold and the story slipped out of focus, would I settle for – risk – actual memory. Anything better than nothing. The awful emptiness and whatever else was down there with it inside of me was the place where I lost her forever."

Celia pauses, removes her glasses. Dr. Daniels is looking at her with an intensity that causes her to begin to sweat. The heat is unbearable, and she has to stop to ask him to open a window. But the slight breeze does nothing to relieve the burning across her shoulders, neck, breasts and cheeks. She concentrates on her associations and this combination – concentration and heat – reminds her of something, a long ago time when she is a young child, perhaps five or six at the oldest, Liz a toddler of two or three. Violet is sitting nearby in the sun, vibrant and gay that summer. They are in a country house for a month in Rye Beach, New York, and Celia is sitting under a large tree with her older friend Lisa who is teaching her how to sift sand. There are elaborate collections of strainers in a neat line before them, and each child has two large pails. They dig up the dirt from under the tree, pour it through the strainers into the pails, then repeat the process over and over until the dirt pours through easily, almost like water, somehow solid and liquid at once. They remain engaged in this for hours until the silky sand is absolutely pure, devoid of pebbles, twigs or leaves. Violet lifts her eyes from her book every so often to watch them, and when the sand is sifted completely, and there is nothing left in the strainers, they get up, shake off the dirt from their shorts and shirts, and rush to Violet's chair to show her what they have made. She is wearing sunglasses, a wide-brimmed hat. She opens her arms wide.

For several sessions in a row Celia reads and sweats. Her face and neck are flushed, her blouse and hair damp, and she is certain he can see all this. Once she has to ask him to turn on the air-conditioner. It embarrasses her, the vigorous sweating, but she keeps reading. She knows she can't shrink from this desire. She will feel the heat when she feels the heat. She will let the walls crumble to dust, sift to liquid sand. She will let the liquid seep and flow.

She dreams she is in a deep cave. Its colors are pink, brown, a pearly salmon lacing through a dark rose. There is a staircase at the end of the cave-room going up to some higher surface. Three little girls are playing with round wooden dolls in the center of the cave and they are making a mess. It's your room, her niece Lia tells her, tell them to get out if you want to. She does, and the girls are gone, leaving her to line the dolls up neatly at the foot of the staircase, to feel the pleasure of being alone in the room.

When she leaves Dr. Daniels' room, she enters a narrow hallway, at the end of which is another door opening into the waiting room in the ordinary world. When she comes into his room from the ordinary world, she closes the first door behind her, walks back down the narrow hallway, closes the inner door and she is in the large interior place the color of flesh beneath the skin. She always wants to be inside, right here with him, the only one. She remembers the feeling of Khoby inside her, the heavy shifting and rolling as he grew too large to fill the space. She hated the fatness, the nausea, the heat of pregnancy, but she loved the shifting and rolling, the feeling that she was filled up with something. She remembers a feeling when she was pregnant, or the absence of a feeling: the nagging threat of the desire to die which had come and gone for as long as she can remember. She couldn't wait to give birth those last weeks, to have it over with, the baby born, her body her own again. But she didn't want to lose it, to let it go and feel the emptiness again. Liz was only four when Violet died, but Celia remembers vaguely the sound of Violet screaming and crying behind a locked door – *I can't take it – the two of them – it's too much for me.* Frank hustling them into their room at the other end of the apartment. Liz was too much for her, she couldn't take it any more. But Celia had been too much too, before Liz was born. Celia moves in and out of all the overlapping stories, trying not to worry about shape and design. "It was terribly hard giving birth," she says, surprised that she is saying this to a man she has known only a little more than a year. He might infer some psychological resistance to her "femaleness." She has fought against such psychological reductionism all her adult life, written articles, books. "It took twenty-four hours," she says. And then, harshly, "A little longer and they would have had to cut him out of me the doctor said."

She wants to be Liz, her thighs twisted over and under Lia's thighs. She wants to be Lia inside of Liz. She wants Lia inside herself. She wants to be back inside Violet before all the losing, the blood rivers, the accident that was not meant to happen. She wants to be inside Dr. Daniels and not just inside his flesh-colored room. She wants him inside herself. But when she is with Luke that night, even when he is inside her, she looks away, toward the sheer white curtain blowing slightly from the lovely breeze, and the words that come into her mind are, I am inside myself and that is the only thing that is only me. She is not with Luke, she supposes, in a way some might consider erotic or healthy. But he enables her tonight to be full of herself, and so she is one with him. She is the corridor, dark and still and dry, a quiet peaceful place and she has left a noisy mess behind.

She is dreaming of open exposed spaces, dangerous ledges surrounded by air. Then she is sucked into a dark interior, cloistered gardens, a cool, damp cave filled with furniture and flowers. Or she is outside the dark gardens and she wants to get in. When the three women come back into her dreams, there is Sonia again. She understands the almost-sister when she thinks of Judith and how like sisters they are. She understands the almost-daughter. "You are almost like my daughter," Lucille used to say to her over and over, in and out of Liz's hearing. But who is this Sonia, the least recognized yet somehow most familiar woman of her dreams?

"Maybe I was almost Frank's daughter," she says out loud to Dr. Daniels. What does she mean by that? That Liz was the real daughter?

"Or did you ever think he wanted a son?" he asks.

Celia laughs at this thought, but then it takes hold. She recalls Frank's joy when Khoby was born, the first time he diapered him shouting, *a penis, a real penis!* Celia and Luke had looked at each other rolling their eyes. Dad! Celia had screamed, alarmed and discomforted by his passionate, private laughter. She shoots back farther in time. "Maybe I thought so," she says. "I was certainly trying to be his heir, do the things he did well, reading, writing, even talking. I wanted him to love me the way he loved Lizzie, but I would take what I could get. I remember wanting him to think I was smart, to praise my words, my school work, the good marks I sometimes got on tests." She hears her voice change suddenly, a reading tone, as though she'd been reading Bettina's section to him out loud. Part of her has always known about wanting to be the perfect daughter/son. So why does she feel as if she's just found it out? Then she feels weary. "When I was a child I had a recurring hallucination. I called it one of 'the feelings.' My arms were so heavy I couldn't lift them. They were exhausted from carrying heavy suitcases for too long." She has the feeling of heavy suitcases in her arms right now.

"You were carrying an impossible burden," he says, amazement opening his eyes wide.

"I can hardly hold my head up," she says, and when she leaves she drags her feet, her shoulders feel round.

The next week she has to miss a session because she and Luke are going to California, to Liz's house, for a birthday celebration. Khoby, in New York for a conference, returns with them to the west coast. In the airport before the flight, she finds her carry-on bag is too heavy, and she asks Khoby to carry it for her. He rolls his eyes, sighs heavily, mutters something about her carrying it herself. She is hurt, angry, and grabs it away from him. Now he feels guilty, as does Luke. They both try to take it from her, but she snarls at them to leave her alone. She will manage on her own. When they arrive in San Francisco, there are crowds everywhere because of reconstruction in the airport. There are long lines for car rentals, and while Luke stands at the Avis counter for what seems like an hour to her but is in reality only about ten minutes, she drags her satchel across the floor. Khoby comes over to lift it for her but even now, seven hours later, she feels the rage, hot and smoldering. When they finally get into the privacy of the car, it ignites. She screams at her grownup son as she used to do at the worst times when he was a child, when she felt she would never be equal to him, his iron will in a small body too formidable for her to bend, that she would never be able to control him, protect him, bring some order to the endless demanding details of motherhood. Now she screams at him so loudly, so high, she loses control of her own voice. Her eyes tear. Her words make no sense. She cannot stop. Luke drives on grimly while she screams. Khoby keeps his eyes on the road, and when she finally pauses, he turns around to her and, with real contempt, he says, "Are you finished now?" Then he begins to analyze with careful moderation and unforgiving accuracy all the elements of her difficult personality that have caused this uproar and, throughout his childhood, so much pain. She listens, as if she is the child. She is contrite. She is genuinely sorry. She agrees with everything he says, and she apologizes in a hoarse voice. She stares out the window for the entire, traffic-laden hour it takes them to drive across the bay.

For weeks afterward, her arms ache, her breasts feel heavy, she has chronic indigestion, her body the mirror of her feelings as surely as the mirror in her room reflects the features on her face. She is only shapely and beautiful when her mouth moves the words from the page into the room. She hears them, sees them move into him, out again, back to her page.

She is glad she is almost done reading, only a few more pages to go. Each time she puts down her work, takes off her glasses, she has to talk about her love, describe the moments when she feels loved in return. Or the other moments, like today, when his silence makes her feel ashamed, certain her story means nothing to anyone but herself, not even to Dr. Daniels, who has been shown all the layers underneath the words. He says nothing, and when she complains of this he says, "You can read my face. You can trust your sense of things." And, "We must be very careful. This is your work, your soul." She likes his use of the religious word, faith and doubt being the emotional trajectory her writing hurtles through with each new project, sometimes each new page. When she leaves the office she has to check the mirror in the hallway near the elevator to make certain her face is acceptable, her hair combed. She looks in, her face close to the glass, afraid she'll see a monster who talks so nakedly of desire and shame. An hour ago, her body felt ordinary when she walked down the street in her new jeans, her loose-fitting brown cotton jacket, the pages to be read folded into her leather shoulder bag. Now, she is enormous, clumsy, her contours are gone, she is fat. She trips, nearly falling off the curb and a young woman reaches out for her.

"I dream I am in a bank on the corner of Greenwich Avenue, where Frank's small account remained after his death. A couple of hundred dollars left to me, the same for Liz, and a few hundred to be split among his 'future grandchildren.' A woman is in a back room where she is taking care of a one armed baby boy. I did not have time to dress, because someone moved all the furniture in my house, nothing was where it was supposed to be, so I am wearing my favorite nightgown, it's both flowing and comfortable, perfectly shaped. It reaches well below my knees, and it is covered with shit."

This is the place where all the bad feelings surface right after the good ones. First the worthiness and beauty, then the shit and shame. They are mind feelings, of being stupid when she is really so smart, and they are body feelings, of being disgusting even though she is really beautiful. Or the opposites: smart when she is really stupid, beautiful when she is really disgusting. They are about being too much, out of control, devouring, enraged.

Let the hungry woman in, he says. What does she want? He thinks he's so brave. He can have no idea of the cave of her hunger and the upside-down rats hanging from the ceiling.

Her hunger right this minute is to know where he is going for a long weekend necessitating a change in her regular session. Dutifully, she expresses every feeling she can find about being abandoned, angry, confused, jealous of his wife, but also excited by what seems the great mystery of his sudden disappearance. She thinks he must be going someplace exotic and romantic. Like where? he asks. Paris, she says, and then tells him about Violet's three trips to Paris, one before Liz was born and two soon after. "I have a photograph," she says, "of Violet in a large square, wearing a fur coat and a black velvet hat. And I have one packet of letters and cards she wrote to us. It was 1948, before easy jet plane travel, so when she left, it was always on a huge ocean liner. My father would take me to the docks to say goodbye. He would hold me up in his arms, Liz too I think when she was two or three, and we would shout goodbye Mommy into the wind. Weeks later, sometimes a whole month, when she returned, we would go back to the dock and meet the boat. Once I was wearing new white boots even though it wasn't raining that day. I shouted to her as she stood on deck – Mommy, look at my new white boots! I remember the sound of my laughter; I can almost hear it in my ear, in the room right now. It was a bit crazed, the kind of laugh that can become a cry of pain in an instant, a crazy laugh. Once I saw a little girl laugh that way when she was really angry with her baby brother. Her mother was holding the little girl in her arms and suddenly her laugh became a bite. She bit her mother on the cheek so the teeth marks showed. Her mother put her down, furious of course, actually crying from the pain, and the daughter was crying too, obviously frightened, shouting, I did a bad thing, I did a bad thing, as if the person who did the bad thing were separate from herself."

He stares at her in a way that makes her worry she has said more than she knows. He says, "To Montauk, for a long weekend, a change of pace. Nothing so romantic as Paris I'm afraid."

From the two-hundred-year-old Montauk lighthouse at the eastern edge of Long Island you can look out over the Atlantic curving toward the beach towns and the highway that leads into the city. Across the road from the inns and motels, which are affordable off season, beyond a thick layer of shrub, the ocean stretches. Some years before, she had gone there with her younger friend Leah, who had once been her student. Something like a daughter to Celia, at other times a mother in her dreams, dark, beautiful and competent, Leah earned her living as a bookkeeper and one April, right after income tax time, taught Celia how to keep track of her finances. She bought Celia a green book with lines and columns for records of bills and debts. "It's just a matter of putting it in order, writing things down," she said. "Now what bills do you pay each month?" To Celia, whose finances at that time were chaotic, it seemed a startlingly simple yet extraordinary piece of magic. She listed for her friend all the credit-card debts, tuition bills for Khoby's school, unpaid doctors' bills, even rent and phone. "Just keep listing them each month," Leah said. "See – you list the creditors here, the payment here," and she drew her pencil swiftly across the horizontal green line and wrote in neat script: paid —, balance —. You bring it all under control and soon the numbers start decreasing, you'll see. It works." They laughed and drank cold white wine on Celia's terrace, where flowers and herbs grew so thickly the pots were mostly hidden, making it look like a real garden. They lifted toasts to each other, to Celia, just past Violet's death age and still alive, to bringing her finances under control, and to Leah, just out of a painful love affair with an abusive and dependent man who kept threatening suicide.

Years later, when Leah was close to Violet's death age herself, and Celia was closing in on fifty, during a spring break from the college where they both taught writing and literature, Celia rented a small motel suite right across from the ocean at Montauk and invited Leah to come with her – five days near the water to write, read, and walk the beach. It was cold, the sky a dense ice blue. They began their walks in turtlenecks and down jackets, heavy socks rolling out of the tops of hiking boots. But each afternoon the sun would break through, and they would lie down on the cold sand, use their down for pillows, roll up their flannel sleeves, open their top buttons, take off the boots and socks and expose some of their shared Mediterranean olive skin to the sun. Both uttered cries of pleasure as the heat caressed their bodies. When the clouds returned and they began walking again, boots and coats on feet and backs again, they talked of what they had written that morning and would read aloud to each other over wine when the sun went down. In the evening, they cooked a simple meal then curled up on the nubby green couch and began to read. Celia was as full as if she had already eaten, yet when dinner came she devoured it, delighted to have these long uninterrupted days with her beautiful, beloved friend with her straight, thick black hair and dark, candid eyes, who had been her student and babysitter when Khoby was small, who considered her a mentor, a great teacher, she often said; who had now become a writer herself. For five days they walked and read, drank wine and, once, took the car to nearby East Hampton with its upscale restaurants and famous, elegant beach. On that cold March Tuesday, Celia and Leah felt it deserved its reputation for beauty; it was broad and empty, the sand white and shell laden. Their own stretch of sand outside the little motel was narrow compared to this, wild and edged with thick grasses and vines through which tiny dirt paths wound and you had to be extremely careful of the poison ivy. Yet they preferred their unkempt beach at the tip of the island where they wore the same flannel shirt day after day and wrote rough drafts.

Some years later, Leah moved to Israel with her husband and baby daughter. For months after she left, Celia was bereft, knowing no one could replace Leah, but she knew her friend was better off in the hot desert land of her birth than in the city she had come to hate so much her body reacted with viruses and allergies all winter long. Celia wrote long narratives in her journal in which she analyzed all her feelings of anger and abandonment, interposing memories of Violet into more recent stories of her friendship with Leah. She wrote and wrote until she felt a sensation of emptiness, or peace, or was merely exhausted in a way she hoped might mean she was cleansed.

Several weeks after Dr. Daniels' extended weekend, Luke and Celia were going to Montauk themselves for a weekend to attend the wedding of a friend's daughter. The motel was a good deal fancier than the one she'd stayed in with Leah – a large semi-circle of neat brick houses with terraces, slanted wooden roofs, kitchenettes and queen size beds. In their rented Toyota, they followed a line of cars down the ocean road toward a wider boulevard and eventually came to a small white church.

The slender bride wore a satin gown that hugged her narrow hips and thighs, then flowed out from her knees in a long lacy train behind her. Her veil, pulled over her face to remind everyone of her purity, the sacred privacy of the place her husband, only he, he alone, would soon penetrate, was kept on her blond head with a crown of white lilies outlined by a few delicate green leaves and stems. When she walked down the aisle to meet the groom, everyone sighed, including Celia who, since she was Jewish, always felt a bit odd in church though she had visited dozens of churches of course – for funerals and weddings, for concerts and lectures, to view works of art and to view the architecture itself. In one great cathedral near her home, Celia had spent countless hours writing in a cool and quiet alcove, escaped there on hot summer days when Khoby was in summer day camp in the city and she had a break from teaching until the fall. Still, when she attended a Christian religious ceremony, and inevitably was asked to bow her head in prayer, and inevitably could not, she felt visibly Jewish, as if everyone could see, and she wanted them to, wanted them to know. Before the vows were taken, the priest took the opportunity to speak out against abortion, homosexuality and premarital sex, to extol sexual faithfulness, not merely as a moral choice but as a reflection of the very nature of love itself. Celia sneered, thinking about reasons for taboos. Luke smiled philosophically – well, that's what people are like – answering his wife with a glance. At the banquet and party, Celia drank a lot of wine, imagining herself reading to Dr. Daniels, sweating and breathless, beautiful and ugly, satiated and then ravenous again. She danced with Luke, with her friend's husband, with the groom, with Khoby, with her friend's son. She was a good dancer. The young people were surprised, since they thought of her as physically shy. She danced to work off the many glasses of wine, the heat of the reading of her beautiful ugly words, the thought that somewhere on the eastern edge of Long Island, Dr. Daniels might be walking the beaches she had once walked with Leah, or sitting on his deck looking out to sea. Then the fast music stopped, and someone announced the bride and groom would have their wedding dance. A circle was formed around them. White satin and lace rustled enticingly, like uncut, wild ocean grass. Even the veil was set aside somewhere, leaving only the pagan crown of flowers and pale green leaves holding the long silken hair in place. The bride came into her husband's arms and the music began. Celia thought of Violet, how she might have danced in Frank's arms once, yet how miserably unhappy she had become; of a story she recalled Lucille telling her after Frank died – she would have to ask her about it the next time she visited her in her lonely apartment on 16th Street – about how Violet had fallen in love with someone else just before she became pregnant with Liz, and she was about to leave Frank for this other man. "I got really angry at her," Lucille had said. "This was already her second marriage, after all. She'd left her first husband for Frank. I said, 'Violet, you can't just keep finding new husbands and leaving the old ones.' She listened to me as she usually did. She adored me, just as I adored her. And soon after that she got pregnant with Liz." Lucille's eyes had filled with tears. "I often thought if she had left Frank – your father was such a – if she had gone off with the other one she'd fallen in love with, maybe – " Celia had coughed, gotten up to get a fresh diet Coke. She wanted and didn't want to hear the old story, the implication about Violet's love or lack of love for Frank, about Liz's birth, the stormy extremities of pregnancy she knew from experience could rock even a stable character into a precarious slide.

The bride and groom were dancing to a traditional wedding song about eternal love. Soon the guests were invited onto the floor, and Celia danced a close one with Luke, her cheek against his neck, her chin on his shoulder wondering about the man Violet had fallen in love with when she was married to Frank. And who was the first husband she'd left for Frank? Nature was the opposite of the priest's injunctions, desire, even erotic love, more like other loves – multiple and fluid. *Once I thought I knew my love, then I saw you.* Celia heard the lyrics of that old song behind the wedding song now being sung by a young man with a soft tenor voice. She swayed to the rhythm of the dance, and the depth of her love for Luke made her close her eyes so she could see Leah more clearly, and Dr. Daniels walking the beach, his slim hips and long legs in jeans, perhaps, instead of his usual blue or gray slacks. He would be gazing out toward the horizon. Perhaps she would cross his mind. He would be thinking of her words.

It was the night to turn the clocks back, and the following morning they had an extra hour to walk the beach themselves. The lighthouse was closed but they could stand and watch it from the long stretch of rocks that lead into the sea. Luke held his hand out to steady her, but Celia walked the rocks gracefully. She was remembering her mother showing her how to find the perfect space between two rocks to rest, her legs thrown over one, her shoulders leaning on another, her bottom floating freely in the air.

"*Refraction*, continued," Celia says as soon as she sits down. "This time the third narrator speaks – Leza. She's the one Bettina has chosen as the reliable witness, someone who might be able to bring all the materials under control:

I have never enjoyed being alone at night when activities and obligations shift to margins of consciousness and feelings can pour out in an uncontrollable flow. I crave solitude during the day, but at night I want the comfort of intimacy with some very familiar soul. Yet, I have promised myself to remain here in my friend's lovely house for as long as it takes me to read the pages Bettina sent me and decide if I can do as she asks. As soon as I wake, I push anxiety to a manageable distance by recording my dreams and associations in a gray notebook. Then I dress, drink coffee, and ride my bike (really my friend's bike) to the bay. As soon as I see the expanse of steel gray, light platinum, jeweled turquoise, changes of color reflecting the light on a particular morning, I feel spacious inside. I ride here even in the rain when the water is a rich navy-blue. I wave hello to the dock-master, talk to him about ferry schedules, the possibility of a storm. The ordinary interchange comforts me, while the water reminds me of my purpose and my tasks. Between the two, I begin to grow calm.

Across the bay I can see the long narrow strip of Fire Island. In the summer, I have taken the ferry over on an afternoon, walked the half-mile bridge through graceful dunes to the small wooden shelter where weathered picnic tables offer shady retreats and shoes are lined up near the stairs. I add mine to the lineup of sandals, sneakers and rubber thongs, and walk barefoot into the sand toward the sea. Sometimes I stay until the last ferry back to the mainland at six o'clock. Sometimes I wonder what would happen if I missed it and stayed all night.

But on these mornings in late February, I just get off my bike and look across to the dunes, catching my breath until the sharpest edge of anxiety fades and I feel time slow down to a normal pace or speed up from an awful other-worldly immobility.

Standing there thinking about the distortions of time with Melissa on my mind, a memory of my son Kai comes back to me. It was February then too, a dark month full of intimate hibernations. Kai was about fifteen, sitting on the edge of my bed, a closed notebook in which he recorded poems, paragraphs, song lyrics, lying in his lap, the heavy white cotton bedspread gathered around his body for warmth, his hair uncombed, sticking out in thick, wiry clumps around his head, its softness catching slivers of reddish light in the dimly lit room. I had turned off the radiator as I could not stand the knocking sound made by the heat coming up, so it was cold and I was lying under my quilt reading when Kai spoke about his destiny, and a fear that he could not measure up to something. 'No one expects anything grander of you than what you are naturally able to do,' I told him, speaking out of my deepest fears, hearing my father's voice, expecting grandeur, finding failure, and Melissa's stories about a childhood filled with the same see saw only even more extreme. Kai did not answer, and in the long silence that followed I experienced one of those moments of maternal impotence I had come to know since my son entered his adolescent years. I wanted to protect him from life itself. A stupid, futile, ultimately deadly hope. Yet, I wanted it, or part of me did – the power to enclose him, imprison him, keep him silent and still and young.

Confusions about one's own power – I feared this above all other confusions. When Melissa was a child she had nearly gone crazy believing she could think, wish, dream her mother back to life, and then began to see signs everywhere that the dead woman was somehow returning. It was a miracle, a revelation, she was certain, and for all those years, until she herself was grown, she had kept the mad conviction to herself. Yet her confusion was not unfamiliar to me. Waiting to hear Kai's key in the door some nights, I fought the fallacy of mistaking my fantasies for reality with lights, hot tea, mostly with books. Reading, I fought off insane voices from my own childhood. Reading, I remembered that Kai was responsible and street smart, and that despite the impression given on the six o'clock news not that many teenaged boys were murdered on a given night.

'It's your life, Kai,' I remember telling him that night. 'Only yours. No one has written a script for you to live up to.' Still wrapped in the white cotton, Kai wormed his way up next to me and for a fleeting, slightly embarrassed moment, he was in my arms.

And remembering this, standing at the edge of the dock looking across the Long Island bay, I know I will do as Bettina had asked and visit Melissa after all these years.

*

The following month I journeyed to the hospital on an island in the middle of the river where Bettina paid a fortune each month to keep her sister in the best possible conditions for someone who had no hope of ever getting well. The landing dock was empty in the early morning when I got out of the cab, and the first ferry had not yet arrived. A group of people – doctors and nurses who worked on the island, I assumed – gathered near the gate, reading newspapers bought from a stand nearby. I looked over the papers, magazines, sandwiches, but ended up buying only some pieces of chocolate I thought I might share with Melissa or eat myself on the way back. I had no idea what she'd be like after nearly twenty years of being locked away. I doubted she'd recognize me, though Bettina said Melissa asked about me whenever she floated into ordinary consciousness, along with questions about other people from her past.

When I boarded the ferry I headed straight for the upper deck and stood outside despite the cold. The interior rooms reeked of stale coffee and roasting hot dogs, and as soon as I entered I felt physically ill. Outside the wind blew fiercely but I huddled near the wall, pulled my down, fur-lined hood over my head, and felt my stomach calm down. I could see the large brick structure throughout the trip, getting closer as we made our way. The ride took only fifteen minutes, and just as I began to enjoy the reverie induced in me by wind, cold and river, we bumped into the dock and were told we could line up to go ashore.

Inside, there were record books to sign, name of patient, name of visitor, time in, time out – making clear this was no ordinary hospital – not exactly a prison, but not a place where one could come and go at will. The atmosphere was dark and severe, but not unpleasant, soothing in a way, as if safety and protection, if not freedom, were assured.

I was told by a pleasant young attendant to wait in an area of dark wood benches and lamps covered in shades of red and purple, creating a comforting, soft light. Red and blue patterned rugs covered large areas of the floor. From my seat I could see the entire main floor with its administrative offices on one side, its guarded and barred elevators on the other – to the patients' quarters, I assumed, where I would be headed presently. But I was wrong, I was told by Melissa's psychiatrist who shook my hand warmly and said good morning, in an old-fashioned and formal tone; he was rather tall and almost bowed. Those elevators lead to the patients' private rooms, he said. We'll go to the visiting room, he said – and cupping my elbow gallantly, he directed me to a large elevator I hadn't noticed with enormous, beautifully inscribed brass doors.

He was a man well past middle age, his hair sparse and white, but he was clearly agile and his face looked youthful with its absence of lines and bright blue eyes. From the first, I felt a kinship with him, an assurance of his gentleness and competence, and I was glad for Melissa. He conveyed none of the arrogance or presumption of special knowledge about other people I've noticed in many others in his profession – as if they possess membership in an exclusive, superior club. We chatted briefly about my past connection to Melissa, our friendship from childhood through our twenties when she began to break down and eventually nearly killed herself by stepping into the street in front of a car. And very soon afterward she broke down for the last time, he said, obviously knowing the whole story, and his voice was filled with sympathy and pain, almost as if he had been the one to suffer the tragic losses and lose his sanity in the end.

When we reached the end of the corridor and entered the visiting room, I saw Melissa sitting at a small round table. A bowl of yellow flowers was neatly placed on a white doily in the center. The windows were barred, yet somehow suggested once again the comfort of protection rather than the constraint of incarceration, like window guards installed to protect a young child. She was heavier than I'd ever seen her – the drugs, the doctor and Bettina had warned – but she was still beautiful, her thick black hair braided neatly into a crown above her head. She wore a black tent dress to cover her bulk, but it was decorated tastefully with a double string of deep blue beads. Someone – or she herself? – had added a gentle pink lipstick and a slight rose blush to her sallow, tan skin.

I sat down and took her hand. She clearly knew me, said my name, ran her fingers down my cheek in a sisterly, or maternal, gesture of love. I found her surprisingly easy to talk to at moments, especially after the doctor left and we were alone except for a few nurses who were either watching over the five or six patients and their guests, or standing guard. Melissa answered my questions with surprising rationality at times. At other times, her answers were non sequiturs and I had no idea what the link for her had been. Two or three times she didn't answer me at all, just looked out into space with an expression of sadness that slowly turned to a kind of sarcastic mockery, and I thought she might lash out at me as I remembered her doing when she first got sick. Her rage came to focus on me for months, and when Bettina finally 'put her away' I found I was shamefully relieved, happy to agree not to visit her all these years. Even now I was afraid of saying the wrong thing, of her getting well enough to know we were working on her notebooks full of her memories, of her being so far from well she'd find a way to kill me as she'd often said she wanted to do. But the angry look passed, and she stared back at

*me calmly, waiting for my next question or some story about my life I found to interest
her. I offered her one of the chocolate bars, and she accepted with a regal smile.*

*After about two hours, the doctor returned and I was relieved to see him.
Melissa and I embraced, and she gathered the two cups we'd used for tea and carried
them carefully to one of the nurses. Then, without looking back at me, she headed for a
door at the other end of the room, clearly knowing just where she was going. Before she
closed the door behind her I saw her heading up some stairs.*

*The doctor escorted me back to the main floor, and again I was struck by his
empathy and his charm. He seemed intensely interested in Melissa, as if, I thought for a
moment, she were his only patient, her fractured mind and chaotic internal life the center
of his life, and then, although when I realized it later I felt foolish, I envied her. When I
reached out my hand to thank him, he kept it in his for a long few minutes while he
assured me Melissa was doing well, was even improving between the drugs and three times
a week therapy with him. 'But,' he said, 'as I'm sure Bettina has told you,' (when he
used Bettina's name with such clear familiarity, I felt a kind of thrill) 'she will probably
never be really well again.' I said I understood, that it was a tragedy, but in addition to
the keen reminder of loss I felt for my old friend, I also felt a disturbing comfort in the
thought that if Melissa's story were not interrupted by some unexpected, miraculous cure,
I'd see the doctor again. I looked very intensely into his eyes when I thanked him and said
goodbye.*

*As the ferry crossed the river to the mainland, standing on the cold deck again,
I thought at first there had been some undeniable erotic connection between Melissa's
doctor and myself, but, by the time we pulled into the dock and I bought some hot coffee
from the magazine and refreshment stand, I wasn't at all sure.*

Journal entry: November, 1996:

What do you think? What do you feel? I echo his questions when I
put the pages down in my lap, take off my glasses. You can see my face, he
tells me, you can read my feelings. But I want the words, unambiguous
declaration, and this desire feels old, and strong – not merely strong, impla-
cable, fundamental, possibly dangerous. What words exactly, he wants to
know, but I don't know them myself. Only that they are there and will save
me. I haven't had the fantasy of killing myself in months, not since I began
this writing, and the words I long for are the words which carry the promise
to keep me from that place. I finished reading the last page I've written
today, and I knew that even though the story was incomplete it was all I
would write for a while. As I spoke the final sentences, I had to pause
between words to catch my breath. Emptiness lies before me; something
unknown. What can I do next? What trick played on destiny, what perfect

performance, might keep me from some half-desired fate? Reading, I felt no need for explanation or interpretation, the act itself sufficient to my purpose. My life so fully in my body reminded me of those moments of reunion with a very young child after even a short separation, when he leaps on you, pastes himself to your body with all his muscles clenched. His arms around your neck and legs around your waist are wrapped so tight you don't have to hold him on. My body's life as dear to me as Khoby's body when he was a small boy. Reading my work to Dr. Daniels, vegetation grew around me, large wet leaves pressing close, damp earth sucking my feet in up to my ankles, keeping me in place. Reading, I was inside myself, making my unique mark in his room where there is room for only me. I felt like I was giving birth, my thighs spread that wide, the dark interior exposed, the blood that dark, that thick. A birth. A rebirth, he said. I was in the room of his body and when he whispered, our time is up, I uttered a small cry, I was nowhere near ready to leave.

3. The Third Person

In the months that follow, during the shortening days of late fall and early winter, she tries to feel connected to her ordinary life, her classes, her husband, even her writing outside of her obsessive record of her work with Dr. Daniels, but she is really only comfortable in the lengthening nights.

One Sunday afternoon, desperate for an escape from the interior, she plans an essay on the artist and the threat of/need for exposure. As usual, she searches for a perfect epigraph, someone else's words to get her started. Once again, she is inspired by Virginia Woolf, and as so often before it is Woolf through her character Lily Briscoe who, in this scene, standing before her unfinished painting, describes the terror of it being seen by one of the other guests who might pass by her easel on the lawn: "But that any other eyes should see the residue of her thirty-three years, the deposit of each day's living mixed with something more secret than she had ever spoken or shown in the course of all those days was an agony. At the same time it was immensely exciting."

She hopes the essay, written in the analytic third person, will open a path to something else, a memoir perhaps, about Violet, Liz and herself. She has only unconnected notes so far. Perhaps it is still too close to the bone.

She walks around a reservoir track with Luke, fast walking for Sunday exercise. The large expanse of water, an urban lake, glistens in the fading sun. A family of ducks from who knows where swims around the edge. She and Luke hold gloved hands. "You seem upset," he says. "Oh, I had disturbing dreams," she tells him and turns her eyes away. She wonders how, when – if – she will try to describe this journey of hers to him, her closest friend, her lover of nearly thirty years, or how much she can expect anyone to comprehend. Perhaps the consequences will be the only part she can share, alterations in her habits nearly imperceptible to others, gigantic inside. At times she opens her journal as if it were an addictive drug, despised and adored. Ideas come, blaze, rock her, fade again.

Journal entry: January 1997

The slow opening that at some point begins to feel unstoppable. And not only memories flashing, sometimes entire scenes, but also constellations of almost lost feelings. Terror; of what? Of some inexpressible ugliness, more than just skin deep, some extraordinary badness offset only through constant effort – to achieve, transform, reshape, hide. A swamp of murky water, surrounding darkness, dangerous and repulsive creatures, outside, inside.

What is this process I am engaged in with commitment bordering on obsession? When I try to escape all metaphor (a journey, an unlayering, an opening) or the clinical vocabulary I try to avoid, (transference, repression, resistance,) and see the thing itself, this room, its ordinary walls and furniture, your high-backed chair supporting your obviously periodically aching back, my chair across the room, the cluttered desk, the lovely tiny sculptures of animals placed on glass end tables and a high shelf, the couch I do not lie down on, and all my words, gestures, movements, words, words, words, then I am left alone with this stunning, paralyzing uncertainty. Who are we to each other? Who are you whom I allow to see these gestures, this stiffening, this slack-jawed focus as if no one were watching me, to hear these halting, naked, unplanned yet effortful words?

Is it possible to be this open? This vulnerable? As if actual fleshy walls of the brain have parted, a dark slit, wet and soft, made of complex cellular mysteries, sounds and shapes formed long before any representation in words? I should have been a painter, or a composer, to try to express these inchoate waves and thunderings, whispers and distant ripples. Words? Synapses? Left brain? The neurological location of memory? Past feelings, vivid again, not *remembered*, no such split; right here, felt now. But perhaps they were never in the past at all – just packed away somewhere, folded into a carefully closed, unmarked box beneath the bed, like children's drawings, a third-grade penmanship notebook, all the years of birthday, Christmas, Valentine's Day cards, *I love you more than all the buildings, Mommy.* Metaphors again, but how else to convey the closeness, right under the bed, of all this, packed away so the teacher can teach, the mother raise children, the sister listen, the wife attend and in some fair and reasonable way expect attention in return. Only the writer is entangled somehow with those layers, and that is the irony; the very one whose *business is words* knows their complete inadequacy. An echo, a color striped across the sky, part real, part illusion.

You are watching me. Somehow, you are aiding and abetting this drawing out of the box, lifting the dusty cover, carefully handling the yellowed drawings, brittle with age. *I'm sorry we had a fight, Mommy. I'll be a good boy.* And knowing now that very likely he was; of course, he was good all along, his anxious, or stressed, or busy, or preoccupied mother the one at fault; no matter, the child will take the blame if love is the offering. So I open, unlayer, expose, and they are here, here in my hands, while you watch, revealing nothing but your sympathy, that lucidity enabling you to feel what I am feeling. That in itself brings these tears. And how do I manage ordinary life in this state? Between the two instantly passing hours a week I sit here, how do I keep myself from weeping on the subway, from shouting at the car turning the corner so fast I am almost hit, from being sucked into unfocused space and fast descent when a student asks a question that cuts too close to the bone?

Now she becomes a daughter/son in all her dreams. Infant boys, boy toddlers lie in her arms, beautiful boys with dark almond skin. At first she thinks they are Khoby, but there is something unlike him, something both familiar and strange. She rescues them from dark caves, once from a swamp where large cows are swimming peacefully, and she wonders why she is afraid of that slow, murky water, why she holds the child so tight. A boy jumps off a high rock wall while she watches, and when he breaks his little leg she mends it with sticks and rags, blots the blood, rushes Luke, who has suddenly had a heart attack, to the cardiac unit of a nearby hospital just in time. The three women return too, standing on an isolated or crowded corner, waiting for her as she walks by, or as she emerges from the ocean. Judith, her almost sister, who is smart and strong. Lia, her almost daughter, who gives her advice. All the baby boys, the men, the sons. Ah, Sonia. *Son*ia. Now she understands.

When Dr. Daniels asks her about old desires to be Violet's son, it is in an ordinary, conversational tone – as he might ask her if she can see him clearly with the afternoon sunlight shining into the room behind his chair, or would she like him to draw the blinds? Did she want at any time she can remember to be her mother's son? He is smiling, imagining possibilities, as if they are experimenting with early versions of a story just coming to mind. Not for the first time she wonders if in his outside life he is also an artist, a musician, she would think, or a poet himself.

"I like it so much better when the blinds are drawn and it's dark in here," she tells him. "I seem to hate the light. I like coming in the late afternoon, especially in the winter, when the sun goes down early and it gets dusky, even nearly dark at times in here, before you turn on the light." She tries to voice her thoughts this way, even when connections seem absent. A painting on the wall of curved shapes around a central layered darkness looks like a tunnel to her, a dark interior. "I wanted to be inside her," she says, remembering the womb dream again, and she feels damp, as if the pleasing grayness of the room were actual fog.

She tells him again, wondering if he is bored by the repetitions, of how words became magical for her, their mystical source in Violet. She tells the old knock-knock joke again. She can see her mother's face clearly now, and her arms dotted with several dark brown beauty marks she allowed Celia to count over and over feeling the slight protrusion from the skin, and her long red, polished nails gently scratching Celia's skin, a delicious tickling and relief, scratch, scratch. She tells him about Frank's stories, the years he worked in the cleaning store and all the people who were described for her and Liz over their Sunday dinners of boiled chicken, canned peas, and malteds from the soda shop down the street. About how words became the currency to earn Frank's love, a facility for language Liz did not possess, or express, or somehow did not need. About how after Frank's death, when they were in their twenties, she and Liz had become closer than they'd been since early childhood and begun a practice of talking to each other every week for hours on the phone.

She tells him about Frank's weekly reading assignments. They would both read the same novel, or essay, and on Sunday night she would discuss the work with him. He wanted her reactions, her analysis; he taught her the word *analysis*. During her recitations he seemed to listen to her more closely than at other times. His instructions were clear – had clearly been thought through. What he didn't want were flights of fancy, he said. This was serious business, training her powers of observation, training her to see the *broader picture*. What about stories of ordinary life, she had wanted to know, confused by his standards. Even stories need *discipline*, he told her, lingering over one of his favorite words. Frank had been forced to quit school in the third grade, educated himself in his youth while working first as a counterman in a cleaning store, next as an assistant manager in a fabrics company where he became active in the union, then a union organizer for years and finally, after his wife died and he could no longer travel, in a cleaning store again. Through it all, he'd read late into the night, never too late to be educated. And if you didn't have certain opportunities, well, that's the breaks, old girl, he would say, can't live your life feeling sorry for yourself. Pile up the books and read them, one by one, no matter how long it takes. When she'd read impressively and found the words to say what she'd learned, he stared at her as if he were seeing her for the first time, as if he were seeing right into her. And if, perhaps, she was Violet to him in some way right then, it no longer mattered. He was staring at her, looking right into her eyes.

"Like I felt with you at times, when I was reading," she says to Dr. Daniels, then adds, "and just as exposed." "Exposed?" he asks, eyes focused sharply on her face. "Yes, as if I were showing off for you, yet afraid that I was not really deserving of this flight of imagination, this making up of Bettina, Leza and Melissa until they feel so real to me. This freedom." She twists uncomfortably in her chair, but then she laughs. "What?" he asks, smiling back at her.

"Okay – once, when Khoby was a teenager, I was convinced he was depressed about something, so I asked him. He denied it – said – in exactly the tone Luke might use – I'm not depressed, just a little sad. It will pass, Mom. I began to suggest symptoms I'd noticed, trying not to scare him but convinced in my heart he was in danger even if he didn't know it, his legacy from Violet, through me. Finally he shouted, Believe me, Mom, it's just your imagination, and you know yourself, your imagination is always running away with you! I left the room feeling so superfluous, so maternally superfluous – the very beginning of a feeling I know a lot about now that he's grown. That night I made a drawing of myself looking haggard, old, a bit like a street beggar. But I was holding the hand of a tall woman in a long, flowing, multi-patterned gown, her hair sensuously curled beneath a wide-brimmed hat, covered with ribbons and flower and veils. She walked a bit ahead, holding the hand of the beggar woman as if she were a child. And I titled it 'Celia With Her Imagination Running Away With Her.'

"There is something about that story I love, and yet it shames me," she says. She wants him to disagree with her about the inherent shamefulness, to rescue her from the self-deprecating slide. "Something to do with how I long to hear your feelings about me," she says, digging deeper. He is silent. Now, she is hot with a vague memory of Violet's magic, the sensuous swoon when her mother softly scratched her back with sharp nails, sang her love songs in the dark: *Let me call you Sweetheart, I'm in love with you. Let me hear you whisper that you love your Mama too.* A pause. The sound of nails scratching. *I love you too, Mama* – a whisper from the bright, hot center of the universe.

"But I remember other times too," she says to break the silence and the mood. "A big family party. Violet has invited Frank's sister, Leza (he smiles, recognizing the name); and his brother Ike and their children; Lucille and her family, Judith and hers. We are all excited – the food cooking, drinks lined up on an oak breakfront covered with a dark green patterned cloth; the translucent sparkling of seltzer in blue bottles, the rich coppery gold of whiskey in a cut-glass decanter – the sliced angles increasing the liquid's shimmering glow. Violet had been planning and cooking for days, yet even though she had the help of her mother and a housekeeper, the demands suddenly become too much for her. Tension rises. You can tell it by the set of her lips, the slight stamp of her walk, the harsh tone of voice when all you did was ask for a drink. I would try to keep my distance – go into the other room with Frank and Liz – but inevitably I would make a mistake, I don't know – talk too loud, get under her feet, demand too much, and she would start screaming at me about how everything was too much for her, she could not be expected to do everything, the guests would be arriving in less than an hour and nothing was finished. Sometimes after she finished screaming she sat down at the kitchen table and wept.

"I look back on it now more as a mother than a child. I remember the tension of our huge family dinners, Luke's and mine, endless lists to remember, needing everything to be perfect, furious at Khoby because he was being a child, dawdling and resisting his chores. Once, when he was about eighteen, he told me he thought I should stop making holiday meals for the family since it upset me so much and was therefore often no pleasure for him. I felt so ashamed, I still do – not to realize how the actual party – which I always ended up enjoying – had been spoiled for him by my mood. Violet must have been overwhelmed, as I was, by the terrible internal pressure about time and the need to make something perfect for some harsh judge."

"But it wasn't just an ordinary mother upset about too much work," he says. The tears begin. And the questions. Why was she so unhappy? Celia chews her lip, then spits out sharply, "I know I must have been angry at her, but I can't remember feeling it."

"You're angry now."

"All I remember as a child is the ruined day, the shame. She shouts at me to get away from her, tells me I am not a goddamn baby. Then I am large, I have the big feeling. I am big. Only much later, at night when it's dark in the room and she's sitting in the rocker by my bed, singing one of her lullabies, do I get small again. She can handle me. I am not too much for her. I am not pushing myself in where I don't belong. She leans over to scratch my back, I let her call me sweetheart and she hypnotizes me into sleep."

Dr. Daniels' voice is interpretive now, instructive. "All these ordinary childhood feelings – ordinary family conflicts – all are made extraordinary by what came later. Nothing developed through stages. It's as if your feelings were frozen and magnified the day you found her dead."

In the late-afternoon dimness of the room, she feels the scratch of nails across her flesh, sees the bright red polish, which reminds her of the bright red ribbons of blood. She whispers, "Pussy cat. Translated into *ketseleh* by my father. Little kitten. Little, small, a baby. She called me baby, too. Yes. Every ordinary sorrow of childhood made gigantic by the day in the bathroom. Her body was lying in that weirdly graceful position on the cold tile floor. Her beautiful face was so empty I am permanently awestruck by the possibility of such absence." She stops speaking and stares at Dr. Daniels, who stares back at her. She feels her neck wet with tears. Then she cringes, as if something disgusting has occurred to her. "What?" he asks instantly. So she tells him about the rats, a word she can hardly say. She hacks it out, like a cough. She finds it hard even to go to the park, she tells him. He knits his brow, and then sees. "The squirrels," he says.

But instead of relating the memory of Frank and the dead mice, she says, "I'm thinking about the dark moles on her arms, the slight protrusion when I ran my fingers over them." She cringes again. Her mouth aches, as it has begun to do at times when she teaches her classes, as if she is trying to speak and keep silent at the same time. She describes her course to him: "Voices of Mothers and Daughters in Fiction by Women," about Jane Eyre's journey to selfhood, Edna Pontellier's mythic swim, Lily Briscoe's transforming vision of the unity of passion and form, Sethe's redemption and Beloved's eternal, haunted wandering. The young women in the class write their own responsive stories, which they read to each other aloud, and many, including Celia, are brought to tears by the students' lives reflecting the themes in great novels, recent and more than one hundred years old. As she feels the minutes move toward the end of the hour what comes to her is a line from the novel she is teaching this week. "I want you to touch me on the inside part," Toni Morrison's ghost-daughter, Beloved, says to her mother's lover, Paul D, "and call me my name." Celia recites the line out loud, to Violet, to Frank, to Dr. Daniels. There are three of them, and all three of them might hear her. She is the fourth, the one whose voice she has heard in cackling whispers and unintelligible echoes for so many years she's given up hoping for clarity, yet here she is, inside the shell of that simple desire, the one who can rise from her chair without tripping, walk through the waiting room into the hallway, the elevator, through the lobby and out onto the street, the one who can walk home without falling, as slow as she likes, savoring unmeasured time, the one who has spoken the words.

4. Prison Visit

The robin's egg blue ceiling covered with constellations of twink-ling stars is restored at last. Brass and wall tile shine again after years of reconstruction and cleaning. She makes her way to Track 28 in Grand Central Station, where, twenty minutes early on this trip, even more than normally anxious that she'll be late, she leans against the gate and reads her book, waiting for the train to come in. During the hour-long ride through upstate towns, she means to continue reading but always ends up staring out the streaked window at the woods and marshes that line the tracks between stations, a city dweller hungry for the spectacle of natural seasonal change. Today birches, oaks and maples are bare amid blue green pines. Thirty or forty miles beyond the city it has snowed heavily and icicles hang from the branches of the trees. When she steps out onto the platform she can see her breath, and she breathes deeply, a sigh of relief. No matter how many times she makes this trip, she is always afraid she will miss her stop, that she has gotten on the wrong train, as if she is in one of her recurring dreams about trains. She walks swiftly to the taxi stand, finds the South American driver she knows by now, and is taken through the lovely village, down a winding road where in the summer leaves of tall trees meet overhead, to the Correctional Facility, the prison where her friend Salina is completing her sixteenth year.

Celia asks the driver three times if he will remember to come pick her up for the three o'clock train back to the city. She tips him an extra dollar, hoping this will ensure his promise, winding her way through dangers familiar from her dreams.

She'd met Salina a year after her arrest for robbing a liquor store. The owner had been killed, and although Salina had been unarmed herself, in fact had been waiting outside as a lookout, she'd been sentenced to twenty years to life under New York State's felony murder law which makes anyone involved in a crime resulting in a death equally responsible, whether or not they pull the actual trigger or plunge in the actual knife. Salina had been addicted to heroin for years, and had a small child when she was arrested. Like Celia, she'd come of age in the 60s in a middle-class family, and after her arrest a mutual friend had asked Celia to join a prison mentoring program enabling Salina to earn a master's degree while incarcerated. They'd been friends now for fifteen years.

Wire in tight sharp patterns surrounds a bleak landscape. A path leads to the Visitor's Door and once inside, a regular by now, she knows there will be forms to sign, lines to wait on, computer searches for her name. She will empty her pockets, her wallet, store most of her belongings in a small steel locker. Arms wide, her watch and belt taken, she is searched with an electronic beeper, as if she were in an airport about to take off for some foreign and dangerous place. She looks over her shoulder, trying to read the guard's mood, or his personality. Some are friendly to the visitors who are nevertheless tainted somehow by their connection to the prisoners. She will be a kind of prisoner too for the next two hours, moving carefully under the eye of an armed guard. Her hand is stamped with a purple mark visible only under ultraviolet light. *An escape pass visible only under ultraviolet light*, she jokes to herself. The guard in the small room between outside and inside looks at her marked hand, and opens one door, allowing her into a small corridor, caged in. Slowly, the interior door opens, and she is even further in, in the prison yard, outdoors again. She opens her mouth, gulps air. Shrubs line the path up to the main building. A truck selling hot dogs, coffee, tacos, and doughnuts is parked at the entrance. Inside again, another signing in – name, address, time in, prisoner to whom she is attached. These guards are usually welcoming, as if allowing her into a protected school for children and like a good child herself, she smiles, thanks, is ingratiating. Then she is in the final place, a large cafeteria-like space filled with small circles of plastic chairs surrounding a table. Each table is numbered and assigned. The last guard, like a vaguely familiar stranger in a dream, is a tall, imposing, elegant woman who sits at a desk on a high platform and looks down at her. Celia presents her pass. Her friend is called. She is given table number 8, where she takes her seat and waits.

There is no longer a prison on the corner near her childhood home. But when she was growing up, the Women's House of Detention covered a square block. The prisoners screamed out of high windows at friends and lovers standing on the street below, and she and Liz could hear them from their bedroom, which faced an open garden in back. Who were the women detained behind bars, their disembodied voices filling the night? Noble victims unjustly taken away from their families? Dangerous women wielding knives and guns who might escape at any moment? An arched corridor separated a double entrance on the street, and you could run in one entrance, through the corridor, out the other, as she often did when dared by Judith, Beth or their brothers. Liz, the youngest girl and frightened, refused to play, and Celia learned to protect her. *No, not Liz, she can't play.* But Celia ran fast, imagining kidnapped victims longing for her to save them, or fierce criminals wielding weapons and chasing her. Or Violet. Perhaps this was the place, ironically near yet impenetrable, to which her mother had been abducted, into whose dark interiors she had disappeared.

     Celia has been waiting for about fifteen minutes when Salina emerges from a locked door at the end of the room. They embrace, as always almost violently. Salina's thick graying hair, still a beautiful corn color over all, has grown longer than usual. Her body is slim and strong, her face lined with stress. Her expression conveys both toughness and warmth, her eyes a blue so dark they seem almost black, especially when she is thinking or listening hard. Celia no longer visits to teach novels and poems. She and Salina are friends, and today they talk about raising sons. Salina has been in constant contact with her son and his adopted mother for all the years of her imprisonment, and he has recently turned fifteen. "Sometimes you just can't find the balance between respecting their boundaries and holding on," Salina says, as might any other mother of an adolescent boy. They talk of their closeness to their sons, the wild passion that remains in the mother even when it has gone underground in the son, that mute longing.

     They break from their easy intensity to walk to the vending machines and get something to drink. Salina is not allowed to handle money, and Celia, as though she were a child confronting mysteries, is awkward and nervous with the many buttons and levers on the machine, so Salina instructs her about where to put the dollar bill, what to press, where to get the change. The room is full now, noisy with the sound of babies crying, children running back and forth, women talking to their visitors. Some sit close to boyfriends or husbands and remain nearly motionless in an extended embrace. Mothers and daughters, or sisters, or friends and lovers hold hands. Salina has been teaching writing and literacy classes to fellow prisoners, but the state has withdrawn the money for the classes now, and so, since she has maintained a connection to her family's privileged world all through her years in prison, she is trying, in addition to her work in the hospital with AIDS patients, to raise private funds for continuing education. "The women's hope is rekindled," she says, "a dangerous thing in here. It's as necessary here as anywhere, but . . ." – she pauses, years of experience etched in her smile – "well, you can't really trust anything in here."

     When they are again seated at the little table sipping their apple juice, Salina begins to talk about when her father left the family, when she was a little girl. He had fallen in love with a woman who eventually became his wife, a good woman, a friend to Salina, and she eventually went to live with them when her own mother died of cancer when Salina was thirteen. "I must have been angry when this happened," Salina says, "but I can't remember feeling angry," and not for the first time, Celia hears her own feelings echoed by this friend. "Yes," she says, "I always picture my mother on the bathroom floor. I walk in and I see her, but a strange silence surrounds me. It's a silence with – well, a kind of texture – a silence that moves, enters . . ." She touches her chest, then her forehead . . . "It fills." Her fingers reach around her own throat. With Salina, she is never embarrassed when her words become more like writing than speaking, her stories more like dreams than experiences in the outside world. Here, layers of meaning are weirdly visible, here, where masks are so obvious a necessity for survival, it is easier to remove the masks. Surrounded by families reunited for only an hour or two, by children running off to play then called back by prisoners who smile apologetically at the guards, surrounded by the soft noise of repeated questions, *so how are you? are you eating okay? how are you?* – the sound of the familiar voice the only real point – the two women stare into each other's eyes and find words for feelings with uncommon ease, as if the bars and rules and weapons and guards make the hard truth the only choice. She tells Salina about nearly getting killed by the taxi, about how that caused her to find Dr. Daniels. "The emotional memory is coming back to me only in the relationship with him. I can't get it simply by telling the old stories over and over. And it's not a one to one analogy, like an allegory. More like a dream."

"I've always loved and envied your comfort with the interior story," Salina says. "I want to explore that myself now, write a memoir about what happened to me. But I'm always afraid that story has no value compared to the need for collective, activist work. There are only so many hours in a day and so much need." She looks around the room.

Celia looks too, and thinks, our fears are the same though we have followed opposite roads, mine into the fear, hers away from it. For all her imprisonment, she is in the world.

"I remember telling everyone I was fine when he left," Salina says again, "and even when I look back now, I only feel the feeling of feeling fine. Yet I was terrified of being alone. I ripped up his books and threw them all over the floor. He kept in very close touch. He adored me, and when I was strung out on drugs, he never abandoned me. When I was arrested he rushed to my side, trying to help in any way he could. Now that he's dead – well, it's pretty hard to feel angry at someone who tried so hard to save your life."

Celia is back in Frank's kitchen, her old home, grown increasingly shabby over the years since her own, then Liz's departure. She was living with Luke in a city nearby; Khoby had just been born and instantly become the apple of his grandfather's eye. Once a week she would commute from her home to a school in New York City where she pursued and never completed a graduate degree in psychology. She'd bring Khoby with her, leave him with Frank when she went to class, then spend the evening with her father, eating one of his thrown-together meals of herring and rye bread, a hard-boiled egg, some cottage cheese, a malted from the corner store for old time's sake. Sitting across from him, their food placed carelessly on the bedraggled black and white checked plastic tablecloth, she relished the sense of reconciliation after long years of childhood and adolescent battling. They talked of the books they were reading, as they had done since she was a small child, of the terrible boredom of his job in the cleaning store, of his depression. He had never remarried after Violet's death though he'd been involved with several women one of whom had remained Celia's friend. She never stopped trying to encourage him to get out more, take a class perhaps, meet people. He dismissed her efforts with a wave of his hand, changing the subject to questions about Luke's studies, Khoby's newest words, even her own defense of the field of psychoanalytic studies whose assumptions, he, an old and still-faithful Marxist, found "exceedingly difficult to comprehend let alone accept." They talked for hours on those nights, and beneath the content of their discussions, with Khoby sleeping in the other room and her husband waiting for her in their own home, she felt a new comfort between them, felt she knew how to talk to him, what to say. And he seemed less irritated by her behavior, by her clothes, although she hadn't much changed the way she dressed since the years when he had criticized her every day it seemed, for a lack of color and flair in her outfits, so unlike the elegance of her mother. Violet had been buried in a beautiful navy-blue suit, Parisian design.

Looking at her aging father across the table, his narrow wrists, pale skin, the deep lines in his forehead, the way his lush hair had begun to recede, Celia remembered his lies. For years he insisted on the lie about Violet's death – that it had been an accident; and then the lie that he had never told that lie. When she was eighteen he had sat down with her and told her she was old enough to know the truth. She thought he was going to acknowledge the years of the first lie, but instead he confronted her with a more disquieting story. In the year before her death, he said, he and Violet had been completely estranged. She spoke to him only politely, stopped yelling and lecturing him about all his failings. Suddenly the battles ceased.

But she became more and more remote. For days at a time she retreated, refusing to see even her mother or her sister Lucille. Only Lucille's husband Max would be allowed to enter her darkened room. Touching her was out of the question, Frank said shyly, and looked away from his daughter's eyes. He never knew why. He begged for explanation, but she insisted in an uncharacteristically cool voice that nothing was wrong. It was all his imagination. She was fine. When she killed herself, he felt he was to blame, and his guilty feelings were subtly confirmed by Lucille. "You never made her happy, Frank," she said, "but it's not your fault."

At eighteen, Celia had hardly known what to make of these stories. Why would her mother see only Max? Why did she become estranged from her husband? Why was Frank telling her these things? She rose from her seat across the table and sat down next to her father. She put her arm around his bony shoulders, letting his head rest against hers. Sitting near him that way reminded her of all the years of hopeless desire, futile efforts when she couldn't be Violet, couldn't be his wife, no matter how much he insisted she looked exactly like her mother. And even if she could have accomplished this dangerous magic, she would have lost the real battle – to possess his love for herself. It would be Celia as Violet he would be loving. But if she remained Celia, she was doomed as well to a partial love, limited by her own inadequacies and by some other mysterious force she could feel but never name.

"Remember that time when I was eighteen and you told me about how hard it was for you and Violet the year before she died?" She asked her father the old haunting question as they sat at the table in the old kitchen. And she repeated the story from memory. But Frank scoffed at her, and said no, he could never have said that because it wasn't true. "Your over active imagination will get you in trouble one day," he said. "You're always making things up."

Something in the harshness of his voice perhaps . . . or now, all these years after his death, the memory of that harshness, and she is at the same table, a little girl having breakfast with her grandmother who in the old country style is dunking pieces of thickly buttered bread into warm coffee, then pushing the delicious mixture into the child's mouth. Frank comes into the room. *Stop it*, he shouts at his mother-in-law, who takes care of his children since Violet's death. *You'll make her fat! She's getting fat already!* Liz is unable to eat regularly, and for years is fed tonics to stimulate her appetite. She is sad and gaunt. Celia, more shamefully, eats too much, slurping down the "dunking," grabbing seconds at even unappetizing meals. She is not obese, will not grow into a fat woman, but has always battled weight, being overweight, the effort as stupendous as the effort to walk in the park with Luke or Khoby when squirrels are running all over, crossing and crisscrossing the path.

Sitting at the small, round table, leaning toward Salina who is talking about her father and how he adored her, she hears Liz's voice again, the day on the beach after they looked at the bloody sculpture, and she feels a familiar and physical longing for her sister, a need to be with her the way she can be with Salina or Judith, a spiritual partner but also a blood relationship rooted thickly in the mysterious materiality of genes. But they cannot. She cannot. As often as they declared their mutual love, declarations which are true if love means devotion and commitment, they cannot talk like this. The deeper stories signal trouble, old conflict and ongoing differences they can never bridge. He made me feel perfectly beautiful, beautifully perfect, Liz had said, but not competitively, rather with an awareness of the surprising unfairness of it. Celia too thinks Liz is perfectly beautiful, her graying blond hair, her slender hips and thighs, the slightly rigid set of her jaw. She looks back at Salina who is beautiful too in Celia's eyes. She wants to run her fingers down those lined cheeks, smooth the furrowed brow. As she and Salina complete their visit, embrace and make plans for a phone call soon, as she reclaims her pass, walks out through the sequence of gates and guards until she is back in the parking lot, waiting ten minutes too early for the taxi to take her back to the station, Celia recalls with a sense of relief the reconciliation in the kitchen during those first years of Khoby's life before Frank died. And this feeling alternates with her admiration for her friend, a prisoner for nearly fifteen years who has accomplished more work for people in need than anyone else Celia knows, yet whose chances for parole, according to the state law pertaining to felony murder, are slight at best.

But on the way back to the city, passing through the sequence of romantically named towns, Valhalla, Crestwood, Pleasantville, Hawthorne, Rye Beach where she always thinks of sifting sand, White Plains and 125th Street, she remembers the long years of criticism that made the reconciliation necessary, the hatred that made the achieved love such a relief. She closes her eyes and hears prison bars clanging; she is handing her papers to elegant guards, moving through ominous tunnels, hearing indecipherable voices. Out on the dark platform of Grand Central Station, hurrying toward the subway, she always feels she's escaped, and she wonders if Salina, living in prison for so many years, still encounters prisons in her dreams.

She is crossing a narrow bridge that stretches across two mountains. Perhaps one is Masada, the famous mountain in Israel she and Luke
once climbed, where the Jews killed themselves and their children rather
than be taken prisoners by the Romans. It was the fathers, she'd read, who
killed the children, then the mothers, then themselves, the fathers who
insisted on the terrible final responsibility, the fathers whose decision to die
carried the day. She is in the middle of the bridge on foot, and she almost
falls off, a downward plunge that will surely kill her. Then she is on a roller
coaster in danger of veering out of control. Years ago, in her thirties, she
had become obsessively attracted to someone and had a series of dreams
about being on a roller coaster in the middle of the night, plunging
downward, blinded to what was ahead. Waking from the dreams the night
after her visit to Salina, she screams and hears Luke say, *Where are you?
Where did you go?* "I'm falling," she tries to shout. "No, you're not," he says,
pulling her into his arms. "You're in the bed." When she is fully awake she
realizes Luke would not say those words: *where are you? where did you go?* He
would say, w*ake up, it's only a dream.* Those are Dr. Daniels' words when she
is plunging down or backing away, slipping off somewhere. It was his
voice, in her head now, she had ascribed to Luke. She remembers the old
dreams of out of control sexual desire. She remembers her talks with her
father about books, the effort to find the words to redeem the ugly clothes
and greedy appetite, the sharp pains in her shoulders as if she'd been
carrying heavy suitcases for too long.

When she tells Dr. Daniels about her visit to the prison, her
memories of Frank, and the dream of the bridge, he repeats her definition
of felony murder: "You haven't actually killed anyone, but the law says you
are just as guilty if you were there, at the scene of the crime." Blood drips
onto white-tiled floors. His eyes grow dark. "I had lost everything," she tells
him. "I knew instantly that now I'd have to fight for a place with Frank. At
the same time I felt eaten up by guilt that I had won my place with him.
She tells him Salina's words about her father, repeats Liz's words about
hers. Her voice grows harsh, harsher than Frank's, she is perfectly
contemptuous as she mocks the women she loves: *My father adored me. He
thought I was perfectly beautiful.* I wanted to spit it back into their faces," she
tells Dr. Daniels, her rage splitting the fog like a gale-force wind. She has
recently eaten but her stomach growls loud enough to be heard by both of
them in the quiet room. She is ashamed again, for her harshness, her envy,
her hunger. The inside pushes her out. The outside pushes her in. There is
too much talking, shouting, lying. Too much feeling, eating, needing.

That night the prison has resumed its old place on the corner, rising up where it belongs, replacing the beautiful garden planted in the empty lot that remained after the House of Detention had been torn down. She and Judith are standing across the street, as the friends of the inmates used to do. A full orchestra is positioned near them, and as Judith and Celia watch, an exquisite cello solo begins. Worshipping and longing, the music weeps for something so fully lost there is no hope left at all except in the music. When she awakens she thinks of a recording she has been listening to recently, Yo-Yo Ma playing "The Swan" from "The Carnival of Animals" by Camille Saint-Saëns. Once, she saw him play it in a televised concert, and with his eyes closed, his neck muscles stretched taut, his mouth opened, he looked like someone having sex. She watched him closely, fascinated and aroused.

She tries to describe the music to Dr. Daniels, but her words are inadequate, and if that is true she is utterly defeated. When he asks her what is happening as she begins to cry, she only shakes her head, staring into the distance yet keeping an eye on his eyes watching her. She wants to be quiet, here, everywhere. She will surface only to breathe, like a large seal.

5. Seals

She is obsessed by her work with Dr. Daniels. (He continues to call it "our work" and now the word *work* provides a shield for her against fears of self-indulgence; Salina is in prison, battling every day the demons of AIDS and illiteracy; in the Bronx, a little girl of ten has died of horrific abuse, her story told in a full-page article in the *Times*.) Between the two hours she is with him, she floats, waits, vigilantly watching time go by, whereas in what she has begun to call The Outside, she is teaching a full load, connected by daily life to her husband, son, friends, attending to problems, small and large. (Her ninety-two-year-old aunt Lucille is diagnosed with lung cancer. She continues to chain smoke, locking herself in her airless apartment for weeks at a time, watching TV and driving her daughter Beth crazy. Celia wishes she could help Beth more as she listens to stories of Lucille's small cruelties and large miseries. She visits her aunt in the old 16th Street apartment intermittently, trying to block out the monsters of her childhood lurking everywhere. But they are her life now. She can't escape them. She is heading deeper down with every passing week.)

She writes down all her thoughts and finds herself trying to memorize them to impress Dr. Daniels, to make him love her back, but also to hold onto the reins of her life, however loosely. She knows it is mad, this writing and memorizing instead of letting her mind roam associationally as it was contracted by their relationship to do. But she can't stop. She sees the dark seals in the zoo, the last stop before Frank took them home where Violet would be waiting for them, then later would never be waiting again. The elephants, the huge pacing cats, sly monkeys, insatiable polar bears, and, always last, the seals. They are sleek and brown, their curves graceful and smooth, their eyes black and huge. She saw wilder seals last summer at the northern California beach with Liz and their families, one or two swimming with the tide toward the lagoon, eyes searching the shore, seeming to stare at her as she walked. Then one magical afternoon, walking past the lagoon, she saw a huge crowd of them sunning on a sandbar exposed by an exceptionally low tide, hundreds of seals turning from black to dusty brown in the sun as they used to in the Central Park Zoo pool where she and Liz watched them with Frank. You have to keep your distance, Liz had warned her last summer. They can be dangerous if you get too close.

Celia offers her memorized perfect words to Dr. Daniels. She tries to assume the seals' indifference to being watched as she feels him watching her. She looks away, suns herself in smooth, dark nakedness on her rock.

Now she does not want to be loved for her scratchy, rehearsed words. She wants to be loved for her sleek, wet body, for the things she cannot help being, because she dives down, then surfaces, swimming and staring at the shore.

"Where are you?" he asks. "Where did you go?" She confesses what she has done, the memorizing, recording the perfect words. "Sonia," she says, "the third daughter." He raises his eyebrows, questioning. Sonia, the word-son she becomes in order to escape the anger of the dark-body-feeling-girl. Sonia compromises, strategizes, will be loved for her words if that is all she can get. Seals can be violent if you get too close.

He doesn't know everything, she notices gratefully. He listens, careful and attentive. He provides gifts of extra minutes when needed, once almost fifteen. And so she is Celia more often – silent, dark, submerged, then on the surface again, finding secrets to tell him, as surprised as he is by the old stories so charged again.

"There is a dead mouse on the floor again and again, although it is possible it only happens once but is so vivid and important – I know it, Liz knows it, – we both remember – it seems to happen again and again. The family, four of us, two parents, two children, are coming home from somewhere. The house is dark. The large kitchen, the room we enter first, is dark. No windows, no lights on. My father clicks on the lamp and there it is, dead on the green linoleum floor. Violet screams, grabs each of us by the hand and runs into the nearby bedroom, where she slams the door and, placing her hands over her ears as if she has heard rather than seen something repulsive and terrifying, keeps on screaming. I can hear my father outside the door as he picks up the mouse, walks to the front door and – he will tell us later – drops it head first down the incinerator, holding it by its awful tail. 'For Pete's sake, Violet,' he shouts. 'You're terrifying them. Act like an adult, for Pete's sake. For someone with so much education . . .' He trails off, this incomprehension of his familiar to us all. How can a young woman of such privileged training and background behave so irrationally? She has come far from the superstitions of the Russian village her own mother lived in for much of her life, where he himself lived until the age of eighteen. She is beautiful, successful, the daughter of a doctor. She is American.

"I hold my mother's hand and take in the terror of mice, which will eventually become rats eating out of walls, appearing suddenly out of nowhere, of rodents of all kinds."

She pauses, says it again, though she knows she has said it before. "Rodents of all kinds." There is something so childish, foolish and vestigial about this fear she wants to emphasize it to him. "The squirrels," he says, a look of pity passing over his face as he remembers.

"But now I remember listening to my father's anger," she continues, "and I feel a strange lightheartedness, a guilty joy." She smiles. "When we emerge from the room, Frank is still angry. Violet walks into her room fast, stamping her feet on the shiny floor. She slams the door. My father takes food out of the refrigerator. A fresh rye bread is on the table. The three of us eat while Violet collects herself, finally emerging in her beautiful pink bathrobe and silver slippers, ready to put us to bed. The mice, the image of rodents of any kind, the words themselves – rats, squirrels, moles – make me jump and cringe." She twists in her chair as she says the words. "Sometimes I cover my eyes with my hand so violently when I see one on TV or in the movies that my own child makes fun of me – now, but even when he was small. When one of them appeared on television, even in a cartoon, he'd shout, Cover your eyes Mom!" She hears Khoby's voice registering the anxiety toward which she feels instant recognition and, when it is her child's worry engendered by her own weakness, deep maternal shame.

"What came to mind then?" he asks her, watching her like a hawk. "Shame," she says, and tells her thoughts about Khoby. He smiles broadly. "For being afraid?" "For being a bad mother," she mumbles. "Oh," he says in his preamble tone to the kind of hearty teasing he offers when he wants her to appreciate her ordinary humanness and special accomplishments. "Oh – a bad mother. To that disturbed failure of a child." She is meant to think about Khoby's many strengths, his relationship with Mari, his commitment to his work, his devotion to his parents. She is meant to separate the threads of the old story from ordinary life.

The next day, as she leans over the bathroom sink washing a light nightgown, she is mesmerized by the blue foam covering the gown, and the dream of lice in the daughter's hair comes back to her. Again she sees the beautiful lesbian mother applying the Quell, carefully picking out the now dead lice. Suddenly her face is not Anna's but the face of the woman with thick, curly hair Violet had taught her to draw. Celia would draw the hair, easy circles and curves, and under it Violet drew the three-quarter face, always the same with its pointy chin, long eye lashes, straight nose, perfectly bowed lips. Then it is not the drawing Celia is remembering, but Violet herself, the shadow of her face, the smell of her breath as she leans over the drawing pad, and the feel, she can remember for a split second and then it is gone, the very particular feel of her shoulder, of a soft breast beneath a cotton nightgown, and the intensity of her scream as they stood behind the door frightened of a mouse, the way her hand clutched Celia's hand, the excitement she'd felt then. But why the lice, she wonders, now that she begins to understand why Violet is a lesbian. She plans to ask Dr. Daniels, knowing he will not answer, that he will open his hands to her as if to say – You tell me – or remark that she will have to wait while he gets out his crystal ball. That is when she may begin to hear her stomach growl, right there in the chair, facing him. Or going home afterward, she may stand in front of the open refrigerator stuffing into her mouth anything she can find.

"I stand in the kitchen in front of the refrigerator and throw food in my mouth," she tells him, "like the zookeeper throwing fish into the mouths of those seals. I wanted my father to love me more than anything or anyone. More than Violet or Liz. I'll get him to love me best, I thought after my mother died. I have to find a way to get him to love me. I remember that thought, that feeling, as vividly as any childhood memory, like the view of the enclosed back yard from my bedroom window, like the special navy blue of the night in our room, like the sound of my mother singing her songs. Wanting him at any cost. Smiling beneath my fear when he was angry at her for her hysteria about mice. But I wanted her too, her dark olive skin with its scattered dark moles along her arms, her arms – her arms – and her voice – and her song lulling me to sleep each night, songs I remember every word of and sang to Khoby until he was too old and could go to sleep by himself. Then I wrote them all into a small leather notebook and gave it to him, in case his memory was not so strengthened and focused by loss. Somehow I couldn't please either one of them. Too intense. Too sloppy for her. Too – something for him."

"Too exuberant," Dr. Daniels translates sweetly, the man who loves children. "And for him – well, there may have been other complexities there – complexities we haven't reached yet."

She leaves with a feeling of relief and security and walks the ten blocks uptown. *Complexities we haven't reached yet.* The words lighten her step. They have a long way to go then. She will surface and dive. She will lie on the rocks exposed to the sun. The journey is nowhere near over. Dr. Daniels is not about to send her away.

6. Hunger Strike

In the college, a group of students, followers of an admired professor whose job is in jeopardy, have begun a hunger strike. Celia supports the strikers, but (her own rhetoric reminding her of the moderate critics she'd hated as a student herself) she disapproves of their methods. Self-starvation, so loaded an action for women under any circumstances, resonating with desire unfulfilled, rage turned against one's own body, should be used only in situations of the greatest extremity, she thinks. Not here, even in a university with more than its share of corporate callousness, or now, to protest the firing of a faculty member no matter how brilliant her thinking or inspiring her classes, no matter how entrancing her long braids and softly draped, richly patterned clothes, no matter how correct her analysis of the hypocrisies of the institution, even no matter that she is a Black woman and this university sends most of its Black faculty members out through a revolving door.

Celia is suspicious of herself, keenly aware that the echoes of hunger in her own life now might be clouding her thinking. Like many, she holds Helene in high esteem. She has attended her lectures, been made to feel a combination of guilt and anger that can sometimes signal a change in consciousness as Helene deftly exposed everyone's complicity in the horrific injustices of global economic colonialism. "Take off your scarf or jacket and look at the label," she'd said calmly. And they all did, reading aloud: *Made in . . .* and then the list of all the places Helene wrote on the board: Ceylon, Indonesia, Guatemala, where factories hired children and underpaid adults to weave fabrics and construct shoes which would then appear in the American chain stores where they all bought their fashionable, over-priced clothing. Helene is powerful, beautiful, deserving of admiration and appreciation. Beneath her calm, analytic exterior is grief at the injustices in the world she studies so carefully, rage at the institution that is denying her employment and denying the students a teacher who is perfectly suited to head a new program in Post-Colonial Studies; a remarkable woman, brilliant, brave, fierce, calm, often seeming unapproachable, it is true, but nevertheless, a woman not given her due. Like Salina, Helene inspires people to act. And even if she lacks Salina's warmth, her life is dedicated to improving other people's lives. Nevertheless, Celia is unable – she recognizes this with genuine regret – to become involved in the struggle between students and administration. Too close to old angers and fears, she cannot risk the inevitable conflicts with Helene and the other leaders about means and ends, the explosions that would surely occur. The shock between inside and outside is intensifying daily. Often, she is left trembling, weeping in transitions, on the subway to and from school. She begins to wear dark glasses, even in the winter, even at dusk.

These days she is grateful for Luke's characteristic silence. Although she suspects he notices nearly everything, he rarely feels the need to express what he notices in words. As if in passing he will communicate some months-old observation or insight, and when she asks him why he hasn't talked to her about it before, he looks confused, surprised himself, and admits it did not occur to him. For months he has been soaking his eyes twice daily with bottled water on the advice of an ophthalmologist who noticed a condition of dried cornea common to middle age. And one day Luke offers her his psychological interpretation, how beneath his daily ablution is the story of a man who never cries and so his eyes become the sign of his character and he must apply Liquid Tears. But he tells her this over the phone, both of them at work in the middle of the day. Soon after he tells her, she notices him crying more frequently, when he talks of his dead brother, when he remembers a childhood experience of humiliation, when he reads a biography of Joe Louis, the great fighter and standard-bearer for democracy who himself was denied democratic rights by racist institutions in the United States.

Still, he never pulls or pushes her into the world, his or anyone's. She may roam the interior for days, sharing only brief words, short meals, silent embraces with her taciturn, kind and comforting husband who makes few demands, voices no criticism, does not weep or shout. At other times this most fundamental aspect of his character, at the heart of his way of loving and of hating, can bring her to the edge of fury as his shells and silences increase in direct proportion to her intensity of need and extremity of expression – a gender arrangement so common, apparently, it has been popularized in several best selling books she does not have to read as she knows every word and silent gesture of the script by heart. But now his quiet presence, his caress of her hair as he reads his newspaper, the absence of questions – all surround her with security, and, especially when she remembers Frank's pacing and weeping, his criticisms and standards, fill her with gratitude.

At school, as the crisis heats up, Celia supports the students when she can but refuses to cancel her classes. Once she tries to explain to Helene her complex and mixed reaction to the hunger-strikers, her support of their general aims but her deep skepticism about the use of self-starvation as a strategy, especially by young women many of whom are prone to eating disorders, all of whom, she knows from the many she has taught in memoir and fiction classes, think they are fat, even the ones who are willowy, even the ones who are bone thin. She navigates carefully, keeping her words pertinent to the political struggle, vigilantly avoiding the narrows and storms, the tides and rip tides of her dreams. Helene is concerned with broad global injustice. She is proposing a narrative about political forces beneath mere personal conflict. She is facing courageously what many, including Celia, recognize as institutionalized fear of strong, outspoken Black women. She is speaking to the longing of people in their twenties for shared community and maternal power. And so she responds coldly, with regal distance, and Celia crawls away (she almost feels her knees on the ground) knowing they could care less about her motivations and doubts, safely distanced from their months-long struggle, but also remembering she is never comfortable with such purity of purpose, the righteous judgments often necessary to political action. Immobilized is how she feels. The perfect opposite of what is called for. Anyway, there is no going back for her. The membrane between outside and inside is too permeable. Experience flows back and forth relentlessly, tropes gathering images and associations like rocks layered with muscles and snails. She behaves respectably on the outside, she hopes, making an effort to be balanced and clear as the hunger strike continues. Inside, she devours details of identification as if they were her own private medicine, her metaphorical meal.

In her dreams she serves food, or food is served to her, inadequate and rotten, and she is lost in the city, night after night wandering in dark, remote neighborhoods, down by the westside docks, in the confusing desolate streets of the Bowery, where homeless people crouch in doorways, their shopping carts parked in front of them to cut down the wind. One night, she is stranded in her childhood home, between her parents' bedroom and her own. The large kitchen is eerie, lit only by a full moon shining through a bare window. "And I am standing there, paralyzed," she tells Dr. Daniels, "stunned – afraid. Then a man appears. He is young, maybe in his thirties. His hair and eyes are dark brown, almost black. Several small dark moles are scattered on the smooth olive skin of his face and hands."

She leans toward him, almost rising from her soft leather chair. "You take me in your arms and hold me. I am so glad you are here, I whisper. I am glad to be here, you whisper back."

This is memory, translated, partial, but resplendent, and the wish she must have lived with all those years for protection of more than one kind, first running into their room each time she heard the scream from one of Violet's nightmares, then when she was gone, running into his room to feel his body alive and warm.

"I remember how his thigh felt beneath the thin cotton of his pale blue pajamas, and his hands rubbing mine when I got the finger feeling, as if they were swollen, gigantic, and had to be massaged down to normal size again."

She is silent then, daring to keep looking into his eyes, and his gaze does not waver. It never has. He takes her in.

She needs courage. Often uncomfortable in her sensuous body, now it is the vessel, her desire the engine, as she uncovers, as if for the first time, the story of her early life. In all the years since she was eighteen of on and off psychoanalysis, of searching through essays, novels and poems to elicit her true story from other people's creations, then her own, none of it had ever come to this. And why? Because she had nearly killed herself, or wanted to for the first time since adolescence, when she no longer had a child to protect, and had lost a coveted promotion she'd assumed was her due? Because she had passed fifty and could see the reality of her own life ending, that sooner or later she would get her old wish to be with Violet, both of them sifted to dust in eternal oblivion, and now that it was in sight she wanted to put it off for as long as she could? Was it possible, then, to be free of that encroaching, seductive past with all its familiar narrative lines and images coalescing into recurring, lifelong dreams? Or was the key, the heart of it all, the singular being of Dr. Daniels, for whom she can no more find satisfactory adjectives than she can find perfect images for this frightening and hopeful descent? He has touched her on the inside part, and she cannot help picturing it as her flesh.

The next time she visits Khoby in L.A., in the middle of the cross-country journey when the flight is at its height, its rhythmic speed most perfectly achieved as it dips in and out of the white blindness of clouds, way up here where the land with all its patterns and colors, mountains and rivers, is suddenly visible then erased again, as she feels herself moving closer and closer to her son while outside the small, thick window all appears to be immobile, she realizes with a start: She is longing for Khoby more than ever as she approaches the west coast. She longs for him when he is far away, and she longs for him when he is sitting across the table from her, always afraid he will be spirited away forever. Because in a way he has been, that small child she took along with her almost everywhere she went, their "travels," they called them then, to California, to New England where Judith lived, to Cape Cod, to the corner store.

You hold onto them all those years with a thousand details of care, a thousand burdens and incomparable intimacies (their flesh, their shit, their fevers, their passionate calls in the night) and then suddenly, except for the limitless love, motherhood as you have known it slips away until there is only the most threadbare veil of it to protect you. That awesome responsibility of naming everything – first people, then birds, trees, colors, numbers, letters, then rights and wrongs, all your brilliantly charged achievements and failures, the power of it is gone; obligations and demands, meals and disciplines, and the lists! All gone, not in the child's mind, perhaps, where it may remain for as long as he lives, but in the mother's, rolled up and crushed like discarded notes for an unfinished story, and you are left only with a blank sheet and a new insidious awkwardness.

She puts on her Walkman to quell the thoughts, and, as she says this to herself, she pauses before she clicks on the piece by Mozart to which she has been listening lately, and she repeats the phrase: *quell the thought*. She thinks of the dream of the daughter-writer with lice in her thick red hair, her scalp alive with something intrusive and hard to extract, even by the beautiful lesbian mother who is pouring Quell, the lice-killing shampoo, into her daughter's flaming hair. Tears spring to Celia's eyes, loss and desire always joined for her, one so close on the heels of the other they can seem indistinguishable at the borders, like seasonal change. This is the thing she's been trying to hide and express forever, hold in and let out into the world, speak and keep silent until her lips ache: this intensity Dr. Daniels seems, oddly, to like so much. It is connected to how much she loves Khoby, to her need to tell stories as close to the truth as possible, her pride in the pages of "Refraction" she keeps in her drawer.

She clicks on the sensuous, romantic sonata and closes her eyes, picturing Dr. Daniels. She is not talking to him, she is dancing with him. They are in a formal ballroom. An orchestra plays. They hold each other at arm's length and gaze into each other's eyes. There is no audience, no one to watch or condemn. He is there, of course, watching her, but even he is not here, in her mind as she imagines the dance. Then she is crying from the old/newness of the feeling, here again after all the years of trying to control it, and suddenly her tears are accompanied by the liquid of a rich, swelling orgasm. When the music is over, she opens her eyes, clicks off the Walkman. A man to her left is playing a computer game on a colored screen. Its blues are pure, its reds dramatic. Before, she'd noticed him reading a huge, hardcover book and wondered, a scholar? a doctor? He has beautiful hands lined with heavy veins, wrists and forearms covered with soft brown hair.

It wasn't Violet's dream, after all, not her desire, not her intrusive thoughts. Dreams are best understood in layers of meaning. She recalls the idea noted in her journal. She is the dark, sensuous lesbian mother as well as the daughter with flaming red hair searching for some protection against all the hot desire, out of control, innocent, indifferently cruel.

But when she returns to the city, after a warm visit with Khoby and Mari, when she is again seated in the leather chair across from Dr. Daniels she is miserable, horribly stuck. She is afraid she will forget everything she means to tell him between sessions, so she keeps writing everything down. She is afraid he forgets her between sessions, so she has to be especially smart, clever and entertaining when she is there. Afraid she will forget, be forgotten, so she keeps up the vigilance, the only thing she has ever been able to do in such circumstances, the obsessive recording. She has created several secure "homes" for herself – in family, in friendship, in writing and teaching, now with him, yet again and again she forgets where she belongs. Walking down a familiar street, she looks up suddenly, momentarily lost. She reads her journal entries over and over to remember what she felt yesterday, where she was the week before.

One day, she walks uptown from her childhood home in Greenwich Village, takes the old route up Seventh Avenue to 16th Street. She will not stop to visit Lucille, however, not this day. She will walk the old circle, leaving out the central event. Up Seventh Avenue from 10th Street, past the few stores still in place after all these years – *Candies 'N Nuts*, a shabby Chinese restaurant, the optometrist's office once owned by the father of a friend of her cousin Beth. Then the gentrified stretch – a huge gallery-store of wicker furniture, an elegant cafe specializing in grilled and raw fish, the Gap. Finally, the corner building that once housed the office of her pediatrician, a woman named Dr. Delman, who once, when Celia was about ten, had invited Frank into the examining room to view Celia's naked body in the earliest stages of budding pubescence, the soft, slight mounds on her chest, the broadening nipples, the few hairs between her parted legs. Well, she has no mother, so I thought you should see, the horrible woman had explained in an afflicted tone. A fast nod from Frank, a blush, and he was out the door again while Celia froze under the doctor's chilling stare. She turns east at the corner of 16th Street, or rather her feet turn east, following old grooves, her mind in the past.

She, Frank and Liz are having dinner with Lucille and her family, a weekly ritual in the early years after Violet's death. Also weekly, before the meal starts, the fight begins. Lucille has prepared a special dish for her son Sam, her favorite child, who refuses almost everything except lean lamb chops and kosher franks. Tonight it is lamb, and Lucille is cutting the meat into tiny bite-sized pieces, although even Liz, six months younger, can eat her meal without help. Everyone else is having chicken, and Celia's uncle Max, at that time in his life a gruff and angry man, attacks Lucille in his sputtering way for spoiling the boy. "Why the hell can't he . . ." the words trail off, he taps his spoon repeatedly on the table. "For everyone else chicken is good enough." Lucille stops cutting. She glares at her husband and begins to lecture him on modern child-rearing practices and their son's sensitive nature. She pauses, changes tone, calls Sam *darling*. Max bangs his silverware down, rips his napkin from his belt and looks to Frank, his brother-in-law, for help. "Calm down, man," says Frank. "What do you care who eats what?" Liz begins to cry, and Frank pulls her over into his lap, shushing her in Yiddish-sounding noises, holding her like a baby, her face buried in his chest, her legs flung over his thigh. Celia is fidgeting under the table, kicking her feet, rolling the fabric of her shirt up and down. When Lucille continues calmly cutting the meat into miniscule pieces and Max begins to sputter and shout again, Beth suddenly gets up from the table, knocking over the chair with her long legs. Crying loudly, she rushes into her room and slams the door. A few seconds later, as soon as she can possibly manage it, Celia gets up and heads into her older, adored cousin's room. Beth is a large girl, tall for her age and plump. What a big girl, people will say to her callously, their eyes traveling to her rounded stomach, their fingers pinching her fleshy cheeks. You're a big girl, everyone says to Celia incessantly since Violet's death. Her grandmother Frieda who sometimes lives with them, sometimes with her eldest daughter, Lucille; friends of the family who come to visit and want to talk to Celia and Liz to see how they are adjusting; Lucille herself; and even Frank, beloved traitor, desired judge: You are a big girl now, Celia, a little mother now, a big girl.

Beth is curled up small at the corner of her bed where the walls meet. She clutches her striped pillow snapping it rhythmically. Celia has never been able to master the wonderful snapping that Beth and Judith can accomplish with such ease. Now the snaps are loud and fast, like Beth's tears and sobs.

Walking slowly toward her aunt's house, Celia remembers the large roundness of Beth's thighs and shoulders, and she recalls a sculpture she's seen the past weekend with Luke at the Guggenheim Museum, Aristide Maillol's seated woman, called "Night," huge, graceful and bronze. Her arms are wrapped around her gigantic calves. Her head rests on her mountainous knees. Celia had walked around and around her, unsettled by the enormous woman, despair etched so plainly into the curved ridges of her spine.

She sits at the edge of Beth's bed, one leg curled under her, the other barely touching the ground. She says nothing and does nothing, just stares at her beloved, big cousin until the snapping and crying subside.

She walks past the old factory, now closed, where she and the other children believed a group of violent conspirators plotted to kidnap small children to aid them in their plans to destroy the world; past the renovated brick houses, pine and ivy bordering their iron gates; past Lucille's building and on to the corner where she turns downtown, heading home on 6th Avenue. The pain in her calves begins. She feels the old desperation. And when she crosses the broad, two-way trafficked thoroughfare of 14th Street, official border between the two neighborhoods of Chelsea and Greenwich Village, she feels the old release of breath, the slowing of time. She hears herself telling Dr. Daniels about the pain in her calves, the anxiety-filled walk, always uptown on 7th Avenue, downtown on 6th, a big girl, too big for her britches, conceited and showing off. She hears Lucille's whispers of praise and possession, how favored Celia is because she is so like Violet, she is sometimes even mistakenly called Violet instead of her own name. She remembers the feeling of walking the street, literally between Frank and Lucille, Lucille's favorite, the best one of all after Sam, before Beth, it is sometimes implied, Lucille's own daughter, before Liz, Celia's beloved and envied sister, before beautiful Judith who imagined all their wonderful games but who Lucille said was ugly and uninteresting, and before Judith's brother, the very last and least loved of all. All of them knew the order for this never-articulated lineup. Here is the old guilt – she loves Beth and Liz, and Judith is her best friend. And the old determination – her marching legs, the pain, from the rush to get home, perhaps this time fast enough to save her mother, but also from this: to escape Lucille, which means she has to figure out a way to win Frank's praise, and until she reaches that goal, which she does not lose sight of for all the years of her childhood, she must try to read the signs, to remember signals and hints, to anticipate the unstated rules and implied expectations. A pattern of compulsive recording and restless observing is formed and woven so tightly into her being that now, a woman past fifty, she is amazed even to imagine an alternative, a temporary letting down of her shoulders, the ability, perhaps, to relish unconsciousness, to live without a plan or a watch.

"Two women are rushing down a long stone stairway in a dark city. One woman is large and strong. The other must be me."

It is a winter afternoon. Dr. Daniels has not turned on the overhead light. His pressed white shirt seems extraordinarily bright. She hopes her recently blemished skin may not be visible. "We are leaping from one stair to the next, more platforms than stairs. The other woman leaps gracefully, but I fall again and again. How do you do that? I ask her. Practice, she says, grimly. She is heading for a large building, a day-care center where she will pick up her child, a boy of two or three. I watch him sleep, his amber skin smooth and luminescent, his black lashes slightly damp, a child of a mixed marriage, I see, like Mari, black and white. The large woman holds him, feels gently inside his diaper to see if he is wet. He opens his eyes slightly and seeing her face closes them again. I see it all so clearly – how exquisitely familiar her face is to him – the brush of her hand, she touches him, confidently, gently, like I touched Khoby when he was a little boy. She lifts him into a beautiful, soft blanket – it's pink and yellow plaid with sparkling golden thread around the borders. She places him in a snug carriage. But outside, the carriage rolls away, faster and faster down the mountain of steps, and I scream at her to notice, to save the child."

A sense memory of touching Khoby's infant back and thighs, so powerful she feels it as if she is Khoby, or she is Khoby's sister, Khoby's brother, Khoby's wife, Khoby's child.

An allegory of desire, so it must be her face, the actual feel of her hand, the delicate wrist unscarred, before it all ends, as it must, in disaster. Perhaps in this dream she is remembering, and since she is not alone, she is with him, and this room too is filled with longing and desire, perhaps something is shifting.

All he says is, "Who is in the carriage?" All she says is, "I suppose it's me."

Men have been banging and lifting all day for weeks. All her furniture is moved to the center of the floor, which is covered with large drop cloths to protect it from the white dust that is everywhere. In all the apartments, old windows are being replaced with tight-fitting new ones, promising to cut down on forty percent of the noise of the street. Between the taking out and the putting in, Celia sits at her dining room table in coat and gloves. Literally, now, the outside is inside, as it takes nearly all day for the new windows to be installed. She reads and comments on student papers, prepares a class about the imagery of darkness in all the novels they have read. Every so often her mind slips, and suddenly the student papers, the books, even the thirty-five degree weather in her living room, are gone. She is filled up with memories and sentences that must be placed somewhere, so she turns to her journal to collect them, lift them out of her mind so she can return to concentrating on her work.

In school, the hunger strike continues. The faculty is split, torn between loyalties and anger. One hunger striker in Celia's class is getting noticeably thin. Deep circles form under her eyes. After class, which she attends religiously, she apologizes to Celia with polite disdain for not having her assignment ready. "Are you okay?" Celia asks, increasingly concerned. "Yes, I'm a bit weak, but fine," the young woman replies, a perfectly modulated understatement. Now, the question of Helene's position has been joined to other issues – the exploitation of maintenance workers and guards (no medical insurance, no raise from minimum wage in several years); the almost complete lack of faculty of color in certain divisions of the university, a situation Celia has fought against for over a decade; yet here she is, this term, a helpless onlooker, as if she is suffering from a terrible illness unknowable to everyone but herself.

At the dining room table, huddled into her coat, she is reading a set of papers on Tillie Olsen's classic story of motherhood, "I Stand Here Ironing." In all her years of teaching, she has never seen a more remarkable set of essays. All the young women, none of them mothers, convey an understanding of maternal guilt and the helplessness so often its twin. When the eldest daughter, who had been sent away to a group home for a period in her childhood, becomes, in adolescence, so good she refuses her mother's eager ministrations in the night and will say only, "Go back to sleep, Mother"; when the working mother of several children is told her daughter is having trouble in school – the eldest child, the helpful, responsible, once frightened, good girl – and the mother cries, "What in me demanded that goodness in her?" the students seem to understand the mutual agony, do not assign the mother easy blame. Celia wonders if this class is one of those happy accidents known to all teachers, a group of eager, talented students all in one place at one time; or if it could be partly her fever, this medicinal breakdown she is living through for some reason resulting in unusually good teaching of the story this term.

Her last windows are installed. The workmen gather their drop cloths and tools, sweep up the top layer of white dust and leave. Celia stares through the improved windows at the now forty percent more silent street, then back at her chaotic room, all the furniture dusty and displaced, as it might be in a dream. She is marveling at Olsen's ability to convey the inside and outside at once in this short story; a mother's lament, a daughter's survival, their pain clearly a consequence at least in part of some social failure, no help for split-up, poor families, and the internal price that is paid. *So all that is in her will not bloom – but in how many does it?* Right now, with all this furniture to move, she is not focused on the echoes and reflections, but only on the way she will begin tomorrow's class. Right now she does not see that Tillie Olsen has articulated the very destiny she is daring to imagine escaping once again.

Often she prefaces her sessions with Dr. Daniels with a caveat. She has much to be thankful for; terrible evils and personal sorrows of greater magnitude than hers exist all around her. Salina. Helene and her brave, hungry students. The abused and murdered child in the Bronx. Yes, her life began with a terrible trauma, and there is no doubt more to be remembered, but often she simply feels she must acknowledge her comparative good luck. She has survived, enjoys privileges, accomplishments, love, and now, since she has been working with him, a return of faith. But she knows she is using her words to clear a path in a way, so she can turn inward again, pay attention to the voices, still alarming, and the memories, still perilous, that permeate every level of her awareness now. She hides her fear, wears the mask of competent adulthood expected of her that also keeps the terror contained. But she is never unaware of it. At the bottom, something old and frightening is always there.

7. Down Here

A little girl in church with Rose, a housekeeper hired to replace the mother who is first working, sometimes in Paris, then dead. Rose is a Catholic woman who believes this child, grieving, people say, like an adult, might be comforted somewhat in church. And she does find the dark wood and stained glass, the low organ music and white stone saints with their kind faces and beckoning hands, comforting. She is taught to sit in a pew, to kneel on a small leather platform, to place her hands together in prayer. And there is something especially comforting about that, tips of fingers joined, hand touching hand, even though both are her own. She is taught to read the 23rd Psalm from the black Bible. She whispers its musical phrases as she looks up at the cross bearing the white stone body that suggests suffering but does not actually suffer. *You leadest me beside the still waters.* She thinks of her father, who can't eat since his wife died, he pushes his plate away, and can't walk, he leans heavily on an old cane, who sings his songs of longing and pain in the dark kitchen at night until she is afraid to go to sleep and afraid to remain awake, Lizzie's soft breathing the only solace, *You anointest my head with oil, my cup runneth over.* Rose hears the whispers, thinks the Jewish child raised in an atheistic home may be naturally religious, and perhaps she is if religion rests partly on the desire for credulity, if that is the beginning of faith, because saying the words on her knees *through the valley of the shadow of death, I will fear no evil,* she is incredulous at the possibility that such faith might exist, and she wants, oh she wants, to believe.

She is lost again, wandering the city. It is cold again and she is naked again. Almost naked. She is covered breast to ankle with a large white towel that keeps slipping off. But there is something next to her body, beneath the towel, a tall narrow thing, as tall as herself. It is stone, it is flesh, and as long as it is there she is safe. She gets on the subway, searching for her home, homeless in the Bowery again – the desolate streets, the wind. She embraces herself, shoulders, chest, the tall narrow something beneath the towel, white stone, olive skin, pink flesh.

"Thy rod and thy staff they comfort me," she had the nerve to say to him after telling him the dream. She cracked a smile, trying to make it into a joke. But then she heard the voice of Rose, almost gone now, barely audible, *don't touch yourself down there.* And remembered the night after being naked on Dr. Delman's table, many nights, reaching down to hold and touch, small palm cupped protectively over soft, smooth skin, feeling her back and shoulders on the firm mattress, the heavy cotton quilt over her, and her hands down there, beneath the quilt in the dark where no one can see, caressing outside, inside, and behind her eyes something dark, opaque, rolling. And remembered standing alone in the dark kitchen. No one is there. No one knows her mother is dead on the bathroom floor. Will never come back even if she begs, *Let me call you sweetheart, I'm in love . . .* And remembered a cruel parody of the old song she'd heard some raucous high-school boys sing when she was fourteen or fifteen, *Let me call you sweetheart because I forgot your name,* and she hated them, shouted at them to shut up – let them think she was crazy. Time is running out with blood. Time has run out. Calves ache. She is all alone, trapped, buried alive. Who were you? Who were you? The story she has wanted to write forever, trying not to forget. And the finger feeling comes. No longer vivid olive brown, her fingers are dead white, and big.

Journal entry: March, 1997.

Finally, the hunger strike has ended. Negotiations with the administration have begun. There is no hope of retaining Helene, but, thanks to her, other concerns will be addressed, certain demands will be granted. Many on the faculty report an end to bouts of insomnia, and I too feel something unlock, am free to breathe easily again.

I realize I have not had the life I thought I had. Not a close family – Luke, Khoby and me. All along I have been living in this other realm, all alone, a single mother of several children. I had to send the eldest to stay with my Aunt Lucille, and I feel very guilty for this, especially since I have failed to visit her, and I am afraid she is angry with me. The child in my dream is Beth when she was a child – plump, a head full of black curls, a very sad child, but a good girl, a too good very sad girl. I am longing to see her but somehow I am prevented from going to her, and so I keep wandering around, up 7th Avenue, down 6th, with no place to go at all.

"This dream gives us a language," he told me today with unusual excitement. "There are two worlds, two realities, and in the other realm you want something from me. This is delicate," he warned, "we must be careful now." *Like a surgical cut, as narrow as a razor slicing flesh until you are looking down on the actual beating heart.* "You have done so much to get to the bottom of it all," he told me. "And there is still something. You are still not satisfied. You are all alone, hungry even though you have so much in the other world. And even with your love of words, you can't find the words for this." His tone was forceful and insistent, nothing more, but when I remember it I hear him screaming. I was quiet, a little afraid, yet oddly comforted. When I remember this session I will see him standing, although in reality he did not leave his chair. I will see him pacing the room, arching over me. "This is the realm of fear," he told me. *Where the earth cracks, where blood ribbons over bleached white bone.* "This is the realm we are in."

I sit in my chair, this journal in my lap, and I hear his words like a tape recording in my brain, no trouble remembering as I write them down with a shaking hand. I listened like a child riveted to a bedtime story in which a secret, waited for, suspected all along, is about to be revealed. Tillie Olsen's sorrowful maternal cry – *What in me demanded that goodness in her?* Toni Morrison's evocation of biblical redemption – *I will call her beloved which was not beloved.*

And now tonight I am cold. The windows are new and tight, but I am sitting here covered with a flannel robe, a blanket over my knees. As a novel unlayers until the deepest voice is heard at last, I am unlayered. In all the years of studying, reading, writing about the way the past is not past, with all the vocabularies I've learned to describe this overlapping of realities, the actual bending of time, with all my favorite passages of prose and poems transcribed into journals, treasured prints framed, albums of symphonies and concertos scratched and worn, works that have actually changed my life, I have never really understood until now, until the language of my dream made me know, made my body know, my mind in my body know, that I live in both worlds. In the other realm, I am always left with Lucille. Violet is dead, Frank is out of my reach, hunger and desolation so powerful I lose my breath. Then I try to remind myself: I am not there now. I am fifty-three. I have a husband, a grown son, work, good fortune. But I have to keep saying it because I am down here where terror stalks. I emerge for long periods, writing, teaching, mothering, but I am always back there – here – waiting for the next time.

Down here many things are clear. Voices are familiar, and all the veils have floated away. Down here it is scary, but it is where I am. The indictments I have heard a million times repeat, criticisms, denunciations, insults. Nothing to do with the other world, I make them up down here. After all these months of trying to expose the shapeless part, hunger unformed into graceful words, here it is, a ravenous longing like nothing I have ever felt before. Nothing but the sounds. Nothing but the threat. Nothing to eat in this dungeon, nothing to trust in this prison, I have made it all up, my mother's life, my father's love, Dr. Daniels. I cannot feel his feelings down here.

3. 16th Street

1.

It is difficult to keep track of time in a story about time frames collapsing. I believe it was in the early autumn of my third year of working with Dr. Daniels that I received the call from Lucille, but it may have been closer to winter, or even early spring. I do know it was after that summer with Judith on the Cape when in an expansive state of mind after the first phase of my journey, I decided to record this story even as it continued to unfold, one of the most difficult and fulfilling labors of my life.

Lucille asked me if I would come for lunch. There were things on her mind, she said – old stories about her childhood, about my mother, pressing again. She wanted to tell them to someone, thinking perhaps they might hold some interest for Sam and Beth, or Liz and me. She had a new tape recorder Sam had given her for Christmas. Could I buy some tapes, she asked. Did I know how to use one of those things? Would I come and help her record the old memories pressing on her mind?

When I told Liz and Beth about it, they scoffed. We've heard her stories all our lives, Liz said. Full of distortions. What's the point of asking again? Go ahead if you want to, but you won't learn anything, Beth said, and with some resentment in her tone: There's no point to it, Celia, believe me, I talk to her every day.

Across the street from her apartment building a car sinks into wet earth. I extricate myself just in time, pull out a small purse just as the opened window is covered with mud. Only the roof and top edges of the doors remain visible once the awful sinking ceases. It is dark, and I have to get all the way uptown to Dr. Daniels' office, so I begin to run, knowing all the while I will never make it in time. When I wake, exhausted from the dream, I gather notebook, pens and new tapes and go downtown to my aunt Lucille's.

The dining-room table we argued around is closed up now, pushed permanently against the wall, and covered with a lace doily and a vase of artificial flowers, as if marking a grave. The rooms are clean and fresh – Beth sees to that – except for the kitchen, its broken tiles and crumbling ceiling plaster, its ancient fixtures and cabinets beyond even Beth's superlative capacities for creating order and cleanliness. Lucille sleeps in Sam's old room, where she and Max slept for years after their children left home, each in a twin bed covered with a blue-ribbed cotton spread. But Max is dead ten years now, and Lucille sleeps alone. Beth's room has long been empty of any life, and when I walk in there, run my finger across the old books on the shelf above the bed, I hear Beth's pillow snapping; I hear voices and cries.

"Darling," Lucille calls from the living room, and I respond quickly, "I'm coming. Just looking around."

Lucille's body is shrunken, so thin even her size-4 clothing hangs off her. Her throat is a pattern of loose skin and fragile chords, her fingers twisted and gnarled by arthritis. Her once thick hair is sparse over the scalp, but still long, washed and combed and braided by a home attendant who comes twice a week to cook a few meals, clean the house and Lucille herself. Lucille leans heavily on a cane when she walks into the narrow kitchen to collect sandwiches and drinks. I rush after her to take out the ice, carry the tray. Although she's been recently diagnosed with lung cancer, Lucille smokes nearly continuously, and I feel my sinuses begin to clog as a slight wave of nausea passes through me, throat to chest.

Or perhaps my thwarted breath and sickly feeling come from being here, and my lungs would resist the ease of their ordinary labor even without the smoke.

Lucille still adores me, so she often says, but the agitation and desire this assertion stimulated in me as a child have turned to angry cynicism now. Though she may adore me, I know she does not love me, does not know me, yet there are mysteries here still drawing me in, and I feel saliva gather at the corners of my mouth, as if I were eight or nine years old again, when she says, "You know I adore you," and tells me she thinks I am still beautiful, although I am nearly old enough to be Violet's mother if you judge Violet's aging as stopped the day she died. (I know I am not ugly – an "attractive woman," I have been called on and off since I passed fifty. But beneath the outer layer of ordinary appearances, I can be large, bent over, my shoulders rounded, breasts hung low, skin pockmarked, hair scraggly and thin, as white as Lucille's. This is how I was when I walked into the old, dilapidated lobby and rang the bell, third from the top on the right. The two large mirrors where I once saw dragons breathing fire are still in place, and I avoided gazing into them out of habit, afraid of that hag I can become, that ugly, fire breathing hag.)

I should visit my aunt more often; help Beth – an angry but dutiful daughter – with the pragmatics of care. But I cannot. All I can manage is a rare visit, a phone call every few weeks, an occasional favor. Today, I have come with the clean tapes for Lucille's new tape recorder so that she can get out the stories pressing on her. I have brought flowers, several new mystery novels for her to read, an almond-lemon tart.

"Of course, none of you may be interested at all," Lucille says, mocking her own hopes. "Why should you be?"

"Of course we're interested. I'm interested, you can be sure of that. How could we not be?" I try to smile encouragingly, turn on the machine, and note a childish pleasure in my aunt's eyes as she inspects the tiny microphone. "This will be Lucille Lotz speaking," I say, using my aunt's maiden name, the one she proudly retained as a young theatrical producer, the one Violet used as a buyer of women's hats for a large department store, both sisters feminists of their time: women who worked and mothered, women who kept their own names. "Now you identify yourself," I say. She does so hesitantly, her voice always gravelly now more so because of the smoke. A wave of pity flows through me, catching in my throat and adding to the already difficult breathing.

"What shall I say?" Lucille asks, still child-like. "Oh, this was a mistake."

"No it wasn't – don't be silly – you wanted to tell some stories." I press the STOP button. "Just pretend you're talking directly to me – Celia – your favorite niece. Tell me," I coax my tiny, aged aunt, keeping any trace of irony from my voice. And I see the younger Lucille walking about the old rooms, hair thick and loose, wearing only underpants, her lovely breasts exposed. The children watch her open the drawers of the chest in the hallway, take out a bra, a filmy black slip, find a dark suit in the closet, a matching scarf.

"Darling," Lucille says, calling me back to present time, tape, smoke, dispersing shadow and mirage. "So, where shall I begin?"

I press ON – "Did you want to start in Norwalk?" – then OFF again, suddenly impatient, as if I think I can get what I want in this sort of interchange simply by demanding it. "Look, Lucille, you know what I'm interested in. Why did she do it? No one has ever come close to explaining it to me. What was she going through all those years of her on and off depression? Why was the last time so irreversible? Did something dramatic happen between her and my father when she returned from Paris in 1948? Is all this part of the story you wanted to record today? I'm thinking about her a lot again. There are things I need to know."

"Why now?" Lucille asks, but I don't want to tell her about the accident, my elaborate suicidal fantasies, or Dr. Daniels. "I don't know why," I say. "Maybe I need to write her story in a new way – maybe it's part of my own aging. I need to know as much about the family as I can."

"Oh, for goodness sakes, it's the past," says Lucille, arguing against her own stated desire.

"Well, you said you have stories pressing," I remind her. "The fact that something is in the past doesn't mean it's erased, or forgotten."

And so she begins with a slightly more detailed version of a story I'd heard many times before. "Well, I always adored your mother, even though she'd been nothing but trouble from the start – temperamental – crying at the slightest injury, at the most ordinary disappointment rushing into Mother's arms. And right up to the end – falling in love, marrying, then falling in love with someone else. Innocent, is how I sometimes thought of her. Dangerously innocent. Of her own power and obvious beauty. Of the way people (not only our mother) adored her." She pauses, drags in smoke, holds it, blows it out. I'm afraid she'll stop at this tantalizing beginning, but she's only having a passing, silent dialogue with herself. "Of course I wondered at times if Violet's insistence on her own weakness and endless fears were false modesty, as if she could never remember her achievements, and Frank was only one of the charismatic, seductive men . . . well he was these things," she admits after a pause to acknowledge the contradiction of her long critique of my father. "Men were instantly attracted to her. And her business success was uncommon for a woman in the 40s – the travels to Europe in elegant circumstances – grand hotels paid for by the company – delicious food, the steady increase in responsibility and salary. Yet she would complain every night on the phone about how awful her life was. We talked every single night, at least once before we went to bed. Max wasn't a jealous husband, but he was jealous of Violet. She'd complain so much, like she was rushing from sorrow to sorrow, and for so many nights in a row, until I began to wish for the other cycles, when she was angry at everyone who crossed her path. The children were selfish, she'd say. Well, they were children, weren't they? Frank was insensitive to her feelings and incapable of passion. I'd tried to warn her about that. He was seductive, but not really sensual, and I suspected it from the first. The sort of man numerous women fell in love with but the few who got into an actual relationship with him knew he didn't like anything close to a steady diet of sex."

Lucille twists her mouth, picks up a cigarette but lays it down in the ashtray unlit. "You sure you want to know all this, Celia? She asks this as if I were learning it for the first time.

"Yes," I say, with as much neutral warmth as I can muster.

"Well, when she was angry, friends and colleagues were not so much guilty of real faults in Violet's mind as they were deserving of contempt for ordinary human foibles, or even qualities of personality some-one else might not view as a fault at all. But I admit it – in the end I preferred her sadness. At least she was vulnerable then, not so critical or mean. But I loved her – maybe I was in love with her like everyone else, if you can say such a thing about a sister. I was always trying to trigger the third mood, the most rare, when her magical intensity – do you remember it, Celia darling? How she could throw an enchanted dust over the world? Max's jealousy wasn't entirely irrational, I guess. But how could I explain such feelings to others? Even to myself?"

Whenever I had heard the story before it had been in a tone of arrogance edged with contempt. Now, aged, sick, or perhaps responding to a passing need, Lucille sounds as if she is looking for the story as she tells it, just as in this record I am doing now. I had turned on the tape recorder when she began describing Violet and now it clicks off, the tape full. I replace it silently while Lucille lights up again. I open the window, breathe, then return to my seat on the brown tweed couch, click ON again. "Was she always depressed on and off?" I ask. This too is a part of the story I have known for years. I remember the periods of depression alternating with her other moods. But I want to hear it all again hoping for some new details, inadvertently let in.

"She'd had bouts of depression since she was about fourteen. She was an enchanting but demanding child, and when she entered puberty she became unbearably moody. And she was gifted – even I, her elder sister with all the normal jealousies could see that. She could draw faces and achieve a remarkable likeness, or layer paint onto a thick sheet of paper in a way that became beautiful when she was done. What is it? Mother would ask. It's nothing, Violet would say, ripping it off the pad before anyone could look at it – just my feelings. I remember wide, uneven brush strokes of brown covering patches of green. And lines of red, I can still see it, like someone had threaded a needle and worked it through a piece of brown wool. Do your faces Violet, Mother would say sharply, shaking her head at the abstractions – you're good at that. My father, on the other hand, had no appreciation of visual art. I don't know what he would have made of Violet's interest in painting if he had lived, or Liz's work for that matter. I forgot about Liz. Never realized before that she must get her talent from her mother. I always think of Violet belonging to you, Lizzie to Frank. She'd tell me again and again, with increasing frequency in the year before she finally took her life: Frank is a good father to Lizzie, but he doesn't understand Celia. Take care of Celia if anything happens to me.

"During the last terrible depression, when she remained in that awful dark room for days on end so that once I actually forced her into a chair, opened the windows and changed the sheets, I felt more anger than pity which I – well, I'm ashamed of it now – even after nearly fifty years. But I had the strangest feeling that she was mocking me, sitting in that chair in her beautiful lace nightgown, holding you in her lap and humming love songs while you sucked your thumb – you were seven already, and still sucking – and I worked on the stifling, messy room."

I recalled the scene in Melissa's narrative. I hadn't known where it came from. I thought I had made it up. All I had was a picture of someone snapping sheets, and I knew the pleasure I always feel in a cool room with white bed linens.

"Later," Lucille whispers after a pause in which she may have been controlling tears, "when she was heavily drugged to control her panic and anger, my love took over again. Sweetheart, I'd whisper. Here's Celia, darling. Here's the baby. Here's Lizzie, dearest. It will be all right. Open your eyes.

"But we saw her in a normal state only one more time, about a week after that worst bout when she seemed to be coming to herself again, a bit distracted but relatively cheerful. I remember she cooked dinner for the family for the first time in months. Lizzie told me in a sad little voice about an hour after we tried to explain to her that her mother was not coming back any more. Mommy cooked, she said. Then, Can I call you Mommy now, Lucille? Of course, I said no.

"I don't know what the point of all this is," she says abruptly. "It's all in the past."

I pat her hand reassuringly, but she looks at me impatiently, stands up with difficulty, and leaning on her cane she limps into the bathroom while I am flooded with more recent memories.

It is the past summer at Stinson Beach, and Khoby and Liz's children are complaining to us one morning of the large blanks in their knowledge of their maternal grandmother although their lives and second-generation memories are rich with stories about Frank. "Well, he lived until we were in our twenties," Liz insists. But we all know the explanation is insufficient.

Luke keeps his eyes on his morning paper as the discussion begins around him. Liz's husband David remains at the stove where he is fixing one of his creative mixtures made up of leftovers from dinner the night before.

"Where are the questions then, in the absence of clear memory?" Lia shouts, looking down and smacking the table where we all sit having breakfast, intermittently keeping our eye on the fog. "Where are the long talks this family supposedly values so much?"

"Right." Khoby backs up his cousin as he holds out his plate for his uncle to share his delicious smelling concoction of foods.

And even Ben, the quiet, still-waters-run-deep one, snorts sarcastically in agreement, then looks up from the sports page to address his sister and cousin, pointedly ignoring his mother and aunt: "I'm like, she's our grandmother. You know what I'm saying? And it's as if she never lived at all."

"No, I'm sorry, Mom . . . Celia," Lia says, pushing her brown hair with its newly dyed wine-red highlights out of her eyes. "It won't work. There's a truly weird silence around your mother. And maybe it was too traumatic. Maybe it's too painful, even now. I understand. But you don't even talk about that!"

Liz and I look at each other, at our children, down at our morning coffee.

"You're right," I finally say. "And Liz and I are both wrestling with the old stories again. We should talk about it all together, as a family."

But Liz looks away from me, then at her daughter impatiently. "I'm sorry, Lia, I don't feel like talking about it with everyone," she says in a tone I always identify as anger, which she always denies. "There are some things that are private. I'm not sure I think everything has to be talked about in a crowd."

A familiar nervousness envelops me as I try to gauge if she is getting upset in general or is perhaps angry at me. Should I have been less quick to offer a family talk? Had I been intrusive, bossy, trying to take up all the space, a tendency Liz has accused me of since we were children? I stare at her eyes, her lips, the set of her jaw. A close reading of her face is the way it comes to me, mixing up my literature classes, some story I am starting to write in my head, and my actual life. Shadows seem to fall on the men at the table as I remember the scene, Lia at the edge of the lit center, Liz and I dead center of a blinding light. Then the time frames open, gates unlock, and behind each gate a picture:

A young girl, six, five, four years old, even three or two: eyes wary, as if she's on the lookout for something bad; lips parted in an ingratiating smile which complicates the wary eyes. She looks up at a woman who is adored. Early in life, as early as the very beginning of words, the child tries to learn to read the woman, but the woman is complex, there are many conflicting layers to the being of this woman. She is passionate, sweeping the child into her arms. She is intriguing, teaching word games and planning adventurous excursions. She is tender, singing haunting love songs at bed-time instead of conventional lullabies: *let me call you sweetheart, I'm in love with you* and *down in a green and shady bed a modest violet* . . . But then she is remote (or perhaps it is indifference), so inaccessible the child will be reminded, much later, of the quarter moon her mother loved. She will try to see into the three quarters of darkness, to imagine the shape of the full circle. Sometimes it seems as if she can see it vaguely outlined in the dark completing the sliver of silver, and the child, then the woman, always mesmerized by quarter moons, will remember the vague smell of her mother, will hear a familiar tone of voice, and sometimes, rarely, but some-times, a phrase – *I'm in love – a green and shady bed* – from the song itself. The mother's remoteness expands over time, or else, worse, becomes a prelude to a sweeping resentment that like a steam roller flattens everything promising or burgeoning in its path. She rails on about her needs and disappointments, about her point of view, which she believes is constantly obliterated by everyone around her. And you can't get in. I remember Frank trying; with Dr. Daniels as partner in this effort to remember and imagine, to recall or construct a story, I begin to remember myself trying as well. I see the precise shape of Violet's body, shoulders slightly stiff, hand movements swift, as she jerks dishes around the table, the slight stamp of her feet as she moves angrily from room to room, and her face: I see myself staring at my mother's eyes, lips, jaw, trying to find a key to unlock the mood. Perhaps if I can be exactly what is wanted at that moment, my mother will become soft again, a warm pleasure will fill the room like a dry riverbed filling with water, and then, who knows, it may fill so deep you can float right in. And always the image: the child looking up at the woman. The child will do anything for her love. She is trying to read the woman's face.

Then I am back in the Stinson Beach kitchen trying to read my sister who is saying in an altered, cheerful tone: "Anyone want to walk on the beach?" Past fights and a few terrible explosions rush through my mind. My sister and I are arguing about some perspective on motherhood over the phone, and without warning we are on a different track from ordinary disagreement. Tension is so thick I feel it through the phone wires, in my back. *Well, I think* . . . I say, my voice becoming a shout. And *Don't shout at me*, she responds. We both try to recover the ordinary track of simple disagreement, but it is inaccessible now. Either we have to agree to hang up instantly or we plunge on, emotions and voices escalating out of control. Once, in the Metropolitan Museum of Art, viewing an exhibit of work by

Anselm Kiefer, a German artist who attempts to confront the Holocaust in large, intense, thickly painted canvases, we begin to differ about some small part of the relationship between politics and art. In essence we agree – that is what is so striking, our views are fundamentally the same – yet right there, in the large, crowded gallery, she raises her voice and begins to lecture me, and I respond in kind, defending my point of view as if we were in fact discussing our different memories of our mother, hers filled with rage and absence, mine with rage and love. Finally I find the self-control to say I must leave, my feet hurt and I have to go home; because we are too far gone on the old track even for a simple statement such as *we had better stop this now, something is wrong*. I might just as easily picture our attachment, rushing into each other's arms at every reunion, each needing the other to know the daily facts and feelings of her life, but just then all this is pushed aside by the many conflicts rushing into my mind. The two of us sitting on her deck, our voices and tension escalating to such a degree that when we look around us we see that everyone else has fled, we are alone, our skins burning in the July afternoon sun, tearing at each other's points of view as if we were scavengers tearing at animal flesh. And once, long before, when the children were very young, fighting with such intensity in my living room that I went into what felt like another realm, hearing my voice from far away as I did when I gave birth and the physical pain had split me into two women, one on her back on the delivery table, the other somewhere at the edge of the room, watching and listening to screams. Khoby still re-members that fight, of course, and tells me how frightened he was, but neither of us remembers the details, or when I do they seem strangely insignificant. Between us, of course, is Violet, but she is not there, and in her absence we have only one place to know our sorrow and our rage.

"I'd love to take a walk," I say, betraying the children, doing anything for love. "Let's go now while the fog is lifted. Look, behind the mountain, the sun is coming out."

Now, I stare at my aunt as she takes her seat again. I feel a mixture of pity and surprise at my own – is it cruelty? Certainly ruthlessness, to push an old woman to revisit the most painful parts of the past. But I can't resist. She is the only one left. Her only brother is dead. Her remaining sister lives in the daze of Alzheimer's, an absence of memory more terrifying even than death. "Who was she, Lucille? Surely you know more than what I've always been told. Beautiful. Brilliant. Often depressed, increasingly so after Liz was born. Who was she really? I want to know. We all want to know." Old, familiar floodgates out of which must pour, I foolishly believe for the moment, the perfect story, a warm current to calm the tides, the true explanation at last promising: if you remember this you will understand.

"Who was she really." Lucille's raised eyebrows and sad smile complete the implication: who can know? Silently, she points to the ON/OFF button, drags on her cigarette, and when the tape is going, begins with a story I have never heard before.

"You know we lived in South Norwalk. It was a big house. There were four children, but your mother – Violet – and I were the closest, even though I was the eldest and she the second to youngest, eight years between us, several miscarriages, and even one abortion, I think. She was our mother's favorite."

"No," she says, and a look of unhappiness passes over her face causing a silence so extended I am alarmed I may lose before I even gain it some new information, even one new detail precious among all the old, encrusted lies. "Oh, come on," I plead. "I understand. It's so uncomfortable. Everyone feels that way telling their stories. But come on – what did the house look like?" She acquiesces, and I rewind, a swift swoosh, then quickly STOP and ON.

"Large, lovely furniture, most of it chosen by my father and his friends who were very sophisticated people. My mother had no taste. She was an ignorant woman – beautiful, but ignorant. But that's not the story I want to tell." She looks off into the distance, back at me, into the distance again. "I was my father's favorite. He adored me. I don't know why. Violet was more beautiful. He loved Rosa, his baby, the youngest in the family, and of course he had a son. But I was his favorite. Something to do with my being smart, I suppose. I was always reading. Even as a child, I could talk with his educated friends. Once – I couldn't have been more than twelve – I made the mistake of telling him I was too shy to talk. He looked at me, very fiercely, and said, Shy? These people come to our house, some of them here for the first time, and you are shy? It's *your* job to make *them* feel comfortable."

I am unsure how to respond to my grandfather's ruthless social training of his eldest daughter. I imagine her, confused, awkward, wanting passionately to please the parent who makes her feel special and loved. But here she is at ninety-three, looking wistful as she recalls the scene. Suddenly, I remember the line in Violet's letter about shyness, how she knew her sister would have gathered everyone around her on the ocean liner heading for Europe. I tell Lucille this story, and I have hit the right note. Lucille smiles and continues.

"So I became his hostess. Mother would be tending to some housework, or the younger children, I really don't know where she was. And I'd be in what we called the parlor with my father and his friends. Oh, I adored him! He was handsome, clever, a doctor who loved literature. He was really saddled with his wife, fell in love with her beauty, I suppose, but they had nothing in common. One day she did a terrible thing to me." She pauses again, lights a new cigarette, purses her lips and straightens them again, in and out in a gesture of nervousness I know as well as my own lip biting. "I don't know. Should I go on?"

"Of course!" I practically shout. "What was the terrible thing?"

Lucille stares at the tape recorder as if it is her partner in the narration. She drags in smoke.

"I'd come home as usual, around four o'clock. I was in high school, about fifteen I think. My father was in New York City for a few days, where he often went for a week at a time, to lecture and see his friends. And my mother greeted me in the hallway, waving a piece of paper at me, screaming – You see! This is the man you so adore! What do you think of him now? She thrust a letter at me and I read it, a love letter from one of his women friends, one of the guests I'd received in the house, an elegant woman, intelligent, and for her day, a feminist. I never forgave my mother for that." Her lips part, meet, part again. Her breathing deepens into a series of sighs. "Turn it off, Celia. I shouldn't have begun." I put my finger on the OFF button but do not press down. The tape rolls. We are quiet for a few minutes, until I ask gently, "And now? Do you feel any sympathy now with your mother? After all these years being a mother and a wife yourself? A grandmother? Now that you're ninety-three?"

Lucille looks at me uncomprehendingly. "No," she says, and the no is hard, a gravestone marking a burial so old only dust and dry bone would remain. I remember the years my grandmother lived with Lucille, for six or seven years before she died, when Lucille's anger filled every room Frieda entered edging out even polite verbal exchange. I had always thought the cause of it was Sam, my grandmother's disapproval of Lucille's indulgence of his whims, her obvious preference and sympathy for her granddaughter, Beth. Like most children, I assumed everything began with the birth of my generation, not old enough to realize that although long past childhood memories can appear to be pounded to dust, flattened and dispersed, they will show up in a hundred vivid translations, a lifetime of disturbing dreams, passed on to the next generation, and the next.

Lucille stands up, takes a deep breath and says, "Come on, let's have a drink. It's late enough for cocktails. Well, almost." I follow her into the kitchen where she opens a bottle of vodka and pours it over ice with shaking hands.

"You never loved her?" I ask Lucille as she hands me a drink. I know the inevitable answer, but also that beneath it, further back, is the burial, because of course Lucille, Frieda's first child, did love her once. I remember Khoby, Lia, Ben, Anna – all the children I have known since birth and helped to raise. They love you passionately. They want you shamelessly. They forgive you and desire you. Their infant mouths suck the fluids from your breasts, they bite your neck and cheeks, their eyes drink you in. They read you, your face, your posture, your mood.

"No," says Lucille. "And she didn't love me. Something never – well – worked between us. I loved my father. My mother loved her son, her baby, Rosa, but most of all Violet, the prettiest one." Then she stops and says again, "This was a mistake," and this time she won't be cajoled by my manipulations. She limps back into the living room and clicks off the recorder herself while I go down the hall to the bathroom.

Its rectangular dark window is painted shut. Tiny squares of white and black tile alternate over the narrow floor space. The sink itself, the view from the toilet of the door that will never quite close, the deep tub worn to gray – all the shapes, colors, the specific smell of it, evoke my childhood fears. Nights when I tried to have "sleepover dates" with Beth, but my panic would rise to such a pitch I'd have to call my father, no matter what the time, and ask him to come get me. One night, after many failed attempts at sleep, Lucille refused to make the call. "What are you so afraid of," she asked, turning on a lamp by the bed, and I answered, "That I won't fall asleep all night." "So?" she said. "So you'll lie there until morning." I stared at her, my body stiff and immobile as the world inside my head shifted and quaked. "What did you think?" she asked. "That I would die," I told my aunt. I was ten years old and had not been able to sleep away from Frank all night since the day I found Violet on the bathroom floor. It would take another forty-five years before I could face the murderous desires keeping that child from sufficiently loosening her hard won and precarious controls to be able to sink into sleep peacefully, without her father on guard in the next room.

Washing my hands under the cold-water tap in Lucille's old scarred sink, looking into the medicine chest mirror, I am in another bathroom, the one in a dream I suddenly remember from the night before. This one is large, its floors and walls covered with a harmonious pattern of pearl white and pale green tile; some of the green tiles are plain, some are etched with a delicate white leaf design. I had dreamed of this bathroom once before, during the middle of my reading to Dr. Daniels. On either side of the room are broad windows. I look out and see a large, attractive woman, her enormous breasts and ample stomach covered by a beautiful fabric of brown and black striped silk. Her thick, graying black hair is pulled off her face into a simple knot. Her cheeks are flushed as she works in her kitchen, eating everything in sight, but comfortable, it seems, in her fat beauty. The room outside the opposite window is dark. Its walls and floor are dark wood. A large, dark wood desk covered by a deep red, richly patterned fabric dominates the space. A thin, harsh-looking woman sits and writes. She wears a red jacket over a black turtleneck shirt. Her short dark hair fits her head like a cap. As she writes, her mouth tightens, she is furious about something. Then the mud street from my other dream replaces the gorgeous bathroom where I turn around and around between hunger and anger and the mud is a swamp, oozing with unidentifiable crawling things. No interpretation, I am thinking as I dry my hands and turn off the overhead light, walk back to the living room where Lucille has turned on the TV and is engrossed in a tennis match, no single narrative in theoretical or clinical vocabulary can adequately name this experience. Some uncompromising mixture of poetry, fiction and literal truth may be the only language adequate to this swift and volatile leaping between time frames Dr. Daniels and I, somehow between the two of us, have set in perpetual motion in me. I am exhausted as I gather my things, kiss my aunt goodbye, promise to return soon.

"Thank you, darling," she says in her low, throaty tone. "I'm sorry it didn't work out."

I give her a small pad and pencil I find on her end table. "Would you write down the address of the house in Norwalk?" I ask her.

"Why?" she asks. "It's not there any more. I think it was torn down."

"It doesn't matter," I insist. "I may go anyway. Just to look at the street. Please write it down." And with painfully twisted fingers, she does.

As I make my way outside I am thinking this desolation, this loneliness goes far beyond deserved punishment; she has suffered enough. But in the midst of my real affection and concern for the frail, aged woman facing a lonely death, I am also aware of a welling hatred for the younger Lucille who – must have – hated us, the children, and hated our mother, the younger sister who came first in their mother's heart, demanding attention from the day of her birth to the day she died, leaving a mess behind to be managed by Lucille. At that moment I want only to escape the depths, the mud-sinking, the world down there. Down *there*, not *here*, I say out loud, angry at myself, at Dr. Daniels, for opening the doors so wide things float and rush out constantly. I'll stay up here, I mutter to myself, tripping on the stoop, and then the phrase *taking the high road* comes into my head, returning me to the very place I am swearing to escape. *You take the high road,* she'd sing, *and I'll take the low road, and I'll be in Scotland afore ye. But me and my true love will never meet again, on the bonny, bonny banks of Loch Lomond.* Scotland, I assumed, although I knew it was a faraway country, must have been also a code word for death. And when she sang that particular song, she was warning me of the separation to come. It must have been so, I remember deciding in the early weeks after her death, because, indeed, we would never meet again. Loch Lomond must mean this world, then, with its bonny banks, and the high road, in sight of but safe from the sea with its waves washing over sharp rocks, must be a clear broad path at the top of a cliff, beautiful and interesting with its variety of flowers and shrubs. But the low road was where I wanted to be, where sea grass grew and tiny scavengers attached themselves to wet black rocks, where she was, down the shadow side of the cliff somewhere, and at the same time winding around the soft gray-rose carpet of Dr. Daniels' room.

"You forget me the moment I walk out the door," I tell him, speaking my feeling as if it were incontestable fact, as a child will do. "I am in the swamp with you." "The swamp?" he asks. "The place where I sink down until I can't breathe. Sucking on disgusting, slimy things. This is what happens to me when I love someone who doesn't love me back." He stares at me gravely, does not reassure me with gesture or word. The coldness, or perhaps the mysterious silent attention, forces me back into my own head, the old refuge where I turn swampy feelings into my very own words.

2.

I try giving Violet my own memories of desperation, the sweet flirtation with death that promises a kind of ultimate control, the most dangerous illusion of all. I try to imagine – but I resist. It may not be a simple fear of the imagination as I have thought. I am afraid of being influenced by popular cultural fashions, the mythology of the quick fix which affects our esthetic choices and preferences, our beliefs about medicine for the body and spirit, and, now with computers as common to family life as television became when I was around ten years old, the rhythm of our daily life and work. Click, you open up a file, delete a crucial letter, replace a draft, transfer money, pay a bill, order a book or a plane ticket. Click, you take a pill to change your mood, so you won't have to wonder why it came about. Click, you explain in a neatly structured and simply shaped novel why a woman killed herself, how despite the fact that she loved deeply and was deeply loved she became so estranged from love she had to migrate frequently to the dark side of the moon. I would rather ask: what do I know, never forgetting that my own needs and wishes will shape the story. And only now, pushed onward and backward by Dr. Daniels' insistence that my mother's death itself and the subsequent years of motherlessness right up to the present moment is the dominant theme of my life, do I begin to see what has been obvious all along. The woman whose walls, anger, passion and sorrows affected me so strongly was a woman people adored. There is much left out of the story I will never know, but Lucille's and Frank's idealizations were not simple lies.

Recently, I was having dinner with Beth's brother who was visiting his mother and who I hadn't seen in a long time. "Do you remember anything about my mother?" I asked him after a few glasses of wine and some fried calamari seemed to lift his spirits. He'd been with Lucille all day. "Yes," he said. "I remember her as elegant, and very kind – what I'd call gracious now. Something special about her. My mother was a wannabe in comparison to Violet. Even as a child I knew that." I felt a twinge of anger in Lucille's behalf that even this adored son saw the sisters that way. Only her own father, apparently, had appreciated her gifts above all others. But maybe that was fantasy too, the creation of a lonely child rejected by her mother, turning a fascinating but callous father into a loving one. Frank may not have been the only charismatic man Lucille had known who falsely promised sensuality and love.

I had been naïve, I saw now, not to realize that Lucille had had a change of heart when I showed up with the tapes. *I'm sorry, it didn't work out,* she had said when I left that day. She had repeated a few old stories and given me a new one. That was true enough. But only one. There must have been others "pressing on her" when she called me. One about Max and Violet, perhaps. She'd always told us Max was jealous of her sister, their closeness and love. But maybe, true to family tradition, the truth had been turned inside out in that story. Perhaps there was something between Max and the woman everyone adored giving Lucille reason to be jealous herself. Such a second-time betrayal would not have to be physical. Desire kept thickly under wraps yet evident to all would be treason enough. There was a photograph on Beth's mantle of her father and my mother, their faces close together, heads touching, both smiling, their expressions sensual and soft. And there was Frank's old story, denied many times in subsequent years, about Violet banishing him in the worst weeks of her depression, on certain days refusing to see even her mother or Lucille, willing to see only Max. Or was this a case of what Khoby called my imagination running away with me? Click, another story of a daughter finally finding herself by discovering the scandalous truth of her mother's life. I cling to my father's stories of ordinary life to mute my mother's love songs, her dramatic transformations and mysterious turnings away. Liz and Celia and Daddy went to the zoo. There they saw the elephants, the monkeys, the hungry seals gulping fish, exposing their backs and underbellies to the sun.

This is what I know: I wanted her, wanted more and more, wanted too much, wanted her madly, as I do at certain moments even now, especially since the time frames have started colliding. I have made up stories all my life, translated her into characters, imposed her on other loves, turned her face into a mask of monstrous power, amputated her body and bloodied her – which is why, perhaps, I saw her that way in Liz's sculpture, laced her into the ocean with its perfect green grasses softening the dunes, made her into life itself. All the stories and substitutions are unsatisfactory in the end. There is too much I don't know, too much you can learn only by living with people, listening to their commonplace voices in the night, in the day, telling stories about themselves. What I have always needed was someone to notice the absence, to listen with me to the roar of the undercurrent of perpetual loss.

Scene: The child is allowed to enter the room. It is nearly dark. She is allowed to lie down next to the woman on the bed. Sheets are white and clean, folded neatly across her mother's breast. Violet is drugged, most likely with powerful tranquilizers. She murmurs, *Darling*. In response to the single word hope rises up in Celia, up to her chest, down her arms, out of her fingers. *Darling Mama*, she responds too loud, and throws her arms across her mother's body, covers her mother's legs, straight and thin under the tight sheet, with her own small, strong legs. She places her chin on her mother's breast, but she must have thrust her chin too hard into the flesh, the bone from refusing food for weeks so close to the skin. She must have been clumsy with her embracing arm and thigh because Violet moans and whispers, *Celia, oh God, that hurts.* Someone is lifting her off then, pulling her away. *That's enough,* someone is saying, and Celia is screaming, *No, don't take me away, please, no, I want her.* But she hears, *it's too much for her, too much, you're too much for her right now, it's enough now.* This is what she hears, or thinks she heard, she remembers hearing it from someone, probably more than once. And the feeling of being lifted off – but not easily, as she remembers Luke lifting Khoby off her body while he slept, his sweaty head on her chest, his stomach pressed against her stomach, his thighs resting on her thighs. When Luke lifted him off it was like lifting a piece of seaweed from the surf, Khoby's body softly bent and hanging gracefully in sleep, back rounded in an arch, legs and arms dangling like leaves on a vine, lips heavy and flaccid, mouth opened as his father gently moved him from Celia's body where he had fallen asleep at last, after a nightmare, or on a late drive home in the car, or watching television after a long and tiring day, in swift efficient movements gathered into his father's arms and then lowered into his own bed where he sighed pleasurably or, at worst, moaned once, then returned to the deepest of sleeps. Celia is lifted off violently. She screams. She hangs on. She clutches the smooth white bed sheet so tightly they cannot pry it from her fingers. She wants more. It is not enough. Nowhere near enough. She cannot remember if she cries *Mama – Don't let them – I love you.* Or, *I hate you.* She can barely remember if Violet's eyes are closed or opened, if Liz is crouching in her bed, clutching her blanket and crying while someone, most likely Frank, in tears himself, tries to calm Celia with his soft shh! shh! She is certain only of this: She is lifted off. She is pried away.

Dr. Daniels' long, unsettling stare is broken when he looks off to the side, as if trying to retrieve some thought nearly slipped away. He closes his eyes for a moment. Bored? Listening even more intensely with the "third ear?" Thinking about a concert he has tickets for that night? I am trying to read his face, to put words to the music in the room. When the time is up he always tells me gently. Well, he says in a soft tone, leaning forward slightly in his chair, We'll stop here . . . he pauses on the up-beat, then adds a lilting reminder . . . For today. Sometimes his expression is clearly that of someone who has been affected by my stories, perhaps as powerfully as I am affected by him. Still, each time, it is as if I have been ripped off my chair. I know I must leave. I am able to maintain a normal demeanor. I have never fallen to my knees begging, let me stay, please let me stay.

For the next several sessions I took refuge in plain talk: a middle-aged woman talking to an older than middle-aged man about the hiding places and incredible longevity of memory. I brought in two photographs that belonged to Violet which are still in their old silver, filigree frames. In one, Liz and I in matching polka-dot dresses with large white collars stare out at the camera, Liz looking shy and sweet, I looking sad. In the other, slightly younger sisters, both bare-chested and sunburned, sit on a couch in front of our mother who leans over us, her arms encircling us, her face set in a mask-like smile. Liz, like her mother, looks slightly posed and uncomfortable in this one, but I look exuberant, downright gleeful, so I like it for its contrast to the first, which caught me in a somber, serious mood. I handed them to Dr. Daniels and when he held them, staring at them for some minutes, commenting on Violet's model-like posture and expression, I felt a thrill, exactly as though he were holding the physical child whose spirit he'd so assiduously invited into his slightly cluttered, peaceful room. I told him of my feeling that for the moment at least, some piece of the old wound felt healed. "What has caused this to happen after all these years," I asked him then, and modestly, he replied, "Well, we don't always know how to describe the process so well when it works." He handed the photographs back to me. I took them home and placed them on a cleared white shelf above my desk. I looked at them periodically as I continued to distinguish what I remembered from what I may have constructed falsely out of driven need. Again and again I tried to find a form that might contain all the pieces, layers and threads. To my left I placed her letters from Paris, the part of the story I knew I'd have to tell next, and I became the little girl with wild red hair again, living things moving around in my head while someone beautiful combs the soothing Quell into my hair so I can think.

3.

It was more than fifteen years before when for the first time I rediscovered the letters our mother wrote home from Europe in 1948. They were buried in a box of mementos of Frank's and what struck me then and strikes me still, more so than the satisfaction of having them, the only letters I possess written in my mother's hand, is the knowledge that I'd read them years before, certainly more than once, and despite their importance I'd completely forgotten their existence.

I had recovered the packet the first time right before Christmas, and when Liz arrived with her family for their annual visit I showed them to her. She was as interested as I was at first, but reading them together, we saw that Violet had not spoken much of her younger child except for general maternal references to us both. Liz's first response was anger, and I began making unconvincing excuses for our mother's ignoring of her younger child. We might as well have been back at 16th Street, standing in the dark rooms of Lucille's apartment, for all the changes we had made in our thirty something years.

Outside, a winter cold had set in. Single-digit temperatures had kept us inside the apartment all day, even New York City steam heat not sufficient to offset the frigid wind, which whistled under my then still inadequate windows. Liz and I were drinking hot tea, wearing heavy socks and sweaters. I don't remember where our children or husbands were, only that I was satisfied to be with her, the two of us alone in my small bedroom where I'd kept the old, dusty box of mementos under the bed, reading over letters from our mother. There were three or four cards to me alone, the rest to Frank with many passionate expressions of love for us all, lush descriptions of Paris and Versailles, the ship, her excitement in the food, theater, opera, her work. There were familiar expressions of maternal guilt at being away so long. *Only four Sundays, Darling, and one of them is crossed off the calendar we made before I left.* And from the ship, the Queen Elizabeth, right after she'd embarked and we, back home on a rainy Sunday, would begin counting the twenty-eight days, then extended to thirty-five, without her: *I have the strangest most detached feeling – it's like a dream – I'm in the middle of nowhere with a huge amount of utter strangers surrounding me – going ahead to some place quite unknown – holding fast to one sure fact – I'll be coming home to you – my dearest – and to our wonderful children – to Mother's warm presence – and all the dear familiar routine. But after you left, I did not return to my room to cry – I became the businesslike Miss Lotz, I watched New York recede into the gray damp mist, then I went straight down to lunch!*

I wondered if the capacity to split herself into her parts had been the quality that first saved, and then destroyed her. But Liz was focusing on another line in one of the letters written to me. It followed a letter in which Violet describes her pain to Frank after a phone call during which I must have cried, missing her, begging her to return, and she must have written to me that very night, desperate to find the words to do what no words could ever do. *I know you are my own big girl – big enough for me to take this long, long trip, big enough to go on weekends to Aunt Lucille and have friends over, and take care of Lizzie and Daddy for me.*

Her face drained of color as she stared past me at the reflecting windowpane, Liz said, "I remember looking at her art books when I was growing up, and when I began to study sculpture thinking happily that my mother had been interested in art. But these letters," she said as she stood up. "I was a baby. Not even two years old. Her baby. But she doesn't seem concerned at all about me. It looks like Lucille has been right all along." And she left the room, close to tears.

I should have followed her. I wish I could have taken her in my arms. I must have been rendered callous by my own need, my own pleasure in revenge for the years of being in second place with Frank. I don't remember trying in any way to comfort her after what must have been a terrible blow. Worse, when I read the letters I never saw what was instantly clear to her, that however innocent our mother's motive may have been to comfort her older child, those words also echoed the old family nightmares lodged in both of our minds. I repacked the letters in their old envelope, and, after the holidays when Liz and her family had gone, Khoby, inheritor of my need to keep family records, asked if he could read them. I was more than happy to give them into his keeping, and soon I forgot them again. Only fifteen years later, because of my taping visit with Lucille, did I suddenly remember them. Then I began looking in all the chests and files I fill with old writings of various kinds, but they were nowhere in my room. I began to wonder if I had made them up, but Liz confirmed their existence, enabling me to think back with greater confidence and recall Khoby's request. When I called him in California, he knew just where in his files he'd left them, and in moments they were in my hands again.

For several months, on and off, I tried to get Lucille to continue her stories, repeatedly offering to come downtown and talk again, but to no avail. She claimed she had nothing more to say, regretted anything she'd said already, had thrown out the tape we'd made. And it must have been soon after that – I know it was summer – I remember the heat – when Liz came alone to the city to see a special show at a museum. I had wanted to show her something beautiful and relatively new in the city of her birth, so one afternoon we took a subway to Battery Park to take a walk down the wide stone paths, through the Japanese gardens and their bridges, close by the river crowded with pleasure boats and ferries. The water provided a cooling breeze that made the sultry heat sensuous rather than oppressive, and we walked for a few miles, weaving in and out of bikes and skate-boards. On a grass hill, a mime dressed in white leotard and tights, his face and hands painted white, a smooth white cap covering his head, stood absolutely motionless, arms bent, head angled upward, legs planted wide, a stone sculpture in the sun. Later, on our way back, we saw him sitting on the grass eating a sandwich, his long brown hair damp with sweat, the tan skin of his chest and forearms exposed.

We stopped for a lunch of cool, delicious soups and salads in an outdoor café, the river only a few feet from us. I stared at my sister's body as I often do with women, especially women I love, drinking in the details, marveling at the graceful curve between neck and shoulder, the gentle triangular indentation at the throat. I observed her fingers, hands I'd written about more than once, an artist's hands, no long nails covered in carefully applied crimson polish but the same long fingers, my sister's ending in short, clipped unpainted fingernails. I wished I could observe her feet as closely without appearing mad, or her thighs, or her breasts. I was satisfied, I thought, with our long meandering talk about marriage, motherhood and art, relishing the visit out of our twenty-year family routine (summer vacation at her house, Christmas in New York,) the day which was somehow entirely free of resentments, tensions and jealousies. I stared at the water thinking how different rivers are from ocean and bay. The water's movement suggests the same possibility of finding what is hidden if you dive down, but here in the city the river seems finite, though its source is in some remote mountain and its mouth is invisible where it meets the sea. The borders of land, which I might have found comforting at some other time, began to make me feel agitated. I felt hopeless, cut off.

When we returned to my apartment and were relaxing with a glass of chilled, white wine, the air-conditioner on, two pairs of bare feet resting on the coffee table, I told her about my recent visit to Lucille's, the taping of stories, and I pulled out the file containing Violet's letters again. "Can we read them together, Lizzie?" I asked, using the childhood diminutive of her name hopefully, remembering particular passages I wanted to read with her, forgetting – or not even realizing then – the pain I'd be resurrecting with my seemingly affectionate request. *Half of me loves this trip, the other rebels against all the time still between me and all of you beloveds. I constantly think of the children. I love them so passionately.* Later in the month, writing from Paris, *Kiss my darling babies.* And in a letter written on the last day before she would embark for home, *I am just plain enjoying everything – I must try to see below the surface because, believe me, the four years I have been here is just a drop in the bucket.* And *four years* is crossed out, *four weeks* written above the mistake that must have reflected in part how long the absence seemed to her.

Children – babies – *plural!* I wanted to shout the words in response to Liz's pain expressed all those years before when we'd initially recovered the letters, wanting to comfort her, wanting her to love Violet with me, retrieve her with me, discard all the stories that kept us from her, from each other too. I kept thinking Liz and I were both mothers now. Surely we could understand the familiar conflict, our mother's casual language trailing desperate messages of her own.

"Let me see them," Liz said. She read through them quickly, a page or paragraph here and there, then said, "I want to copy these and take them home with me." I agreed immediately, saying we'd Xerox them the next morning. "I don't think I'm ready to read them out loud though – together – right now," she said. Her cheeks flushed pink. "It would be such a relief if we could talk about her more candidly," I said, and Liz responded softly, "Well, maybe someday we can."

16th Street circled my living room like a freezing wind seeping under the windows, filling my comfortable space of red and brown fabrics, dark wood chests and bright white shelves, with its faded colors and dank smell, its smoke, the weight of all its erasures and lies, and I saw Lizzie there. She is only four or five, standing in a doorway or next to Frank, her body pasted to his side or her hand on his knee. Her pink plaid dress with the ruffles up the back is wrinkled from her playing constantly with the material, folding and unfolding creases. Then she is ten, eleven, a gawky twelve; her jeans are rolled up at the cuffs, her mouth twisted as she bites her cheeks in what has become a compulsive gesture of unending distress. Liz hardly speaks at all when we are at 16th Street, unless she is in the room with Sam and Judith's brother. Then I hear her laughing or talking in a comfortable tone. When our uncle Max enters a room she cringes, even more than the rest of us. She darts her eyes at me and I take her hand. I see Judith too, her clever jokes and pretty eyes erased in Lucille's vision, which, spoken and unspoken, dominates us all, including the other adults, Judith's parents and my father. They permit Lucille's destructive narratives with joking dismissals or, at best, half-hearted attempts to interrupt her hierarchies of our virtues and faults. "Oh, come on, Lucille, enough of that,"

I'd hear my father say from time to time when Lucille began deriding Judith's obviously superior intellectual gifts so that she'd fall beneath Sam. But Lucille never acknowledged her cruelty if confronted. She'd assume a pained expression, as if she were the one who had been hurt and unjustly accused. So Frank and the others would change the subject, ignoring her or leaving the room if she began again. And even in our adulthood, when I developed a friendship with Judith's mother Kay, and asked her why and how they could have allowed Lucille to do what she did, Kay echoed Frank's old words. "Oh, come on, Celia," she said dismissively. "That was just Lucille. No one took her seriously." Although by then it had been made clear by at least a few of us that we had taken it very seriously, that some of us had in some way spent a good part of our lives trying to liberate our images of ourselves from her judgments and preferences, the dark interior of her unconscious having cloaked each of us in turn with the roaming, dominating ghosts of her childhood more than fifty years before.

I see Lucille: sensuous, bare-breasted in her hallway, or haughty at dinner as she rings for a maid to clear the table with a loathsome little bell; the frail and sad old woman I now knew, thinking she might finally release the burden of the stories to her niece and a tape recorder, then realizing she did not possess the words, or the courage, or even at this late date, perhaps, the memories themselves; and I see the child in Norwalk, a large house I have been told, an old-fashioned country kitchen where her mother stands, shouting about the treachery of her beloved father. She is only fourteen. Her mother holds her younger sister Violet, only five years old, with one hand, and in the other she balls up a letter written on pale blue stationery and throws at her first born, her eldest daughter who has become, who perhaps has been forced to become, her father's child.

"There is another letter somewhere, from another time, and I can't find it," she tells Dr. Daniels one afternoon. "I know I read it. I couldn't have made it up. My father had volunteered to go to war, even though he had a partly deaf ear that could have gotten him out. It was 1941, I think. In the letter – I suppose I must have found it among his papers when he died – it was from her – she was apologizing for being so weak, crying in secret the day before he was to leave. When you found me hidden in our closet, she said, and I with the sleeves of your jacket wrapped around me, I felt so ashamed. I didn't want you to think me weak when you were the one going to war.

"Years after she died my father became involved with a woman — I've told you about her — Sharon — the only serious affair we ever knew him to have. She died herself, last month, remember?"

Dr. Daniels smiles as her question, a wordless reminder of her belief that he forgets her and all her stories from session to session, that he cannot hold on to her reality in his mind, as if he were completely inaccessible, he once suggested, like a person who is clinically depressed.

"Well, I remained friends with Sharon until her death. She was a person who was full of joy, flamboyant, loved to laugh, a wonderful influence on me. She lived near me, a few blocks uptown, and one day we were having dinner in an Italian restaurant on Broadway and I asked her, probably for the hundredth time, to tell me about my father. She was an honest woman, but not a vindictive one . . ." Celia pauses. "Did I tell you this? I must have."

Dr. Daniels gestures ambiguously and says, "It doesn't matter — you're telling me now."

"Sharon spoke to me hesitantly that day, with a certain reticence, but I assured her anything she said could only help me learn what I needed to know. So she began to tell me how Frank was a charismatic man — using that word Lucille always used. Then she described some of his anxieties and insecurities. It was not easy to sustain a relationship with him, she said. That's why she left. From the way she looked at me, then quickly away, I suspected she was talking about sex but didn't want to go any further than I would be comfortable with, so I asked directly — are you talking about sex? And she said — I remember her exact words — yes I am, Celia. He was a man who thought of himself as ardent, but he was deeply uncomfortable with sex, with women's bodies, with anything besides, well — and she giggled — the straight and narrow. Then she told me she had always assumed my mother was as unhappy in this way as she had been — or maybe she was as repressed as he was — or he may have loved her more passionately than he loved me, she said. One never knows, she said. It's true. One never knows."

She stares away from him, down at the rug. "Where did you go," he asks gently after a few silent moments have passed, and the often-heard question coaxes her feelings once again into words, but it is not her father's sex coming to mind. "I remember the passion of those letters. And her naked body — taking a bath with her — or sitting on the closed toilet watching her bathe. When she was done she'd stand up and reach for a towel. I stared at her olive skin, the dark nipples of her breasts, the lush black hair between her thighs. I wanted . . . and . . ." But there are no more words, only surprising, copious, unstoppable tears and sobs that sound like an animal barking, or someone very ill coughing up phlegm.

For weeks her dreams have remained subterranean, waking her with strong emotions but leaving no images, no trace of a scene or a face. But that night they return, several remembered each morning, sequences of dreams, recurring images, disguises as flimsy as those narrow black Halloween masks that cover only the eyes, leaving the face exposed, easily recognized, instantly known.

Celia's friend Leah is pregnant and tells Celia she is having an abortion. But you already have a child, Celia says nonsensically and sees with horror that Leah has forgotten her first daughter's existence. Then a familiar man walks into the room. He is a recurring figure in Celia's dreams – a tall, powerful, white-haired man with a sinister smile. He is Celia's lover, but as she walks toward him for an embrace she sees he is the father of Leah's child.

She is making love with Luke, or perhaps it is someone else, a stranger, or someone she has not seen in a long time. As she becomes more and more aroused, she turns her head and sees the lush black hair under his lifted arm. She kisses it, nuzzles her face into it, smells it, and feels a powerful orgasm gathering which ceases instantly as she wakes, her mind filled with the lush black hair, and then, like faded but still visible footprints back in time, with the moss green triangles of her former dreams.

Violet herself enters Celia's dreams undisguised, her face and body as vivid as if she died just the day before. And her voice – her voice is low toned, edged with a sharp sorrow, well known. Or perhaps, Celia thinks, when she retells the dreams to Dr. Daniels, it is Liz's voice.

One night Violet is cast in a play, and Celia is watching a rehearsal, but Violet is so frightened of not being able to remember the script she is going to kill herself. Then she is gone, she is dead, and Celia is asking the stage manager, a kindly, observant man with jet black eyes, why she had to die. She was just exhausted, he tells her, from always trying to remember her lines. Can you tell me then, she asks, touching his arm, what was she like? Was she like her sister Lucille? He looks into the distance and says sadly, Well, yes and no.

In the morning when Celia remembers this and writes it down, she recalls a second dream with another recurring character, a young woman of some exotic mixed heritage who reminds her of Mari except that this woman's brown skin is marked with deep scars. Still, she is beautiful, her thick black hair pulled away from her face and falling down to her shoulders in a cape of curls. She sits on a bus crowded with people, and she is shouting at Liz: Psychoanalysis isn't a science! It's more like art, or like love! Everyone gets off the bus, but the young woman is left, staring angrily and passionately at Liz who looks back at her silently, as if she cannot or will not speak.

Later that day, when Celia is being crushed by bodies on a crowded subway car heading uptown, she sees an older woman whose wavy hair and elegant brown velvet hat remind her of Sharon, and suddenly she realizes there was a third dream the night before. She was in a dark, circular room with a high, domed ceiling. There were marble statues, stained glass windows, banks of candles, a beautiful tile floor of white, gold and blue. It must have been a church, and Sharon's daughter, with whom Celia shares a warm if episodic connection, was walking toward her. My mother is dead, the daughter said, but she smiled.

During all the next day, waiting impatiently for her session, Celia thinks of the triptych of dreams. She sees them horizontally, spread out before her like Violet's three-part mirror she remembers so well, as if all three dreams appeared simultaneously instead of unfolding in linear sequence as most dreams do. Violet dying because she is exhausted from trying to remember the script. Celia in the guise of the young Black woman shouting at Liz on the bus. And in the center, Sharon's death announced in a peaceful, beautiful place, a sanctuary.

"I can't think why I'd be shouting those words at Liz," she tells Dr. Daniels, and as soon as he smiles she sees it is him she is shouting at about love and art. He is the one she longs to penetrate. Beneath his arm she longs to take swooning refuge. He is the treacherous lover who has impregnated her friend.

"But no," she says. "It's Violet, it's my father, it's Luke, or maybe it *is* Liz." She looks at the wall separating this room from his living quarters, and she feels the anger of her dream. "Paris," she says bitterly. "Where she went when she left me. Paris. On the other side of that wall."

"Yes, well it's a real dilemma. You want to break it down, but then you'd have to relinquish your analysis." His tone is sad, or she hears it that way. His eyes look full of sorrow to her. He must be feeling what she is feeling, a dangerous, measureless passion precariously and carefully contained within the boundaries of their odd, asymmetrical relationship. Or else, he only senses and mirrors her emotion, does not desire what she wishes him to, for himself.

4.

Dreams of murdering and being murdered. An enormous mad dog left in my care and I am shouting at Judith's daughter Anna, at Lia, my niece – No, I will not take care of this creature! I will not be left alone with this mad dog!

I am so frightened by these dreams and their obvious message I begin writing down all my feelings again. I draw detailed maps of the streets of Norwalk, a dark X where the house might still be. I plan the trip to the nearby Connecticut town as if it is a continent or an ocean away. I call Lucille to ask her for the name of the cemetery where my mother is buried as no one can find the old records and I have been there only once when Liz and I scattered our father's ashes on our mother's grave. But Lucille says, "I don't know, Celia. Max would have known. Anyway, what's the difference? She's dead." So I write to the Department of Health for her death certificate, on which the place of burial will be indicated, Luke assures me. Yet with all my recording and research I seem to float around a central emptiness, and I wonder how my life would have been different if there had been someone like Dr. Daniels when I was a child, someone who understood the kindness of acknowledging the impossibility of substitutes, that healing does not lie only in compensatory happiness, of which there is much, but in facing absence itself. "I am not her," he says gently once. And another time, "But I am alive." And once, joking, "I'm the wrong gender." Then, in a voice as soft as Cape air on a quiet, gray day, "Somehow I feel no words I might say would suffice. The child wants the real thing."

I go over and over what he says. I think and I write, trying to unravel and perhaps banish feelings by turning them into words. Now my love for Dr. Daniels feels like a prison, not a road. It reminds me of waiting for Salina in the prison waiting room. I wait up to an hour sometimes, and no one comes and tells me why Salina is so late. I sit in Dr. Daniels' tiny waiting room when there is some delay, and I stare at the door locked against me. Later, while he waits silently for my words, I want to stand up, walk to his chair and lean over him, trap him there while I trace his features with my fingers, touch his wide lips, his flushed cheeks, unbutton his shirt and caress his chest, the fleshy curves I can see through the fabric. I want to kiss him, but I am imprisoned in the chair, action restricted to words.

She emerges from shadows. She is walking down the avenue. I see her face. I hear her voice clearly as I emerge from sleep. Then, over the phone, when I am talking to Liz, I remember, or hear, her actual voice in

Liz's voice. Voices are directly genetic, I have read somewhere, and I've noticed the remarkable sameness in the voices of Luke and Khoby, Anna and Judith, Lia and Liz. Now, I listen to my sister's voice and know I am hearing my mother's, and I hear my own voice too.

All this memory, I hope, all this researching, is a way of letting go. I repeat the popular phrase, *let them go* (the children), *let it go* (the past), the implication of ease and untroubled liberation stunning me. I am ripping off layers of skin; like a paring knife digs into the core of a fruit I am cutting out the center of my life, risking an unimaginable emptiness. I try to imagine Frank and Violet as characters in a story, to intuit somehow what became of their love. Then my imagining is cut off by anger at the cruel and terrible way they split their children between them, the mother's child soon to be bereft and desperate, a powerful, frightened father left to seduce and please; the father's child, adored and adoring, but forever partly unmoored, afloat in a terrain of watery ground, banks of fog where clear horizons ought to be. I feel old rage at Lizzie rise and fall over the phone wires, spoken, unspoken, then on a yearly visit threatening to explode and disrupt the family reunion everyone has looked forward to for months. I map the spaces between us, seemingly immense at times. Then suddenly her voice deepens and I hear its echoes in her mother's voice, in my own. During one conversation she is feeling sad about something and talking in that low, rich tone. I remember Lucille's words about loving Violet's sad voice, and I actually close my eyes trying to move from present time into memory, and as she continues to speak, so soft she can't possibly hear me, I murmur *Liz, Liz.*

Periodically, I take out the slip of paper on which I wrote the Norwalk address the day I visited Lucille, and I wonder if the old house still stands, if somehow the stories I so require would reveal themselves if I were walking through its rooms. Or if this formidable emptiness will persist, must persist, and I must learn to let it be.

I would have waited for Liz's next visit, but Liz said she did not want to go. I would have gone with Beth, but Beth called the whole plan foolish. Why would anyone want to rake up that old past?

It was something like a dream anyway, sitting in the back seat of a rented car, Luke driving, Khoby, home for a visit sitting up front where there was more space for his long legs. He played tapes, music he and his father loved, but careful to compromise with my taste for blues and ballads too – it was my trip, after all, my journey – we listened to Stevie Wonder, Louis Armstrong, Bob Marley. I sang softly to myself, my face directly in the wind, as once I had sung the song about the modest violet. We knew South Norwalk was about an hour north on 95, though once off the highway we had no idea where Main Street, or Number 47 might be. But only several blocks after Exit 14, down a hill and to the left, following the maps Liz and David had found on the Internet and faxed to us, there it was.

A wide street cuts through what looks more like an old-fashioned village than a modern suburban center. On one side, small industrial buildings typical of early twentieth-century architecture. Yellow brick, dark shutters, a large brass plate indicating *Harris Mercantile Building* on one door. On the other side of the street a wood frame house with a front lawn stretches to a small red brick apartment house, number 51, which extends without a break to number 49, both dwellings locked, the windows on the front door yellowed with age so that I have to press my face against them to see a dilapidated hallway, a stairway in bad need of repair. I have already noticed that the next part of the block is empty of buildings, a large parking lot where number 47 might have been.

By this time Luke and Khoby have parked the car, and as I stand in the emptiness of the large parking lot, knees weakening, feeling as alone as I've ever been, I realize I am in fact alone. Luke and Khoby have remained in the car. Listening to the remainder of the tapes, I think angrily, and I send a snarling look in their direction. Instantly catching my meaning, Khoby leaps out of the car, jogs to my side and puts his arm around me. I suppress my anger and lean against my son, but anger moves through me and extends within me like Stinson fog. Meanwhile, Luke walks to the back of the lot where an apparently unlived-in yellow wood frame house is hidden behind the small apartment buildings, numbers 49 and 51. Khoby and I follow him, walking around it several times, but we can find no number on its doors.

"It's old enough to be their house," Khoby says, "but it seems more likely it was torn down, like Aunt Lucille said. That it was here, where this parking lot is now."

At the far edge of the asphalt is a narrow border of trees and behind the trees an old railroad track. I am picturing Lucille, Violet, Rosa and their brother as children. I see them in the brown tinted colors of the old photographs in our albums at home. Violet is wearing a jacket with large, round buttons over a short skirt. Ankle-high laced boots and thick white leggings cover her feet and legs. You can see the folds where the leggings gather at the knees. The dark border of a round tam reaches almost to her eyes. Her face is very clear, and, except that it is the face of a child about five years old, it is Violet's face as I have seen it in dozens of photographs of her as a young woman. The eyes are small and dark and look out at the photographer intensely. The wide mouth suggests my own, Khoby's. There is no smile. The expression conveys warmth and thoughtfulness. Recalling the photograph, now framed above my desk next to the ones of Liz and myself in our varying moods, and the tiny black wood statues of a horse and an elephant Luke gave me for my birthday this past year, I mentally transfer the child to a path that runs alongside the railroad track. She is standing there with her brother and her older sister, Lucille. Despite the shadows of maternal preference for herself, paternal preference for her sister, despite the anger toward her father she sometimes feels rising up from her gut to where they say her heart is, her admiration for him mixing with the fear that somehow she has proven herself to be inadequate, despite what she knows is her older sister's justifiable anger at her for being her mother's guilty favorite and for reasons as mysterious as the reasons for her father's indifference or dislike, despite it all, she eagerly grips her sister's hand. The train is rumbling by. They hear its whistle. It is heading for New York City, which seems as far away to her as Paris, the elegant place she's read about in books. But in the sensuous excitement of the sound of the whistle, the rapid, loud passing of the long black train, she imagines both places, New York, Paris, and she feels certain she will get there some day.

I become aware of the story I am constructing when I accidentally bite my tongue. I am furious at my grandfather, who was dead long before I was born, for his ruthless rejection of his younger daughter. What arrogance, I think, recalling the piercing eyes in the photograph Lucille once gave to all the grandchildren of her beloved "Papa." How could he not have loved the beautiful child in her loose leggings and large tam, with her wide lips and dark eyes more like his features than her mother's? Both sisters resembled their father, but Lucille had said once that if anyone commented that she had her mother's eyes, Frieda would respond angrily, No, she looks like him! How complex it must have been for Violet, the favorite of a childish, envious mother, the grandmother I remember as an embittered, self-pitying woman communicating her resentments of Frank to Liz and me after our mother died. He's an untrustworthy man, she'd whisper out of his hearing, echoing her daughter Lucille's sentiments. He's going to put you in an orphanage, she said more than once, frightened of her own banishment from her son-in-law's home. How lonely it must have been for the younger sister, preferred by a mother who neither cared about nor understood the feelings she tried to express in paint. How chronically angry and culpable she must have felt, driven into early cycles of depression which would last into adulthood and eventually, perhaps, since she cannot please her sexually ambivalent husband (it must be her fault) she might find herself falling in love with her sister's husband, Max.

Angrily, I kick some stones across the lot. "What's wrong?" Khoby asks, and I confess my anger at my grandfather for causing my mother such pain. "Hasn't he been dead a long time?" Khoby asks in a purposefully innocent tone. "And one thing I've learned from my practice. You can't take any one person's story for the truth. You can only focus on that person's feelings. You don't really *know* what went on here, Mom. In the house that used to be here. You only have Aunt Lucille's point of view."

His gentle intelligence intensifies my bitterness, which wells up in me with such sour taste I nearly spit. But it is Frank's face, not my grandfather's, filling my head. I am very young, then older, and he is criticizing me for eating too much, dressing too sloppily, spending too much time staring at paintings or blank walls. I am eight, and strangers have come to take my mother away. I stand in the hallway in the throes of that most vivid memory of my childhood, the least faded by time. Frank's hand on my shoulder. Hearing his sobs. Thinking, now I will have to make my daddy love me like he loves Liz. And the memory's instant twin: He tries to hold me. He is weeping. But I resist him. I run to Aunt Lucille. Then, years later, I am at the kitchen table with him, or in the living room watching him read *The New York Times*, and I remember him crying out to me, I don't know where you get all these ideas, Celia, I love you very much. I always have. All his declarations run together. The early ones that made me feel distrustful, then ecstatic and a little afraid; the later ones when I am married and Khoby is a baby, when some space, or wind, was let in to the hot, thick steam between us.

I return to the present, the parking lot and Khoby when I realize Luke is no longer at my side. He has gone off exploring the rest of the street. Khoby is embracing me gently, saying, "Don't cry, Mom." And so I realize I am crying. I wipe my eyes and listen to my son, a grown man visiting his mother and father and no doubt missing his lover in L.A. "You're not that little girl, Mommy," I am told by my son, the child psychologist, his now rarely used endearing name for me reminding me of years of history and so confirming perfectly the truth of what he says.

I recall a few lines from one of Violet's letters from Paris to Frank: *Sunday on the telephone you seemed so genuinely worried I felt I should come right home. I feel like a real failure – my heart nearly broke when I heard Celia cry.*

Recently, when Khoby and I were walking on a southern California beach having one of our long talks, Luke and Mari walking up ahead, he began to describe the children he worked with – their traumas, the internal confusions that could derail their lives even without dramatic loss or abuse. "They remind me of your childhood," he had said, "and of Mari's. You're both such strong women, but I remember seeing you sad so often too when I was a little boy. You may not have realized it but I was always trying to heal your wounds, and I knew I couldn't. But now, I feel I can do something to heal Mari's." "She had no father," I had said, understanding in a new way why this competent woman was so in love with my strong, passionate son. "And the wounds of the children who come to me," Khoby continued, "some of them as young as Mari was, or you were, when your parents died." Then he'd told me he and Mari were planning to marry the following fall. I had embraced him, feeling the future open, a place in my life, as well as his, to be chartered new. I anticipated telling Luke, celebrating, but first I said, "No one has done more to heal my wounds than you. And that you are a wound-healer of others is a part of what you have done for me."

On South Main Street where number 47 used to be, I tell him about the image of Violet I'd had, an excited little girl watching trains. Khoby looks out toward the tracks. His eyes light up then fill with tears. "Yeah," he says softly. "She must have stood right near here, filled with dreams. She must have watched that train come around that bend and pass by fast, heading for the city . . ." He laughs, wipes his eyes and points to Luke who has come toward us, his arms filled with old maps of the city, a book on "Historic Norwalk," and four lovely white tiles each with a green leaf design which we will inlay on a shelf in our kitchen next to the stove.

5.

Compared to the surprise of our next trip, my visit to Norwalk shone with admirable intention. I thought this as Luke and I drank coffee during the proscribed hour in the Air France terminal, waiting to board the flight to Paris; though why the word *admirable* should come to me in this context I did not know. Was I still laboring under the illusion, after all this time, that the aim and effect of psychoanalysis was to eliminate the unconscious rather than coming to know its power with greater respect, its language with greater diffidence? I'd joked when I told Dr. Daniels about Luke's surprise gift of a five-day journey to Paris to celebrate our thirtieth anniversary, nodding at his wall. "I'm finally going to her city," I had said, smiling mischievously. But he focused his comments on the present. "Have a wonderful, romantic time," he said. In response to the word *romantic* I had a strange, silent association, an experience from a year before, never confessed to him.

On one of his visits home, Khoby had been playing basketball with friends and hurt his back so badly he couldn't move. After receiving the call at home, Luke and I rushed to the hospital emergency room where we found Khoby lying on a stretcher, unable to move and terrified. Surrounded by a crowded ward of patients, many of them shouting and moaning in pain in English and Spanish, I pulled the inadequate curtains around my son's bed, trying to soothe him as we waited a long two hours for the x-ray that would diagnose his injury. On the next bed an older man was speaking loudly to his doctor about his abdominal pain and diarrhea. As the pain subsided a bit, and Khoby could move his legs a bit, we dared to relax slightly, and I made funny faces of exaggerated disgust, hoping to help him tolerate the disturbing scene while enduring his own pain. Then a nurse rolled the old man out through the wide opening between the curtains, and I was stunned by his beauty, his expressive brilliant blue eyes, his pale skin, the way deep sunken cavities around his collar bones made his shoulders and neck seem fragile and vulnerable. How comfortably and unselfconsciously he sat there, I thought and, since a resident had come to ask Khoby some questions I thought he might want to answer in privacy, unobserved by the harried medical staff and distressed patient, I walked near the stretcher for a few yards, observing the old man's beautiful chest, listening to him discuss the consistency of his bowels. Something in his voice, a tone of self-mocking yet dignified humor in his story of biology gone awry, moved me deeply. When I held the doors opened for the nurse to push him into the corridor for his x-ray, I noticed his nipples. He must have been cold because they were long and erect and lovely. Then I turned and walked back to Khoby. I'd been gone only two or three minutes, but the nurses were there at last, readying him for his x-rays. I followed them all into the corridor, and when they were out of sight terror rose up unmasked and I began to cry. A woman who was mopping the linoleum floor noticed me, left her pail and returned with a glass of water, murmuring, don't worry, honey, he'll be okay, I saw him, he's a big strong boy. And only when the kind woman had been proven correct, almost an hour later, and we were on our way home, Khoby in pain and on crutches but suffering only from a slipped disc which would heal in a matter of weeks, did I remember the man, and how, surrounded by cries of anguish in English and Spanish, my beloved son nearly immobilized in pain and possibly in terrible danger, I had been attacked – it felt like an attack – by the power of sexual desire.

"What came to mind?" Dr. Daniels asked in his usual way, but once more I decided against telling him. "Paris, that maybe mysteries will be solved," I said, and reminded him of Violet's knock-knock jokes. "After she died, I sometimes thought she'd recovered from her wounds in a hospital and gone to Paris on some secret mission which somehow couldn't be revealed to us. I've told you this many times before, I know." But the often-repeated words filled me with a strange excitement. I looked at his wall again where three small, intricate collages hung over the couch, as if I could see through the plaster if my gaze were sharp enough.

Looking back, after the trip and what it led to, I recalled the beautiful old man in the hospital as a sign of the devouring power of unconscious forces. Then I'd think as well of the experience on the plane which seemed like another perfectly foreshadowing metaphor. It had been the weekend of the Paris marathon, and the plane was filled with runners – French runners returning home, Spanish and English-speaking runners, a large group talking in loud, excited tones in Japanese. I felt irritated, intruded on, even with earphones on and Mozart's clarinet quintet in my ears, increasingly disturbed by their constant movement, the party atmosphere they were creating on the plane for much of the night. But I knew the real reason for my annoyance was that I couldn't understand their words.

"Close your eyes. Listen to your music," Luke said with no sympathy in his voice. And his irritation with my "overly sensitive reactions to everything" might have warned me as well – if this had been a story and I a reader – of the conflict to come.

For the first two days, the excitement of viewing magnificent sites previously only read about engrossed us. We took no time to sleep the first day but walked right to the Seine, to the Île de la Cité and Notre-Dame. We walked all day, carrying umbrellas, and I taught Luke to say, *il pleut tous les jours*. He knew no French, but took great pleasure in trying to communicate with Parisians, referring constantly to his pocket dictionary. He prefaced every interchange, as French friends had instructed, with *Bonjour, Monsieur, Madame, parlez-vous Anglais?* – never assuming a knowledge of English in the language-proud Parisians, and the simple ritual seemed to work. We encountered mostly helpful, pleasant strangers, avoided the famous French disdain for Americans who spoke only their native tongue.

Nevertheless, since my high school French was returning to me in surprising spurts of long forgotten vocabulary and phrase, I did most of the communicating, requesting directions, reading maps and ordering food. This small reversal in our usual roles – Luke ordinarily the leader in any social or public situation – pleased me, and I thought it might be pleasing to him too. Of everyone in the world, past and present, I felt most secure with Luke. With everyone else, I tried to keep a steady, conscious eye on myself, ever vigilant for unintentional exposure of failures, faults and mistakes. His love was something never questioned, and I was long and keenly aware of this as a gift, never to be taken for granted. I wanted him to be proud of me, and I knew he valued a certain risky independence. I even wished – as I remembered Khoby wished once in an adolescent explosion of frustration – that I could "change my personality" for my husband, who had provided so much support and reliable love for thirty years. So I read the map and lead him through the Métro line from the Place de l'Opéra, the station nearest our hotel, to the Latin Quarter on the left bank, from museum to museum and garden to monument. In the Marais, after walking in the rain for what seemed like hours, we finally found the Rue des Rosiers in the old Jewish quarter and the middle-eastern restaurant where we'd been told we'd get the best falafel in the world, including Cairo and Jerusalem. The tiny restaurant was closed, but the sympathetic, Arabic-speaking owner pitied us and opened her doors. We ate the delectable condiments, warmed pita and superb falafel greedily, excited and pleased with ourselves, while Luke recounted some of the World War II history of Paris, how the Nazis had sought to humiliate the French by marching up the Champs-Élysées as if they owned the great boulevard, famous for its elegance and its historical significance between the two great monuments of the city.

"I feel very Jewish here," I told him. "In this neighborhood it's suddenly clear how much of an outsider I feel as a Jew in the rest of the city."

"It's different, being a Jew in Europe," Luke said, and although he was not Jewish, especially so, I felt warmed by his empathy and later that afternoon, when we were walking down the Champs-Élysées, I remembered – *a Jew in Europe* – his perfect words.

By the third day, after struggling with my minimal French with pedestrians, waiters and guards in the cool, dark churches, when Luke suggested a day tour to Chartres, I jumped at the opportunity not only to see the famous cathedral but also to relax in the care of an English-speaking guide named Marie. She explained to all the tourists on our bus how to "read the windows" with their famous blue glass, unique to Chartres. When they were built, hardly anyone could read so the story of Christ was represented in consecutive pictures cut into the glass. In the large sanctuary, she showed us the labyrinth where pilgrims, who had walked all the way from Paris, walked these last yards on their knees to complete their submission to God. Throughout the day, I felt energized and liberated, and later, back in the hotel, I tried to explain this feeling to Luke.

"I feel exhausted by having no competent language," I told him as we bathed together in the large, old tub, and dressed for dinner at a highly recommended neighborhood restaurant on the left bank. "It's a source of stress I hadn't anticipated – and I felt the absence of today – able to ask all my questions in English, not reduced to *bonjour,* and *òu est la Boulevard St. Germain,* or *la salle de bain.*"

Luke grimaced and responded in an impatient tone. "Why stress? How can anyone be stressed in this wonderful city? It's exciting to try to speak the language."

"Sometimes the stress makes me want to stay right here, in the room," I told him, growing angrier as he failed to understand.

Later that night, after a tense dinner and a tiring walk back to the hotel, I brought it up again. "You don't care about words. You don't need to talk about everything, so it doesn't bother you," I accused. "But I feel grief-stricken without words."

We were both undressed, lying side by side under the warm, white quilt, a pale gray light from the windows across the courtyard filling the room, when he said, "Sometimes I get so tired of your extreme reactions. Grief-stricken. Why not mildly inconvenienced? And why inconvenienced at all? Why not just excited by the adventure?"

Perhaps my strong desire to please him converged with my hunger to be understood, I would think later, wondering at the intensity of my anger. I'd been trying hard for days to act as I thought he wanted me to – trekking uncomplainingly through the rain from neighborhood to neighborhood, museum to monument, plunging headlong into the unfamiliar world of the Métro rather than relying on cabs, agreeing to ask a stranger to snap our photo while we kissed on a footbridge over the Seine, though the stranger and the posed tourist kiss embarrassed me. After thirty years there had been no need for him to tell me what he wanted of me on this trip, and since the near argument on the plane, I had tried to give him what he wanted. Away from our city, our home, our bed, I felt liberated, too, from the dailyness of marriage. I saw him differently – a handsome, dark skinned, middle-aged man in his woolen beret and black trench coat, with an engaging smile, a remarkable confidence and an infectious love of the world. Perhaps, I would think later, I wanted him to see me as he must have when he fell in love half a lifetime ago – an intense woman, full of layers of emotion that intrigued him, making him want to penetrate, comfort, be taken in.

And had not my love of words, my need for language in all its forms, always been my deepest need, almost as primal and fundamental as a young child's need for love? So when I spoke to him of grief, of the more than superficial relief when I could use English for a day, was I not expressing, in a sense, the same sentiment as when I spoke about feeling Jewish on the Rue des Rosiers, which he had understood so well?

We argued for several hours, until it was after 3 a.m. and each of us had said things the other knew perfectly well but had never been said before. And with these long-known, but carefully unsaid feelings spoken out loud, something old threatened to break, perhaps beyond repair. After a silence of close to an hour, I began to cry. He got up and went into the bathroom. I heard the water running, heard him rummaging through the bottles and pills in his toiletry kit.

"What did you do?" I asked when he returned to bed, something in the quality of his silence distressing and unfamiliar.

"I took one of those sleeping pills I got for the flight," he said. And this act was so uncharacteristic of Luke, for whom instant sleep was an always-reliable escape from every stress, that I became alarmed. The alarm separated me from my husband of thirty years and even from the attractive stranger on the footbridge, and, as I had wanted to do since we embarked on this anniversary journey, I saw the man himself, Luke, and I was afraid of losing him. I turned to him and held him, and we made a strange kind of intimate, sorrowful love. I saw, as if in a painting, a visual metaphor as clear and powerful as Monet's vast *Water Lilies* we'd seen the morning before, the vast spaces between us, and I knew, even before he said, "I forget how much I love you Celia until I'm afraid of losing you," even though the harsh truth of his words made me flinch in recognition and pain, that no, I would never really question it again, I was bound to him for life. Then softly into his ear, as if someone might overhear an oath too sacred for ordinary tones, I whispered the words spoken with a certain casual infatuation long ago, this time with a depth born of each and every conflict between us, each and every piece of knowledge painfully or easily gained, *till death do us part,* with both resignation and gratitude for everything relinquished forever and everything kept somehow in place. *Till death–,* he whispered in return.

The next day we walked to the Musée d'Orsay, then over to the famous district where Simone de Beauvoir, Sartre and Camus had lived and wrote, and we tried to order café au lait in the now famous Les Deux Magots, where crowds of tourists took refuge from the latest downpour. A waiter spoke harshly to Luke who had accidentally bumped his arm, and back out on the street, preferring the rain to the stifling absence of air inside, Luke became so enraged I had to plead with him not to go back in and start a fight. When the rain intensified, we crossed the street to the old church of St. Germain-des-Prés and sat for nearly an hour in a dark wood pew, silently holding hands.

When we returned to the right bank, the rain had finally stopped. We rested on a damp bench in the Tuileries and I wrote in my journal, page after page of description of Chartres, le Marais, of gardens, baguettes, the beautiful tile designs in the Bastille Métro station, of omelets with brie, a rude waiter that morning in a brasserie. I wrote a portrait of a beggar woman I'd seen crouched in front of Notre-Dame, her entire face and body hidden in black veils and coat, one hand extended outward to passersby, pleading silently for a frank. And I described Monet's *Water Lilies,* remembering that it was when I saw the photograph of the actual flowers on the pond in Giverny, the thing itself that human emotion, craft and art had transformed into the monumental creations covering the curved walls in the adjoining rooms, that I began to cry. Then I remembered two dreams from the few hours I'd slept the night before. An old man in bed with me pulls out a razor and is about to cut my throat for a crime I committed against him years before. I scream my innocence, but he is impenetrable and I think, I will jump out the window, I would rather kill myself than let him kill me. And a dark night full of stars; I am floating on a dark lake looking up at the stars as Beethoven had done in his dream in a film I'd seen recently about his life. As the chorus of *Ode to Joy* grows louder and louder I, he, falls upward into the stars, or the dark lake beneath him and the dark sky above him become one. While Luke studies his travel books, pausing every so often to look at me lovingly, I write on and on in my journal, as always finding a sanctuary in words.

On our last night, the night of our actual anniversary, after a sumptuous meal of roast duck and soufflé flambé served by attentive waiters, we take a bus tour around the city to see the monuments lit up. And in the midst of the thrill of the lights on Notre-Dame, the Arc de Triomphe and especially the Eiffel Tower, I am conscious of a surprising, though not unpleasant, absence of a sense of magic. When the tour bus returns to the station, we walk several blocks back to the hotel, and I remember Violet's card to me from Paris in 1948, when I was four and a half years old. *Here is a picture of the city of Paris,* she wrote, *right near where I live when I am in Paris.* And the photo is of the Place de l'Opéra, the old opera house now home to the Paris Ballet, a large ornate building of arches, domes, winged sculptured women reaching for the sky. We are there, right there in the square in front of the old opera house, because it is two blocks away from our hotel. We had been staying where she had stayed all along. The longing begins, for her body, the sound of her voice, for words, but she is nowhere, of course. I actually look around. She is not here after all. Like the emptiness of the lot where perhaps 47 South Main Street used to be, I am filled with a wordless emptiness, a silence that is somehow the opposite of the deafening strains of *Ode to Joy,* and in that silent emptiness there is something perfectly ordinary, some extraordinary relief.

6.

Before her first session following the trip, there is a day of school, classes and meetings to attend. By this time, years after the failure that preceded what she now sees as a breakdown and the start of her work with Dr. Daniels, she thought she had made peace with that disappointment for good. But the insults and pain caused to people she admires, and to herself as well, escalate regularly, more so since the upheaval involving Helene which was supported by many of the faculty members now being marginalized, their jobs threatened. That first day, she is presented with a proposal written by one of the eminent men of the university for a redesigned program in creative writing and literature which makes no reference to the curricular work she and her colleagues have accomplished, calls for the hiring of celebrities whose salaries will diminish the incomes and increments of many others, some of whom, for all of the decades of imaginative work sustaining the institution, will be fired or, in the euphemism of academic discourse, not be rehired after their next reviews. She knows the depth of her rage is measured by her impotence, but something is obliterated, outside and inside, and she seems to slip off her feet, just as she had that day years before when she'd nearly been hit by the cab.

When she first sees Dr. Daniels it is not Paris but this burning anger she describes. They talk about the corporatizing of American institutions, including American universities, so that individual need, service and accomplishment are everywhere subsumed by structural revisions and administrative policies designed to maximize profits through the gathering of stars, thus reducing the number of people – artists, scientists, scholars, teachers – who can earn a living by doing the work they've been trained to do. Institutions she has made her life within converge, and like millions of others she must face and endure it, find ways of protecting herself within this new world. This, she realizes, is not a problem for psychoanalysis, or any other therapy, to solve. Nevertheless, Dr. Daniels' empathic understanding and shared human values strengthen her.

She pauses for a moment, intends to turn to a description of her trip to Paris, but she cannot find adequate words. Only the broadest categorical signs seem sufficiently suggestive: Paris; walls. She describes the fight with Luke in general terms, but she doesn't feel like going into detail, afraid to present herself as a spoiler of what was supposed to have been "a romantic time." She tries to get him, for perhaps the hundredth time, to express in words what he feels about her. Gently, yet severely, he refuses. She is very angry, but she has been angry about this conflict between them so many times before she resists speaking her anger again. She is fatigued by its repetitiveness, its apparently inescapable intensity. Instead, as she sits there, she recalls a passage from that favorite of all books, *To the Lighthouse*, this time Lily's words about William Banks: *Then up rose in a fume the essence of his being . . . she felt herself transfixed by the intensity of her perception; it was his severity; his goodness.* She recites the words out loud, and Dr. Daniels responds with his darkest stare, as if words might indeed pour irresistibly out of his mouth, as if the burden on his eyes might shatter their delicate corneas like tiny splinters of glass. She wonders again if she will ever find words for this journey, or if it matters to its destination if she does, and again she wishes she were a musician. Then she tells him of the dream about Beethoven's *Ode to Joy* and connects it to a woman named Joy she'd known as a child. "She was a psychotic who wandered the roads of the country town where Frank took us for summers after our mother's death. She always wore strange outfits, mismatched socks, bright-colored blouses. She wrapped herself in torn shawls. She was enormously fat, and we mocked her. We'd shout – here comes Old Crazy Joy! – following her as she walked down the road. We were cruel."

Dr. Daniels looks alarmed for a moment, and with uncharacteristic directness he interprets her dream. "The water melding with the night – it's a sign of death," he tells her, cautioning. "And you describe a feeling of ecstasy."

Beneath the story of her trip to Paris, of course, it had been there all along. She was going to find Violet, her image of Violet, to be Violet, Frank's Violet, the Celia/Violet she'd always wanted to be. A dark, old story wish. A death wish. She stares back at Dr. Daniels with sudden comprehension. She feels the protection of his powerful concern and uncompromising vision as if she is rocked in his arms.

And so that night she prepares a fresh draft of "Refraction: an Unfinished Story," this time with a new closing passage about silence and language in her own undisguised, autobiographical voice, different from Melissa and Bettina, but different from Leza too – a fourth narrator, the writer, almost but not quite herself. She writes about 16th Street, its dark haunting place in her soul. She prefaces the work with the passage from Woolf about severity and goodness and the dream of the horse and the elephant. She covers the pages in a clear, plastic binding, tinted blue. But when she holds it out to him he raises his hand as if to stop her and says kindly but strictly, "Let's wait. Keep it for a while. Let's talk about it. What would it mean if you gave it to me, and if you did not?"

Voices inside her head shout in a deafening cacophony of contradiction. She knows he would never intentionally hurt her, so there must be something here she is intended to see that she cannot see. Yet she hates his rigorous philosophy that shuts her out and keeps her from the surely innocent and healing pleasure she is seeking in his love. She knows his "method," which must be an expression of himself, has brought her this far, but she feels some old sense of humiliation and rage that nearly stops all speech. "Tell me what you're feeling right now," he says, leaning forward in his chair. But instantly she loses her anger and feels only the desire to reassure him of her trust. Hoping to counteract the rapid heartbeat and sweaty palms, the sharp pain in her back, she evades his question, instead telling him of an experience from the week before, right before she left for Paris.

She had been walking past her old childhood home, a small building, shabbier than it once was but still kept up. She could see plants hanging in the second floor windows of their old living room, a curtain blocking her view of the room in which both her parents died. A woman had been cleaning the outer lobby, and Celia, identifying herself as a former tenant, asked if she could look into the small garden and sitting area in the back. The woman agreed, and Celia found herself under the windows of her and Liz's old room, turning to look at all the well-known corners and spaces, yet not slipping back in time. She saw the stone benches now broken into pieces, deep cracks filled with dirt and overgrown grass. "It's a shame they don't take care of this place," she said to the woman who had followed her into the yard and now leaned on the mop, observing her. "No one cares," she said. "No one uses it any more." Turning around again, Celia saw the steep steps down to the dark basement, its stone walls still uncovered by plaster or paint, another place where she and Liz and their cousins and friends from 16th Street had believed monsters lurked. Yes, she'd thought, standing there quite still, firmly in the present, I know what happened here. She felt as if she were standing at the edge of a cliff, looking down but the ground firm beneath her, as if she had reached some crucial stopping place and could rest before she took off again. Yes, she said again, this time in a soft whisper, I know what happened here now.

They are silent. Perhaps he can feel her confused rage, as well as her effort to save them with a reminder of how far they have come together. She looks down at her manuscript, traces her finger across its cover of shimmering blue. For an instant he looks doubtful, as if he might bend. She pleads with angry eyes. When he breaks the silence it is to reassure her of his understanding of how important the story is.

"I could, in ordinary circumstances, welcome the pleasure of receiving a wonderful gift," he tells her. "But it would deprive us of your experience, the feelings we have access to now." His words assuage her temporarily – the idea of resisted pleasure, of fierce protectiveness offered despite his desires, or hers.

When she leaves the office she believes, and presumes he does as well, that they will weather this crisis next time, as they have done with such reliable continuity so many times in the past. He walks her to the door. "We'll work it out," he says, promising her with his eyes.

7.

Slowly her surroundings clarify: doctors, nurses, orderlies in the constant rush that suggests a hospital emergency room. Bright lights. Luke sitting next to her looking at her with an expression of intense anxiety, holding her hand. His presence soothes her. She is not frightened, only confused. I suppose I was hit by a car after all, she thinks, and here I am – something is broken – perhaps more than one thing – many things are broken – but I am here, and Luke is here, and I seem to be alive. It does seem to her that time has passed since that near accident; images rush her but nothing she can quite place. I must have been dreaming all this time, she thinks. I must have been unconscious after being hit by the car. She smiles at Luke who smiles back and wipes his eyes. She feels for her legs. They are there as usual, no bandages or splints under her hospital gown.

"Do you remember coming here?" Luke asks, and when he asks the question, she does. In a taxi late at night. "Do you remember why we're here?" She shakes her head, laughs at her own stupidity. "Do you remember where we went on our trip?" he asks. No, she has no knowledge of a trip.

Now she is being wheeled into another room, warned in careful tones that it will only take several minutes. A black mask is placed over her eyes. She hears the calming tones of a piano and violin – she remembers that – through earphones placed gently around her head. And when she is inside the tubular machine, she feels the exquisitely familiar touch of Luke's hands massaging her feet, which are sticking out in the cold air. Later, back in the crowded, brightly lit emergency room, a woman doctor with exhausted eyes and thick brown hair falling into her face warns her that something might hurt. She is asked to sit up, bend over her knees, and although everything is muted by the strange blank areas spreading into large, still whiteness in her mind, she is aware of a pain in the base of her spine so dramatic it encompasses her entire body for a few moments, her entire conscious mind, including the cool white space, and she moans, but without fear somehow, rather with a feeling that this pain is the very thing, the place she's been afraid of, yet somehow seeking too, all of her life. 16th Street, the smell or the shadows of its buildings are somehow there in the huge lit-up hospital emergency room, and she is so special she gets to have the pain, so special she can bear it, lost in crowds so thick, yet utterly alone.

Luke holds her against him when the doctor is done. The pain is gone for now, and she asks him, "Where am I, Luke? What happened to me?"

"You lost your memory," he says in a faraway voice.

She pulls back – a feeling of alarm so primeval she almost laughs. She smacks her forehead with an open palm. "Oh, my god," she shouts, "I lost my memory?"

And he tells her, "Yes, at home. Right after dinner you said you felt dizzy. You fell asleep on the couch and when you woke up you vomited for a long time."

Prodded by his reminders, she sees herself, or remembers, walking into the kitchen from the bathroom, wanting a glass of water. Everything looked odd. There were many things she didn't recognize that she felt she ought to know. And Luke seemed to be walking toward her in slow motion. What's wrong Celia, he kept repeating and, where am I, she must have said, or something like it, because he began questioning her. Where did those flowers come from? Where did we go on our trip? What is this? – holding a bunch of pages covered in shiny blue plastic in his hand. And she thought – I know him perfectly well. That is my husband, Luke. But she was sorry to disappoint him, she wanted to cooperate, but she couldn't remember anything else.

4. The Fourth Narrator

1.

Summer, 1999
What would it mean if I gave it to him, and if I did not?

I've heard his question repeating in my head for over a year. Absentmindedly I write it again in my journal opened before me where I sit looking out from the cool porch, a respite of wind blowing off the water on this hot afternoon. The huge salt marsh, its watery land at low tide a dark rich green, stretches behind a line of shrub dotted with rose hip Judith will probably use later in the summer to make jam. After that bitter childhood in New York City, she's become a country woman in the twenty years she's lived in a small New England town, knowledgeable about gardens, storm windows, bird feeders, jams. Each year she seems to become more competent in the woods, like her daughter Anna, physically strong.

At high tide, the water will cover the grasses of the marsh. A kayak or canoe will appear, winding its way through the tributaries of the Pamet River. Far in the distance, I see hills, dunes and tucked into their sides, gray Cape houses overlooking the bay. All winter I remember the purple and green brush of this land, the deep blue and tans of its waters and beaches, the atmosphere of every house Judith and I have rented together for the past fifteen years. Now, one year later, it is difficult to believe that in one night I actually lost three years of memories, and several hours before that may never be fully reclaimed.

"Transient global amnesia is the term for a sudden episode of severe memory loss and confusion that generally happens for no apparent reason . . . The condition is rare and usually occurs in middle-aged and older adults. Its cause is a mystery."
    --Health Oasis, Mayo Clinic

Several days after the return of her memory, she is in Dr. Daniels' room, holding an ice pack to her neck where excruciating pain from the spinal tap returns every time she is vertical allowing fluid to flow out of the tiny hole the harassed doctor mistakenly made. In her other hand is the story in its blue plastic cover, and as she talks she smacks it periodically against her thigh and the arm of the chair. "It's fucking Anna O all over again," she shouts. "Here I am on the verge of the fucking millennium, clinically hysterical because of silent, thwarted rage. It's humiliating. It's disgusting." She remembers the neurologist in the hospital who was certain she had something called Transient Global Amnesia, but said frankly they had no idea what that really was. Once Celia's memory returned, he theorized she'd had a "hysterical reaction" and asked if she were in "treatment," wondering if he could confer with her therapist since he was doing research on the condition. Celia relayed the question to Dr. Daniels, who without a beat of hesitation refused. You can talk for yourself, was what he said.

"Why do you hate the story?" he asks, interrupting a passionate diatribe against herself for offering him the story in the first place. And for some reason rats come to mind, the terror she feels when she thinks of them, and the fear of the fear. "It's exactly like when I was a child," she shouts. *What's wrong, Mama? Why are you sad? Why are you angry? I'm fine,* she'd say, anger absolutely dripping from her mouth, shooting out of her eyes – *nothing's wrong.* And Frank – *Mommy's just tired. Mommy's been working hard.* And now you. Silent. Impenetrable." This is the under-layer, the well inside where black water undulates and rats may be swimming, where the bricks lining the shaft of the well are loose, slimy, precarious. She knows she is in it. She knows the smell. "You refused my gift," she accuses with furious eyes.

"Choose a passage to read to me now," he says.

She reads the very last section, a passage written by the fourth narrator about all the three women being herself, Melissa, the crazy one, Leza, the story teller, Bettina, who maintains control – all three names derivations of "Elizabeth," the full name Frank and Violet might have but did not give Liz. Then she reads him an extended memory of talking to Frank alone in a lit room, Violet dead, Liz gone to sleep, the shame when her words are clumsy and wrong, and, when they are perfect, the ecstasy. And who is this fourth narrator, she wonders, listening to her own voice – no longer Sonia, the girl who trades words for love, no one purely imaginary but no one exactly real either. The words gather and make up stories. Stories fill and shape her voice. They are her. They are not her.

When she comes to the last line, her soft crying threatening to become sobs, she asks, "Do you see how important words are?" He nods once, his chin touching his chest where it remains for a moment, his eyes closed, but this time she feels no absence or exclusion from the closed eyes; what she feels is closer to a sexual arousal so profound you close your eyes so you can bear the intimacy; or the opposite, because with eyes closed the presence of the other is even more intense.

She is cradling the story in her hands. "Bring it back next time," he says, as they are way over time. "We'll talk more." But with her glasses still on and everything blurred but the print right in front of her, she cannot read his face.

For the rest of the week Celia remains horizontal as often as she can so the spinal fluid will not leak. One afternoon, in a state of reverie between sleep and waking, she is back in the hospital. Someone is standing over her, possibly Dr. Daniels, or maybe someone she doesn't know. He warns her he is going to give her something that will cause pain. But it's a good kind of pain, he says, a pain that will help bring you back to health – what do think I have? My mother's heart, she asks in response. A rat? No, he says, it's a story, a powerful work. I have it here, and he holds it out to her. But it's not mine, it's yours. The blue covers are stained dark purple, covered with blood. She cringes and says, is that blood? He says yes, it's your life blood. So it's good blood, she asks, and he nods. She feels him bending over her, and then the work is in her hands.

As she comes further into ordinary consciousness a fantasy takes over, unbidden though it must be created by some part of herself. She is in the midst of a session, and she says to him, Tell me in clinical psychoanalytic language what happened to me. She thinks he's going to say something about the ego going away temporarily in order to protect itself from a dangerous onslaught. (You were on overload, you went into the breakdown lane, Judith had said.) Tell me, she presses him, but he says, You know I won't do that. Wait until you hear my reasons before you decide, she says, that's the rule, and patiently she explains her tendency to make up elaborate stories too far from the truth, so it's always better for her to know the truth, basic, honest and simple. But before he can respond the phone rings, and from the way he is talking she can tell it is someone in his family, wife or daughter, someone close. Not quite yet, he says into the phone. She gets up, ready to leave, realizing her session has run way over time and his family is either worried or annoyed. Wait, he says, I didn't say the session was over, and she tells him, You're not the boss of the world.

For months she is shifted by changing patterns, as if she exists somewhere behind a kaleidoscopic chaos of fragments held within a frame. Never has therapy been so agitating. She repeats and repeats. Her father's desire sweeps over her and the waves leave her frightened, excited, ashamed, slightly blinded, the world blurred. Then some criticism from him – a movement of her shoulders evoking Violet, or a gesture too different from hers, or possibly, she begins to see, she is too disturbing a mirror of Frank himself. Then she is nothing again, she dreams of shit again, she is an awkward, angry, shit-covered child.

Again and again he wants her to describe what happens if he takes the story, reads it, keeps it, what happens if he does not.

One day she remembers a frightening experience when Khoby was a toddler. They were walking home in the evening on a street covered with ice, Khoby on Luke's shoulders, when Luke slipped, Khoby fell backward and hit his head on the sidewalk. When they spoke to the doctor, he reassured them that the fact that Khoby was moving and acting normally, his head cushioned, it seemed, by the snowsuit and woolen cap, was a good sign. If he vomits call me back, the doctor said. If you vomit, it means you've been badly hurt. She will never remember the vomiting that preceded the memory loss, but Luke tells her it was a long, violent bout. She only recalls unconnected flashes of its aftermath, the living room looking unfamiliar and on the coffee table a manuscript covered in a crass, vulgar blue.

During that period, a week in the middle of February, she travels to Los Angeles where she's been invited to speak at a conference held not far from Khoby's and Mari's house. It is the week of a pilot slowdown and flights are cancelled or indefinitely delayed. There are no flights to California until late that night, she is told and, surprised by the old extremity of her reaction, she is in the midst of a full-blown panic attack. She rushes from the terminal to the street to get a cab home as it is only noon. But perhaps because everyone else is waiting inside for rescheduled flights, the street outside the terminal is as eerily desolate as one of her nightmares. She paces back and forth, repeatedly ringing the phone at the taxi stand with increasing desperation, nearly shouting at the operator who responds with cordial patience – I'm trying to get one, Madam. At last, the taxi appears like a phantom at the edge of the ramp, and a handsome young man approaches her, a pilot who tips his captain's hat and asks if he can help. She thanks him, says she will be all right as she gets into the taxi and then, between the forces of her panic and the man's kindness, she cries quietly all the way home.

It is six in the morning, local time, when she is in her hotel room in L.A. trying to calm her nerves with a huge breakfast and a call to her sister up north. As the phone rings, she is thinking of an article she'd read recently in the *Times* about panic attacks, how one terrifying experience can form an emotional memory "difficult to erase"; that "the metaphor of the unconscious is real and accurate in terms of the cartography of the brain." When she describes her experience of the past twenty hours, Liz immediately understands. "The feeling of being lost," she says, and they compare notes – empty streets, unfamiliar buildings – "even familiar ones if no one is around," Liz says. And Celia tells her about her recurring "wandering" dreams. "I have them too," her sister says, "the same ones."

For months after she returns, she has sudden memories of Violet. Scenes explode into her head, then disappear. Violet crying at the kitchen table, coldly inquiring why Celia is disturbing her dinner before she and Frank have called the children into the room, reading wonderful stories at night, embracing her in the bathroom, lying in bed horribly still, staring, not seeming to hear when Celia, standing in the doorway, calls her name.

She speaks to Dr. Daniels of her anger and pain quietly, distantly, almost as if she is in the third person. She offers a fantasy of his indifference and cruelty: "I am not cherished or valued. Just a patient who takes up two hours of your time, a source of income to pay for your new house." But she says this in an ironic tone, as though they are colleagues analyzing a difficult case. Only through dreams, faithfully recorded and reported, is she able to withstand the new clarity of the emotions he calls up in her.

Once again, she is in the old house where the mad dog threatened, where she shouted at Anna and Lia not to leave her alone. Now she hears movement upstairs and with some trepidation she inches up to the second floor. There in a sparse room bathed in afternoon light sits a cruel doctor. He is opening his black medical bag, packing away a whip. Then he takes it out again, runs his fingers down the leather strap. She begins screaming at him to get out, calls loudly for Luke to help her, but Luke is out of earshot. She will have to get rid of the man; she keeps an eye on him, biding her time.

She is with him, Dr. Daniels himself. They climb around the terraces and up the rickety staircase of an old building, behind a huge, locked gate, which he pulls open. They walk onto a precarious ledge and have to jump several floors to the street. He jumps easily but she is frightened, barefoot, looking at the debris and broken glass below. She swings down and grabs a window guard to break her fall, but it tears off the window as she lands. A woman with thick wavy hair and rich mahogany skin who reminds her of Bettina as Celia has always imagined her comes to the window. Celia says, I'm so sorry. I grabbed it because I was so afraid I would fall. But the woman isn't angry, and she pulls the guardrail easily back into place.

"Years ago," she tells him the day after these dreams, "I wrote a novel called *Mourning Him* about the death of several fathers, including mine. When I reread it now I see I "knew" all this then, twenty years ago, but like the existence of my mother's letters, I forgot what I knew, or what

I wrote, and now I have to learn it all over again. When I finished that novel I experienced a period of elation that lasted for several weeks as I revised – over and over – my increasingly well-chosen words. Now my words are – somewhere – I don't know where at times. " But for the first time she feels the absence of language not as nightmare but as rest, and understands – astonished at the risk, his faith in her – that if he had taken her story as a gift when she first offered it, she would have been Sonia again, smiling and proud, feeling a powerful, transitory pleasure that would have left her unchanged. How hard this is, she thinks, how very hard.

"Where did you go?" he asks.

She stares at him silently, does not want to break her stare with a sound.

When she returns home she lies down and listens to music, imagining Dr. Daniels in his office, in his kitchen, babysitting for his grandchildren, mentoring his trainees. She is with him in his mind over time, on the surface of his consciousness, then beneath it, then surfacing again. She forgets many of the details of her sessions. She does not reach for meaning nor does she want to write.

Toward the end of the school year, as the summer approaches, he tells her, "We've done our work about the amnesia and the story. If you still want to give it to me, I'd be honored to accept."

"It still isn't finished," she tells him as she stands to leave.

He shrugs, and says, "No."

If she were to write it all over now, from the beginning, she would structure it differently: from Bettina's letter, to Leza's journey across the river, to Melissa's narrative, the innermost story of all. Then she would move out again, from Melissa to Leza and back to the frame of Bettina who, having received Leza's version of Melissa's story wonders if she still wants to try to publish it or if she would prefer to return it to a box in her closet with Melissa's other things. And thinking of Mary Shelley, that other motherless fourth narrator she has sometimes taught in her "Mothers and Daughters in Fiction" course, Celia wonders what she will do with her three part story – leave it with Dr. Daniels, attempt another draft, fashion a new ending, cut out her own voice, make it all simpler, or only an introduction to something else?

That night she floats in a dark lake surrounded by grassy banks, naked and fast asleep in the water. Soon she wakes, walks to the shore and puts on a white nightgown – the kind she and Judith like to wear during their summers at the Cape. In the morning, they put old, soft, denim work shirts over the nightgowns, and this becomes a family-wide uniform Anna will adopt at times. Many familiar figures stand on the shore in the dream: the beautiful dark-haired lesbian mother, the young woman of mixed race with skin scarred from adolescent acne, Bettina, as she looked framed by the window, the Lia and Anna of her dreams. Any of these people can help me find my way home, she says aloud, or even that stranger standing close to the water on the narrow beach.

2.

I read my description of the aftermath of amnesia and wonder about the ritual of fiction, for that is not how it really happened if *really* means an inclusion of all the parts. Have I recaptured the essence of the story? And how to describe the space that develops between the first person and the third: an enactment, symbolic and theatrical, exaggerated, then elliptical, complete with costumes and masks. What am I after, making my way through that calm space as smoothly as the canoe makes its way through the marsh to the river? Would I today, if the elevator broke again, be able to find my way through Dr. Daniels' apartment to the waiting room, this time with the self-contained confidence of the woman in green? Am I – this woman on the porch who dutifully, or compulsively, records – the same one who unconsciously seduced the old stories into the outside world? And have the stories been changed?

Often, during this time, I think of a close friend and former student, a young French Jew whose considerable psychological pain did not seem to include a shred of self-pity or anger, but whose anxiety was so cyclical and fierce he tried twice, before the final successful time, to end his young life. His sister was a cello player, and on one of her albums she plays a Jewish chant so lyrical and sad I must put down whatever I am doing when it begins, sit still, listen and wait. She had been the one to call and tell me of her brother's death. We spoke of his kindness, his intelligence, the boundless grief of their parents whose only son had killed himself.

I come across a passage in *Love, Hate and Reparation*, by Melanie Klein and Joan Riviere, in which they speak of the dangers of greedy retaliation as one path to suicide – of hatred of life and everything in it as the emotion that dominates such an extreme choice.

Was such anger and contempt part of my friend's story, contradicted – repressed? – by everything visible in his being, everything I thought I knew? *Suicide* must be a name for multiple acts understandable only in multiple stories. Yet I admit, my own desires for self-destruction have always been laced with rage.

I read scientific articles that posit biochemical imbalances and remedies, suggesting that failure of cure is a matter of incomplete knowledge, and suicide will very likely be explained in time as a neurological event, like many other problems we think of as experiential or spiritual now. I read literary memoirs that focus only on symptoms and pain, as if the absence of clear cause in the realm of experience should make us shy away from any thought of psychological cause at all. I study certain poststructural, psychoanalytic essays, enjoying the dense, image-laden language but eventually feel these works are only a more obscure, less resonant poetry than the poems I have read over many years, and soon I return to the three women who wrote until writing could no longer save them.

Virginia Woolf, whose last letter to her husband extolling his goodness and seeking to protect them both from the return of her "madness" deepens my sense of the mystery of suffering even as it reminds me of the periodic inescapability of despair. For what finally drove her into the river, pockets filled with stones? There is no one story to suffice.

Sylvia Plath, whose capacity to inspire a following of critics and scholars searching for definition of her genius and meaning in her self-destruction does not take anything away from the purity and freedom of the language of her death poems. Someone, unnamed, is "done for." The aura of unpredictability, and tenderness, contradicted by the inevitability of loss, remains with me for days.

I see the *Beware* sign at the edge of the unlifeguarded ocean on the northern California coast, the *Swim At Your Own Risk* sign at the top of Long Nook's highest dune, words I will always see flashing above the image of the accident that might have killed me.

And the most dangerous idea of all: lies masquerading as imagination, as if imagination and truth were opposites, until words are drained and flat, meaning reduced to mere designation, story to plot, and the echoing layers of language to mechanical cliché. Stories filled with truth are mirrors, not masks. They are reflections from different angles, refractions of color and shape. In the rearrangement of parts, we hope to see more clearly, to become more brave.

I have no more words, my mother had written in her last note, as if the absence of words could explain her abandonment instead of ensuring that we would never know her story, we who needed it so much.

Angrily, I turn to Anne Sexton again, uncompromising poet who spoke coldly of tools. But I find these words: "My mother died / unrocked, unrocked . . ." And in a last letter to her daughter, Linda, confessing a love too linked to pain: "I lied, Linda. I did love my mother and she loved me. She never held me but I miss her – so that I have to deny I ever loved her – or she me! Silly Anne! So there!"

"Talk to my poems and talk to your heart," she wrote in that last letter to her daughter. "I am in both."

Lucky daughter, I write in the margin of the page. Four hundred and twenty-one pages of letters! And I have only ten. Fear that I may never escape the impact of her death and the forever silenced stories surrounding it nearly stops my breath. I get up and walk outside the porch, across the small stretch of yard and into a circle of trees where an old hammock is strung. I swing on it for a few moments until I recover the rhythm of ordinary breathing. I recall the lines from Sexton's poem I memorized long ago, and I recite them out loud: "My business is words. Words are like labels. / Or coins, or better, like swarming bees. / I confess I am broken only by the source of things."

Kicking my feet in the air I feel the surge of relief that always comes with the last line, in the humility rooted in the word *broken*, and the small promise of the *only*.

3.

Light clouds are coming in, but there is no sign of rain. Soon a path will emerge on the outskirts of the marsh and we will be able to walk all the way to the tiny harbor where the river flows into the open sea. I gaze at the peaceful scene as I wait for Luke and Judith to return from their run, read their papers and eat their muffins before the three of us go for a promised walk. Every few minutes I look down at my journal, this "death notebook" volume, in which I've recorded poems, passages, memories about suicide. And as if for the first time, thinking of that last letter to us all – perhaps because I had tried in a different way to obliterate myself – my experience, my memories, my work – to punish someone I loved in one perfectly symbolic act – I hear again and am shocked by the cruelty in my mother's words before she left us forever. *I can't bear the emptiness any longer – there is nothing to live for.*

So different from Lucille whose suicide at ninety-four seemed to be an act of consolation, a facing up to reality and needs long denied. When I heard from Beth that Lucille was dying, and probably by her own choice, memory rushed in like a sea storm. Old images of blood, white tile, a woman's angry face and nightmare screams. More recent images of a taxi turning a corner, and I shuddered as if I were just getting up from the street where I'd fallen years before. Then in an instant I saw all the places I'd been, all in some sense consecutive, so that if I followed them backwards I could come to the beginning again. Paris. Norwalk. 16th Street. The prison. Point Reyes with its dangerous ocean and hushed lagoon. Dr. Daniels' flesh-colored room. Still to come, the cemetery, my mother's grave, and, always, the waters of the Cape. Then I was dizzy for a minute in places not easily seen but as real in a way – a childhood street filled with mud, a prison torn down yet its inmates' screams still audible, a dark, odorous room, its smells captured in memory. "I dreamed of Max last night," Lucille had said on her last conscious day to the home attendant who had helped her cook, clean and dress herself for several years. "He was standing somewhere dark and very familiar, and he said to me, what is taking you so long? I'm waiting for you."

There had been no note at all, only instructions for her burial, the disbursement of her savings to her children and grandchildren (nothing to Celia and Liz) and a version of her resume for an obituary in the *Times*.

Beth's husband was out of town, her daughter due to return from Europe in a few days, so I had rushed to the hospital to join my cousin as soon as I heard. Lucille lay on her back under a sheet, an oxygen mask covering her face, her long white braid falling over her shoulder. The nurse on duty suggested we speak to her about dying on the chance she could still hear. There was no hope she'd survive the large numbers of pills Beth had counted missing from the bedside lineup of bottles, even if they pumped her stomach which everyone agreed would amount to cruelty, not rescue. We went to her bedside. Beth was silent as she straightened the sheet, adjusted the tube of the oxygen mask, but she did not touch the body, which was still alive. I traced my fingers across her forehead, down the soft braid, and whispered, as I'd been taught to do at other deathbeds, "We're here, Lucille, Beth and Celia. You can go now. It will be all right." Less than an hour later, moved from the emergency ward to a semi-private room, she was gone. "She's dead," Beth said. "There's no breath." And she removed the mask. Now she stroked her mother's head and arms, touched her feet and her fingers, remaining near her for quite some time. Then she turned to me and, crossing the space long between us, in a sisterly intimacy not felt this strongly since those days in her bedroom when I witnessed her crying and snapping her pillow, we fell into a long embrace.

And who can say what Lucille may have understood about the truths of her life that morning after she'd heard her husband calling her. All we know is she did not say she'd heard her father call, or her sister. She'd heard Max.

Late that afternoon, we take the long walk to the bay, single file, Judith first, Luke behind me. The dry, narrow path at the edge of the marsh winds around puddles and streams filled with moving botanical and animal life – insects, crabs, snails, tiny fish, oysters, sea worms marked by iridescent silver streaks; at one point a large snake slithers across the path, nearly frightening Luke and me out of our wits until Judith assures us it isn't the dangerous kind. The salt marsh has been called "the origin of life," she says – life itself may have begun in places such as this, perhaps this place. The only thing I have to be frightened of, she warns, is poison ivy. We leap over creeks and pools, river-filled even at this lowest of tides, and soon we reach the tiny harbor. Boats are beached in a dark mud so layered with stones and shells we decide to wear our sneakers over the sultry, wide expanse and into the river itself. The distance between us lengthens. Judith moves quickly toward the dune. Luke hugs the river's shore, water rippling around his muscular calves, the brim of his old pink running hat covering his eyes; when he has to go deeper to cross over to the dune, water darkens his light beige t-shirt to a deep gray brown. I watch him as I take up the rear relishing the deepening, quickening currents as the water reaches my waist,

covers my shoulders, for a moment my head. Then – quickly and dramatically – it is shallow again as the riverbed inclines toward the enormous
sandbars I've always loved but never approached from this direction, the
river's path, always before walking with Judith down the bay beach. I walk
over the extraterrestrial seeming places, which are in reality profoundly
earthy. Only a few fishermen stand out in the bay, swinging their nets or
holding their poles over the still water. No one is on this sandbar, although
on the next one, further toward the beach, a few young families gather, the
gentle water perfect for small children's play while tired parents are free to
lounge and stare, undisturbed. I remember a particular low tide at Fire
Island when Khoby was two. Each afternoon a soft shallow stream would
form between the banks of beach and sand bar, the un-bounded and
dangerous ocean an uncrossable distance for his small legs. I'd sit in the
wet sand, the tops of my thighs and my shoulders darkening in the sun,
while he painted himself with mud and caught tiny sea creatures in his
faded pink pail.

When I reach the edge of the sandbar, Judith and Luke are seated
in the water, laughing. Clams are literally floating into their laps, pushed by
the tide, and, despite the prohibitions on picking them without a license,
Judith is gathering dozens into Luke's backpack with an eye to steamers and
sauce. I walk far into the bay but the water reaches only to my thighs. I
begin a slow breaststroke. If I lower my hands and knees to the ground I
can crawl, so I turn on my back to float. I feel a mixture of awareness of my
direction – not wanting to float out too far – and a sense that I could lose
all consciousness here, the soft waters drowning me. And then I realize it is
the same feeling – only now I am naming it – I'd had a month before at my
mother's grave.

The death certificate had arrived in the mail almost unexpectedly
one day. It had taken so long for a response I'd stopped looking for it and
suddenly there it was, in my hands like any ordinary piece of official paper
received in the afternoon post. I read it several times while walking to my
session with Dr. Daniels, and when I got there I read it to him. How could
it be after all this time, holding an official document in shaking hands, the
date: March 1, 1951, as ingrained in my memory as my own birthdate, that I
finally knew in an entirely new way that Violet, my mother, was dead? The
doctor had signed a short passage certifying that her death was indeed a
suicide, but there were no records I had been able to find of autopsy or
treatment prior to or after the fatal attempt. It was too late, I had been told
by three different officials at the Department of Health, there were no

records kept prior to 1955. In this, as in my other stories of her life, I'd be left with fragments, uncertain in the place where memory and imagination converge. The doctor had indicated six o'clock at night as the time of her death, and above his signature, the heart-breaking line: Last seen alive by her doctor at 4:30 p.m. He had come to visit her, I supposed, that very afternoon. Perhaps she had spoken to him in the suddenly energetic way suicides are reported to do right before their last, successful act. Perhaps he had been worried, or encouraged, or had given up the idea there was anything he could do. If someone really wants to die, I've been told by several therapists and doctors, even in this time of psychotropic drugs, there is nothing anyone can do short of shackling them to the bed or medicating them into unconsciousness.

Now I knew. At 4:30 p.m. on March 1, 1951, Violet had been alive. He had seen her. The scene in the bathroom filled my head. I had screamed. Rose lifted me into her arms. Then it was hours later. Frank and Lucille were there. I saw them from the open doorway when the doctors came, wrapped her in a white sheet and a dark bag and took her away. Frank turned to me, got down on his knees and tried to hold me while he sobbed. I reached for Lucille. Only a few moments later, beginning the pitiless disjoining of her from her mother they would all echo and repeat for the next forty years, they tried to explain it to Liz and when she stared at them, stunned and clearly aware of the meaning of the statement, *Mommy isn't coming back any more,* Lucille said to us all, "She doesn't understand. She's too young."

I stared for a long moment at the paper, then at Dr. Daniels. "She is dead now," I said to him. "But once she was alive." Stating the two facts so simply I remembered all the patterns of word and phrase I had used as a child to escape the mystery of the first, the astonishing simplicity of the second. "I can see her," I told him, "her red nail polish, her dark shining hair, the smooth beige of her skin, the dark moles scattered on her arms, I can hear her scream when we saw the dead mouse, her angry shout when I did something wrong, her passionate shout when we went to the Hudson River Docks in the rain to meet her ship arriving from Le Havre, her painful sigh when I hurt her thin chest with my chin, her songs, every one of them, every single line, I could sing them right now, to you," I said. Pausing in the recitation of my well-known list, I contented myself with speaking the one favorite line, *let me call you Sweetheart, I'm in love with you.* Then I told him that as soon as Khoby arrived for his next visit, which happened to be scheduled for the next week, I was ready to visit her grave for the second time in the forty-eight years since her death.

4.

The night before we were to drive out to the Long Island cemetery, I dreamed Lucille was sitting in a wheelchair on the corner of Seventh Avenue and 16th Street in front of Dr. Delman's office where I remembered feeling so exposed. I had never seen Lucille in a wheelchair but once I'd suggested getting one for her. Beth and I would be able to take her to the park, I urged, or for a walk in the neighborhood. She wouldn't be cooped up in the apartment for weeks, even months at a time. She reacted with furious dismissal. "I don't need a wheelchair. Nor do I need you to come downtown just to take me out." Seeing I'd offended her and angry myself, I never raised it again. In my dream I'd just stood next to her, staring at her frightened angry face, wanting to help her more than anything else in the world. When I woke and got out of bed my leg was aching so badly I could hardly walk, and as I limped down the hallway the uneven sound of my feet hitting the floor reminded me of Frank walking from room to room after Violet's death, leaning on his cane. So I knew it had been Violet in the wheelchair, and I was remembering trying to save her. And I knew that the full depth of my anger at her could be known only in translation, in Melissa's rage, in the extremity of amnesia, in a dream about Lucille. If I tried to take it in too nakedly, arrogantly assuming anything at all can be incorporated into a perfect reparative unity rather than understanding the need for mirrors, the various pieces of myself might clash and break. And I knew too, as I massaged my leg and dressed for our drive to the cemetery, that the love I received from Lucille, however twisted and broken into cutting, hurtful layers, however guilty it could still make me feel when I thought of Judith, Liz, or even Beth, had also helped to get me through.

The enormous cemetery is one of many in a tiny town outside of Babylon, Long Island. There are two posts leading into Section 3, Block 8, where many old graves crowd so closely they almost touch. On one post is written in carved letters, Always Beloved, in English and Hebrew. Her grave is a few rows in and to the right, visible, once you know where it is, from the path. I had created a loose ritual in my mind, including some words from Virginia Woolf. I carried two small pots of violets, a large bunch of daisies, Frank's favorite, a rose for Liz and one for me, and a bouquet of baby's breath just because it was pretty and invoked infancy when, presumably, all of this began.

Luke, Khoby and I stood in the sun in a wonderful cool breeze, in front of a thick, high hedge of pine that almost came to the top of her stone where the *Violet* was just visible. Khoby took large rubbings of her name and dates as Liz had done many years before when we came here together, a less complicated or a less conscious time, to bury our father's ashes in the earth of our mother's grave. I scattered and arranged the flowers, some on the top ledge of the stone, some leaning up against it, stuck in the high branches. I planted the violets in a tiny square of earth near the overgrown shrub. Then I drew a picture of the scene and mapped the site so we wouldn't lose it again. I have a file now in which I am keeping all the information I gather so that Khoby, who is interested in genealogies and family history, Lia, who has begun to write stories and journals, and Ben who with his quiet attention may be taking in more than we know, will not have to feel so cut off from history as Liz and I have felt.

Next I read three passages from *To the Lighthouse*. Woolf wrote in a short memoir, *Sketch of the Past*, that only after writing this novel, when she was in her late forties, did she cease being haunted by her mother who had died when Virginia was thirteen. She said she thought writing it had perhaps done for her what psychoanalysts do for their patients, that after writing it she no longer heard her mother's voice, she no longer saw her. The passages, all in the final part of the novel, are the thoughts of Lily Briscoe – the daughter figure, the solitary artist, the character based on Woolf herself – as she tries to complete her painting of Mrs. Ramsay (a faithful portrait of Woolf's mother) who died some time before.

For how could one express in words these emotions of the body? Express that emptiness there? (She was looking at the drawing-room steps; they looked extraordinarily empty.) It was one's body feeling, not one's mind. The physical sensations that went with the bare look of the steps had become suddenly extremely unpleasant. To want and not to have, sent all up her body a hardness, a hollowness, a strain. And then to want and not to have – to want and want – how that wrung the heart, and wrung it again and again.

I paused, breathed in and continued reading. *She addressed old Mr. Carmichael again. What was it then? What did it mean? Could things thrust their hands up and grip one; could the blade cut; the fist grasp? Was there no safety? No learning by heart of the ways of the world? No guide, no shelter, but all was miracle, and leaping from the pinnacle of a tower into the air? Could it be, even for elderly people, that this was life? – startling, unexpected, unknown? For one moment she felt that if they both got up, here, now on the lawn, and demanded an explanation, why was it so short, why was it so inexplicable, said it with violence, as two fully equipped human beings from whom nothing should be hid might speak, then, beauty would roll itself up; the space would fill; those empty flourishes would form into shape; if they shouted loud enough,*

Mrs. Ramsay would return. "Mrs. Ramsay!" she said aloud, "Mrs. Ramsay!" The tears ran down her face.

I saw tears on Luke's cheeks and in Khoby's eyes, and thought this must be the saddest part for them; to hear at last so perfectly described the inarticulate and probably mysterious longing they had always known as the center of my life.

Then the last: *"Mrs. Ramsay! Mrs. Ramsay!" she cried – feeling the old horror come back – to want and want and not to have. Could she inflict that still? And then, quietly, as if she refrained, that too became part of ordinary experience, was on a level with the chair, with the table. Mrs. Ramsay – it was part of her perfect goodness – sat there quite simply, in the chair, flicked her needles to and fro, knitted her reddish-brown stocking, cast her shadow on the step. There she sat.*

Forever afterward, whenever I thought or talked or wrote about the experience, I would slip and say, *the day of the funeral,* or *the day we buried my mother,* but the end of my eulogy that day was about Frank. When we were children, I said, looking more at Khoby than at Luke, our father could never give up grieving, so I had to keep grieving too, partly because that is where he was, that is what we did. No one understood that their over-lapping, contradictory, fragmentary stories honestly told would have been the very thing to heal us and allow us to go on.

But perhaps that is not what they wanted – to heal – perhaps their lifelong grief was a tonic for their repressions and denials as I once thought Frank's stories were a tonic for endless grief. The loss in my life will never be undone. No other love, no aunt, or maternal friend, or husband, or sister, or child, however beloved, no book, not even an analyst can ever change that reality. Yet, I have come to say goodbye to my mother who I will never completely remember, yet who I do remember sometimes in flashes with a burning flame I will always adore. I feel strange now. For forty-eight years, and before that when she lived, she and my longing for her have been the center of my life. Now there is emptiness, bright and clear and ordinary.

No, I said, speaking out loud again to my husband and son, as if they'd heard the thoughts in between. Not emptiness. Love.

We placed small stones on the tombstone to record our visit. Then I crawled under the thick brush so I could touch the dirt of her actual grave where I'd scattered and buried my father's ashes so many years before. I felt the cool, damp, magnetic pull of the earth above their bones, and that is when I experienced the mixed feeling of awareness and drowning I remembered as I floated in the bay.

5.

Later that day, Luke left the Cape for New York. As he drove away I felt a familiar tearing away I experience even when he leaves for work in the morning (unless we have been fighting, then I am glad to see the back of him.) But I can sleep alone now happily, even if I wake in the night. I moved my room to another empty one to reinforce my solitude, so I'd be less likely to reach for his body and feel its absence when my guard was down. I chose a smaller room, decorated in pinks and browns. An old double bed stood close to a window overlooking the front yard. There was a lovely dark wood chest and matching chair on one side. A slanted roof met a low wall of flowered wallpaper, reminding me of rooms in girlhood novels I'd always imagined and never before inhabited.

Judith and I, joined by Anna, who had come for several days, sat on the porch as the salt marsh filled up with the tide. The soil and grasses disappeared again, and a canoe arrived on the horizon, making its slow, graceful way to the river.

"You promised to show me the letters from Violet," Judith said, so I retrieved them from my suitcase upstairs and handed them to her. She read silently for some time while I sat near her on an old day bed, Anna's head resting on my legs. I treasured these rare moments with Anna who, like Lia, is passionate and expressive and loves to have her skin stroked, her hair gently braided and unbraided as she dozes in a maternal lap. "Mmmm," she murmured every so often as she read her novel, and then lifted her eyes to stare out at the water; and, missing Khoby, I began to hum one of Violet's bedtime songs. Soon I was interrupted by soft noises, sighs, quick intakes of breaths, exclamations of emotion from Judith.

"These are magnificent," she said. "What an amazing person she was, so full of conflict and intensity."

"You mean the maternal guilt?" I asked. Judith's blue eyes narrowed. She shrugged her beautifully curved shoulders in a movement I knew meant she'd had something else in mind. Then she began to read passages from my mother's letters out loud.

"'My own darlings,'" she read. "'My head is really in a whirl – I've seen so much – done so much in these two days – this is without a doubt the most beautiful, most vast, most fascinating city in the world – Now I can understand people being in love with Paris! Yesterday, I started out at 9 a.m. and didn't get back to the hotel until 7:30!

"'I was taken to dinner by two business colleagues. They escorted me here to the Ritz and is it ritzy!! Wow! I have a large room – a palatial bathroom, four closets, a writing desk with a silver topped inkwell and on and on!'

"And she traveled to Italy, too," Judith said, her voice ringing with excitement as if it were Anna traveling the world and we were reading letters home from her.

"'I was mad about Florence – narrow streets, marble palaces, horse drawn cabs, the museum which was the palace of the Medici filled with fantastic treasures of art, tapestries. I stood on the stones under which Michelangelo, Raphael, Rosetti and dozens more were buried.'

"She's so young," Judith said, shaking her head. "I can see her wide open eyes taking it all in – these letters are wonderful, Celia." Then she moved another page to the back of her pile and read again. "'Darling, I'm so happy that I didn't have to forego this trip – it's been so rich in experiences and sights – I try to see below the surface of things. I've been to the Luxembourg Gardens and Notre-Dame and Versailles and eaten in the district of Montmartre and spent Saturday afternoon in the country. If I didn't have a family I'd never get home. I can't tell you how I long for Lizzie and Celia – just the feel of them. I adore you.'"

"What happened to her?" I managed to whisper, for I was crying now, hearing in Judith's familiar, resonant voice a part of things I had not heard before. Anna sat up on the couch staring at me and was holding my hand.

Judith shook her head. "We'll never know. They're all dead, and not much left behind. Even 16th Street's gone now."

I saw the empty rooms, bare and cleaned out. Sam driving away in a truck loaded with saved pieces for various members of the family – a black wooden chair for me, the old brass samovar lamp for Beth, a tea table and a cabinet carefully disassembled and packed for shipping to Sam's home on the west coast to keep for his daughter who was setting up her own house. Beth's daughter walked through the apartment with her camera taking photographs of the bare rooms and of her own reflection in the mirrors left attached to the walls. I imagined the emptiness for her was painful yet straightforward, a permanence of absence I began to comprehend right after my father died and I saw the emptiness of his favorite chair. I made a charcoal drawing titled The Emptiness of Chairs, trying to evoke that uncanny absence where the most solid, seemingly immutable presence had been – and trying also, I suppose, to evoke my mother within me by drawing, trying to remember her in the early days following my father's death.

"I loved and battled Frank before he died," I said to Judith. "The loss of him was keen. It still fills me with unambivalent sorrow and regret. The loss of my mother seems – it will take me a lifetime to fully comprehend. But the death of Lucille and the "16th Street" she stood for is different. I feel the end of something, the closing of a part of my history. When I think of the apartment on 16th Street – it's most likely renovated by now by some much higher paying tenant – probably replaced the kitchen appliances – opened up those stuck living room windows – painted the old gray shelves in the hallway – when I think we are all – *all of us* – gone from that place, I feel the absence of a weight behind me. I don't think I could have relinquished it while she lived."

"I feel it too – a striking emptiness now that it's gone, but I can't fill it up yet," Judith said. "I thought by coming to the memorial I'd feel a resolution of something."

"You should have heard your mother," I told Anna. "Her usual perfect words. She talked about how deeply her mother, your grandmother, loved Lucille. It was a kind of marriage, your mom said, one as complex and resilient as her marriage to her husband. At times it seemed she loved Lucille more than anyone, even more than her own children. Those were your mother's words," I told Anna, "a eulogy of praise to most of the audience, but I can tell you – Beth and Sam and I didn't miss her point."

"I was glad my brother and Liz weren't there when the grand-children began talking about what a brilliant, loving woman she had been," Judith said. "They wouldn't have been able to take it I'm afraid."

Anna pulled her dog up onto her lap and nuzzled her face into his. "There's a lot about it all I still don't understand. Why was she so mean to you? When I used to visit her and Grandma in Florida – when they lived together there during the winter? She seemed so funny, and so smart."

Judith and I smiled, neither of us knowing what to say, where to begin. Then Judith read the line from Violet's letter I had fixed on when I first discovered them what seemed like years before: "I have the strangest, most detached feeling – its like a dream – I'm in the middle of nowhere with a huge amount of utter strangers surrounding me – going ahead to some place quite unknown . . ." She looked up at us with a smile, as if there were something in those words that might answer Anna's question, care-fully refolded the old letters and returned them to the envelope. Late that evening we drove to a favorite ice cream parlor in the village of North Truro and ordered hot fudge sundaes with all the trimmings. Anna drove home, Judith next to her. I felt dreamy and satiated in the back seat.

"Those letters," Judith said. "I can't stop hearing her voice."

I hear Judith's voice again giving actual sound to my mother's words, and in a sudden movement around me, as if the darkness is tangible and weighty, I see Liz, her hands sculpting, her eyes growing bright when she walks through the halls of museums or talks about her work.

6.

February, 2000

　　Several consecutive snowfalls have layered Central Park in hills of white. Ice in shimmering layers and watery shapes covers lakes, branches of trees, the crests of rocks and the edges of street signs. She is riding uptown in a taxi at night through the park drive. The whiteness is illuminated by yellow lights: first the lamp posts, behind them windows in the buildings facing the park, and last, lights from even taller skyscrapers lining avenues farther west. The snow, ice, lights in intricate patterns remind her of Melissa saying, I see the world in layers, and I hear a thousand voices, each with a different point of view. The voices of the women in her stories and dreams seem audible in the air around her as they drive toward the west side where a garden of royal blue light is suddenly visible within the stretches of yellow and white. She knows these are the winter trees surrounding a famous restaurant in the park, their every branch strung with bright blue bulbs. Yet the scene seems to promise something more: strings of Christmas lights, ordinary and mundane, woven around the branches of trees by some patient and meticulous soul, but like the actual water lilies at Giverny, or like the European cities her mother saw for the first time, made over into a landscape of some place quite unknown.

　　Some dreams linger. Their meanings unfold and change over years. She has not thought of the dream of the horse and the elephant for some time, but now, hearing the echo of Judith's voice reading Violet's letters out loud, Celia feels a nightmarish quality to the dream – the gigantic power of those magnificent creatures emerging from the sea, making her feel beautiful, but also awestruck and small. She thinks of Frank, not at this moment of his magnetism or his lies, but of his goodness; and of Violet, not of her anger or her mystery but her passion. She can see them – Frank, his large hands holding hers as they watch the magnificent elephants lift their trunks to the sky, then his face drawn and aging fast from relentless grief; and Violet, laughing in the back seat of a carriage drawn by a black horse, angry and desperate in a room of vague shadows and rancid smells, then a shy young woman bravely crossing an ocean toward an unknown world.

　　Suddenly she feels a jolt, as if the taxi has stopped short and almost thrown her into the glass behind the driver's seat. Like her mother's, her own story is incomplete, fragmented, full of the ordinary chaos and in-triguing confusion of a life untransformed into art. Even her story with Dr.

Daniels is only at the end of its first phase, and who knows what unpredictable plot turns lie ahead? She opens the window, tries to catch her breath, sucking in the cold night air. Khoby comes to mind – his honest, empathic eyes, his love for Mari, his desire to heal the wounds of the world. She has written a fictional memoir, a novel, a story. She is a writer whose genres get mixed up. It seems obvious: she is Bettina, Melissa, Leza. She imagines, dreams, remembers experiences, situations, scenes that are closer to the truth than the literal truth, but sometimes they are the literal truth. This is what she teaches her students: this is the meaning of metaphor. And this is why her characters stay with her for so long. She never forgets them or lets them go, any more than she *lets Khoby go,* though he lives his very own life three thousand miles away. They remain within her, their faces as vivid and present as her own in the mirror, their voices as clear as her own monologues when she talks to herself.

As the taxi continues on its way toward the exit drive, she observes the circular road, the circle of trees around the restaurant. She thinks about the circle of stories whose trails she's been following and remembers circling her room. She had been looking into the mirror. She took her finger and tried to touch the reflection of her face, but her finger met its own reflection where she placed it against the glass. Only by touching her actual flesh could she see what she wanted so much to see: her reflected finger touching her reflected mouth, her reflected eyes staring back at her.

Acknowledgments

I am grateful for permission to quote from:

Anne Sexton: A Self-Portrait in Letters edited by Linda Grey Sexton and Lois Ames. Copyright © 1977 by Linda Grey Sexton and Loring Conant Jr., executors of the will of Anne Sexton. Reprinted by permission of Houghton Mifflin Company. All rights reserved.

"The Death Baby," from *The Death Notebooks* by Anne Sexton. Copyright © 1974 by Anne Sexton, renewed 2002 by Linda G. Sexton. Reprinted by permission of Houghton Mifflin Harcourt Publishing Company. All rights reserved.

"Wanting to Die," from *Live or Die* by Anne Sexton. Copyright © 1966 by Anne Sexton, renewed 1994 by Linda G. Sexton. Reprinted by permission of Houghton Mifflin Harcourt Publishing Company. All rights reserved.

"Said the Poet to the Analyst," from *To Bedlam and Part Way Back* by Anne Sexton. Copyright © 1960 by Anne Sexton, renewed 1988 by Linda G. Sexton. Reprinted by permission of Houghton Mifflin Harcourt Publishing Company. All rights reserved.

Mrs. Dalloway by Virginia Woolf. Copyright © 1925 by Houghton Mifflin Harcourt Publishing company and renewed 1953 by Leonard Woolf, reprinted by permission of the publisher.

To the Lighthouse by Virginia Woolf, copyright © 1927 by Houghton Mifflin Harcourt Publishing Company and renewed 1954 by Leonard Woolf, reprinted by permission of the publisher.

I Stand Here Ironing by Tillie Olsen, copyright © 1956 Tillie Olsen. Reprinted by permission of The Francis Goldin Literary Agency.

Several chapters of this novel were originally published in slightly different forms in *Mothers Who Think*, Eds. Camille Peri and Kate Moses, and *What Do Mothers Want?*, Ed. Sheila F. Brown, The Analytic Press.

I want to thank the members of Hamilton Stone Editions for their faith in me and commitment to this work. I especially appreciate the support of

Carole Rosenthal, Lynda Schor, Meredith Sue Willis, Halvard Johnson, whose reliable attention, humor and technical expertise got me through, and Lou Robinson, who created the beautiful cover.

Long-standing appreciation for responses and help in many ways in the early years of the making of this novel goes to Edith Konecky, the late Rebecca Kavaler, and my agent, Wendy Weil, for her early support of this work and many others.

Ruth Charney's support of my work is unique in my life.

I thank my students Claire Basescu, Sally Donaldson and Sarah Stemp, three gifted writers and psychoanalysts for their readings and incisive comments on this work in its next-to-final stage.

I thank my niece, Sarah Lazarre-Bloom for her attentive reading, and my sister, Emily Lazarre, whose work is often inspiration to my own.

Most recently, and with special gratitude, I thank the wonderful writers of my writing group: Jan Clausen, Beverly Gologorsky and Jocelyn Lieu. Thank you for your attention and for your work.

I am as grateful as ever to my patient and devoted husband, Douglas White, my sons – consistent readers and dear friends – Adam Lazarre-White and Khary Lazarre-White. Without your love and support, everything would be diminished.

For all the years of encouragement and education that have affected my life and my work in countless ways, I will always be grateful to Dr. Louis Lauro.

Although this is a work of fiction, and the character of Violet is imagined, I have used actual passages of letters from my mother, Tullah Deitz Lazarre, written from Europe in 1948.

Some Comments on Jane Lazarre's Books:

on *Inheritance* [not yet published]:

"A powerful and poetic narrative that seems to float on a shifting surface of emotion. Memory seems buried, or drowned. Yet it breaks through. The novel strengthened my hope that art can stiffen our spines and shape up our thinking and feeling around race. Desire and love are radical and dangerous, and the ongoing effort to write seems like a rescue mission, a deep diving and life saving mission."

> Sekou Sundiata, prize-winning poet and playwright, "The 51st (Dream) State," "Blessing the Boats," and many other works.

"This book is simply wonderful. Lazarre has woven a rich tapestry in which the past insists on itself in the lives of several American families. Beautifully orchestrated, her white characters must confront racism because of their love for black husbands, children, sisters, friends and teachers. Their journey from slavery to the present is unforgettably rendered. A fierce and honest novel that once again proves the searing truth of fiction."

> Beverly Gologorsky, author, *The Things We Do To Make It Home*," a *New York Times* Notable Book

"*Persimmon Tree*, an on-line magazine for older women, published quarterly in association with Mills College, is honored to include in its premier issue an excerpt from Jane Lazarre's unpublished novel, *Inheritance*. This beautifully written story reveals the subtleties of emotion that exist between white and Black people who love each other but have to navigate the incomprehensibility and ugliness of racial discrimination. A gripping story, it shows how the themes of race play out in the most personal ways."

> Nan Gefen, Publisher, *Persimmon Tree*

on *The Mother Knot*

"A wholly original and important book . . . I cannot imagine a woman who would not be moved, or a man who would not be enlightened."

> Adrienne Rich

"Beautifully written – *The Mother Knot* says the unsayable, crackling with insights . . . at once profoundly consoling and terrifying, her finds are universal."

Barbara Seaman, *Washington Post Book World*

on *On Loving Men*

"A very contemporary document. Meditative, often lyrical . . . compassionate and honest.

The New York Times Book Review

"I've read so many books by now in which women have written in blood and bitterness about their experience with men that it came as a relief to see how someone is managing to reconcile conflicting feelings without rancour. I saw myself and a dozen of my friends in the woman she writes about."

Rosellen Brown

on *Some Kind of Innocence*

" . . . a perfect matching of subject and form . . . The dignity, spareness, the fairness and compassion for everyone in the story make it a delight to read . . . At her best, Lazarre takes chances which few of today's fiction writers, more mannered and strategic, would."

Philip Lopate

on *The Powers of Charlotte*

"There is a marvelous amplitude, a sensual, moral, caring dimension, a dense substance to this life embracing novel. As expected of the author of the pioneering *The Mother Knot*, mothering, children, are present with immediacy, depth, truth, almost no other writers summon, but this is far more. Those children, the young, the ripening, the coming to be old, the successor young are evoked for us – as is Charlotte herself – through the saga of her erotic, emotional, intellectual artist-being – a wonderful achievement. Set into the changing societal context bordered by mystery,

beauty and death, the result is rare to come out of literature; tenderness for
life, respect for human beings – power indeed."
　　　　　　Tillie Olsen

　　　　"A beautifully written tour de force of a novel in the spirit of Doris
Lessing and Margaret Atwood."
　　　　　　American Book Review

on *Worlds Beyond My Control*

　　　　"Jane Lazarre's new book is a special sort of literary adventure. It
has the rich, dense texture of life itself."
　　　　　　Lynne Sharon Schwartz

　　　　". . . Lazarre combines the genres of fiction and memoir to weave
a work that is quite unique. Maybe sublime."
　　　　　　Lynda Schor

on *Beyond the Whiteness of Whiteness*

　　　　"An important affirmation of a white woman's love of her black
sons. Jane Lazarre, warrior mom, has crossed over."
　　　　　　Alice Walker

　　　　"Through the profoundly human caring of this book; its luminous
beauty, passionate authenticity, truth and power; its multi-lensed and
sourced hard-wrung wisdom – and yes, through the art with which it is
written – we see, we feel, understand what we never have before, the ways
of the Whiteness of Whiteness; and we are challenged, enlarged, and
enabled, as was Jane Lazarre, to move beyond."
　　　　　　Tillie Olsen

　　　　'*Beyond the Whiteness of Whiteness* will be the classic Lazarre's *The
Mother Knot* has become, a book in which a piece of American experience
gets its full telling, a necessary book."
　　　　　　　　Ann Snitow, Critic, Writer, Professor of Literature, the
　　　　　　　　New School

"A beautifully written, deeply thoughtful journey into the worlds of self and other."
Kirkus Reviews

"Lazarre's voice is artful and measured . . . substantial food for thought for both white and black perspectives on the murky issue of race in America."
Publishers Weekly

on *Wet Earth and Dreams: A Narrative of Grief and Recovery*

"She has it right! Perhaps even workers in the field will learn something about how patients feel. Thank you, Jane Lazarre, from all of us."
Lucille Clifton

"Jane Lazarre has always been one of our bravest writers. She once again makes an art of raw, fierce honesty, as she moves through encounters with pain, loss, illness and death. Inspired by the urgent desire to know and be known, she has created an intensely gripping and profoundly moving work."
Jessica Benjamin, author of *The Bonds of Love*

Jane Lazarre has received awards in fiction from the National Endowment for the Arts and the New York Foundation for the Arts. Her essays and reviews have been widely published and anthologized. In 2005, she retired from the full-time faculty in Creative Writing at the Eugene Lang College of The New School, where for many years she directed the undergraduate writing program. In 1995, she was given the University Award for Excellence in Teaching. She serves on the Board of Directors of The Brotherhood/Sister Sol, an organization that serves New York City Black and Latino children and youth. She is also on the Advisory Board of *Persimmon Tree*, an online literary journal.